FEATHERWEIGHT

Also by Mick Kitson

Sal

FEATHERWEIGHT

MICK KITSON

CANONGATE

First published in Great Britain, the USA and Canada in 2021
by Canongate Books Ltd, 14 High Street, Edinburgh EH1 1TE

Distributed in the USA by Publishers Group West and in
Canada by Publishers Group Canada

canongate.co.uk

1

Frontispiece illustration courtesy of Florilegius / Alamy Stock Photo

British Library Cataloguing-in-Publication Data
A catalogue record for this book is available on
request from the British Library

ISBN 978 1 83885 191 0
Export ISBN 978 1 83885 192 7

Typeset in Granjon LT Std by Palimpsest Book Production Ltd,
Falkirk, Stirlingshire

Printed and bound in Great Britain by Clays Ltd, Elcograf S.p.A.

MIX
Paper from
responsible sources
FSC® C018072

For my brother, Jim Kitson

On the

Farefield at Hallow Heath,

in the County of Worcestershire,
at the annual Horse Fair adjacent to the
new Birmingham Canal.

On this day September 12th in the Year of Our Lord
EIGHTEEN HUNDRED AND THIRTY-EIGHT

A MOST ANTICIPATED
BOUT OF THE NOBLE

ART
OF

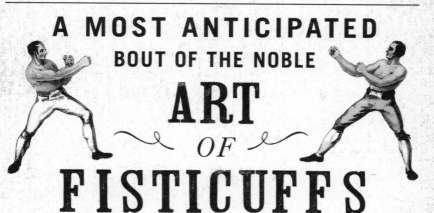

FISTICUFFS

A RE-MATCH OF THE HARPENDEN ENCOUNTER
OF TEN YEARS AGO.

CERTAIN GENTLEMEN *are to be* COMMENDED
FOR THE ORGANISATION AND DISPOSAL OF THIS
REMARKABLE *and* HISTORIC RE-MATCH.

The NOBLE *and* MOST HONOURABLE PURSUIT *of*
A PRIZE THAT SHALL NOT EXCEED THIRTY
GUINEAS FOR THE WINNER.

And a **Double Purse of Twenty Guineas** for the Loser
all provided by a most Excellent and well-known
Personage of the Local Gentry.

Spectators shall see
the great and undefeated Staffordshire Champion

MR WILLIAM PERRY,

also known as Bill Perry, also known as the

TIPTON SLASHER

Engage and test his Skill and Fists of Staffordshire Iron

AGAINST HIS OPPONENT,

known as the

IRISH HURRICANE

MR TIMOTHY HEANEY,

who in that Kingdom and at various Fields of Sport in England
has proved himself a most **Worthy** and **Terrible** opponent.

Sporting Gentlemen will enjoy the MANY Opportunities
occasioned by this HISTORIC PRIZE BOUT.

Ladies are requested to ensure that they prepare themselves
for the Might and Majesty of these two Giants of the Ring.

The Bout shall commence after the last Sale at near 12 noon.
A Hat will be passed for Contributions to Subscriptions for
the two NOBLE Sportsmen.

BUT *this* ENTERTAINMENT *is* FREE TO THOSE
WHO CAN STEEL THEMSELVES FOR THE FURY
and SPORTING PROWESS *of the* CHALLENGERS.

JACK BROUGHTON RULES *SHALL BE OBSERVED*
WITH THE ATTENTION of a WELL-APPOINTED
REFEREE MR EVANS and TIMEKEEPER
MR BARROWMAN.

Prologue

Ithan, Pennsylvania
1906

Jeannie Brand stood before the Missus and wondered at the rare curiosity of her being called up from the scullery at eleven on a fine autumn morning. Odd she should be called up at any time at all.

It was only the second time she had seen the inside of the drawing room. It was the first time ever she had been spoken to by the Missus. The old lady dealt only with Uncle Kenny. And it was Uncle Kenny who had rushed into the canhouse where Jeannie was crimping tops onto jars of stewed apple and called in an amazed voice, 'Jean, the Missus wishes to speak to you.'

He held out his hands, as perplexed as she at the sudden strangeness of the request, but he knew that the Missus had begun to take queer fancies in the past months. He had seen Sullivan the lawyer's trap outside the big house three times since the start of October.

Now he was troubled that the child he had brought over from his family in Fife a year past had been called so sudden and untoward. Not much happened at the big house that the Missus didn't discuss with Kenny. But the old lady seemed to know things. Things about the servants and the works and the comings and goings of the village that no soul could've told her.

Kenny stopped for a moment and looked at his niece. She was tall, taller than he, with the same bright flashing eyes and sharp temper as his mother. Only last week the girl had wrestled and punched a big Welsh woman after they had words in the bakery line. 'She certainly don't act like no Scotch lady, Mr Ken,' said Trapper Dan White as he told Kenny of the scene that unfolded before him while he waited atop the gig as Jeannie ran the morning messages.

And the girl sang so as she moved about the house. She had a sweet voice and she sang the songs of Rabbie Burns and it was a pleasure to hear for Kenny. It reminded him of the tiny village perched on a hill overlooking the Forth where he grew in the years before he came to America, where the men worked the pits and the women scoured and bleached linen in the fields. The girl's voice was warm and delicate as a summer shower, but Kenny fretted that it annoyed the Missus when it wafted through the lower corridors to the parlour above.

'I only hope she has had no word of your disgraceful behaviour at the bakery Tuesday past,' he grumbled at Jeannie as they hurried up the back stair, she swatting at the dust and apple flakes on her apron. 'Or you're vexing her with your warbling songs all the hours of the day.'

'She'll no' have an idea of the bakery wifie, Kenny . . . how would she?'

'You don't know her, lassie, and it's my reputation at stake. I vouched for you and got you here, remember that.' He shoved her towards the drawing-room door saying, 'God help you if she's displeased, and you don't mention I know about the rammy at the bakery line.'

Jeannie knocked and heard the low gruff voice from within call, 'Come on.'

The Missus was seated by the window. The bright morning sun from behind rendered her a silhouette with a fine slim neck and

2

hair pinned in a tight bun. Jeannie stepped into the room and made a clumsy curtsey. 'You wished to see me, Missus,' she said quietly.

The old lady turned and her face was in black shadow. 'Come closer, girl,' she said and Jeannie moved towards her.

'Here and take me hands,' said the Missus. Jeannie wanted to shudder as she lightly clasped the two gnarled and twisted things. They shone like polished mahogany and each was cut with thousands of tiny lines yet they seemed to weigh nothing, as light and insubstantial as goose feathers. The knuckles were jagged and ridged like a miniature mountain range, and from beneath the stretched toffee-brown skin the old grey bone jutted and shone. Holding the old woman's hands, Jeannie's smooth white fingers were like spring blossom settled on a midden.

The Missus said, 'These are all I have ever had, girl.'

Jeannie tried to smile and said, 'Yes, Missus.'

The Missus said, 'These are a pretty pair, child. Mine were like these once a long time ago. Mine were me fate and me fortune.'

Jeannie looked into the old woman's face; her eyes were the fearsome dark green of a deep mill pond. She tried to think and hear that voice. What was that voice? That queer way of speaking the Missus had. It was not Scots, nor Irish, nor Welsh. It was not American, nor had it the zees and zeds of the Germans or the Dutch. There was no lilt and music like the Italians nor the guttural shudder of the Jews. There was none of the drawl and laughter she heard in the speech of the Negroes, nor the clipped and assured chatter of the English.

The Missus closed her eyes and held her head back and said, nodding slightly, 'I seen you, Jeannie Brand, walloping the big wench in the bakery line.'

Jeannie flushed and twisted, but the Missus was laughing, her thin body shaking with a delighted wheezing.

3

'She got what-for, dint she? You remind me of a fair and lovely wench I knew long back. Long long back.'

'I apologise, Missus. I have a temper, I do. But our Kenny knows nothing of it. The lassie was braiding me for being Scots and I saw red. I am so sorry for any trouble I have brought you, Missus.'

The Missus's smile showed good white teeth and she patted Jeannie's hand. 'Big fat thing, weren't she?'

Emboldened by the mischievous smile on the old lady's face, Jeannie said, 'She was, aye, Missus, great fat cruel mouth on her. The vicious things she said, Missus . . .'

'Well, it's as well you wiped it for her, wench. I expect you are fast with your fists. You've a fair reach on ya.'

Jeannie was puzzled for a second. The old lady said, 'Ya did no wrong. A woman has to fight sometimes. It's as well ya know how.'

Then the old lady leaned forward and fixed Jeannie with her dark green eyes. The morning sun was hot in the room and dust motes sparkled in the air. 'What are your people?' she said.

'My father was a miner, Missus. He was killed two years past when the shafts flooded. My mother died the year after of fever and so too my wee sister. That's why Kenny sent for me. And many thanks to you, Missus, for letting me come.'

'Kenny is too good a man to leave in me foundry and if you are his blood then you must be a good un too. And so sweet and pretty, you do me old eyes good just being about the place. And I hear your songs too, child.'

Jeannie put her hand to her mouth. 'I apologise. I shall quieten if it vexes you, Missus. Where I come from we sing all the time.'

'Don't you never apologise for poetry, young wench. And never apologise for Mr Burns. He is the loveliest of all, and his poor heart so badly broken. I fancy it was a pretty Scotch lassie just like you as wronged him, Jeannie Brand.'

The girl tried to smile but she was baffled by the old lady's strange talk and was glad when the Missus shifted and held out her arm and said, 'Help me to the chair. I am sore with sitting here.'

The girl took the Missus by the arm and supported her as she edged across the room. Her tiny frame felt as weightless as her gnarled hands and she seemed to float as she took Jeannie's forearm to be guided to the chair next to the fire. There was a heavy dark-oak cabinet with a shining glass front. And as the older woman settled like an April snowflake Jeannie glanced at the cabinet. There she saw no knick knacks or china, no Meissen or Staffordshire. Instead, at the centre of the only shelf, placed carefully on a fine linen doily, was a small bronze ring. And next to it a scrap of faded red ribbon. The things were dwarfed by the span and volume of the glass shelf they sat upon and hung as if suspended in mid-air.

The old lady was smiling still as the girl's gaze returned to her. The window end of the quiet room glowed gold in the slanting sunbeams and was suddenly airy and full of dancing light.

The Missus said, 'Go and call Kenny to fetch us some tea. I should like to have a talk with you.'

And as Jeannie moved towards the door the old woman said, aloud and to the general air of the room, 'I am the last one. I have nobody left. They are just old songs now.'

I

When I was a babby I spoke Black Country and I dint speak much neither. Then nor now. They said I was a moody mare and I was always scowling and I walked slow and heavy and leaning like I was a Punch barge-hauling coal. I still walk like that, but slow now because of the years and sore bones and puffy swelling knuckles where once they were sharp and cut fast.

We sometime spoke Romi on the road but that's all gone now too. All gone from my voice and my head. All knocked out and spilled on the lanes and alehouses and farefields. But there are still songs I got from all over in my head and they come in waves sometimes, sometimes a word or a sound or the way an American says a word I know like he is Black Country, and the words tumble back and the tunes and the sounds and the voices I heard that shouted and sang when I was a little wench and got offered up and bought by Billy Perry. The thud of the barge on the wharfside. The hiss of the rope on the bridge corner. The old Shire's soft clopping on the path. My mammy crying the day I walked down into the fair holding our Tommy's hand.

Before that walk, in the years my people roamed and wandered them lanes and fields in that country all over, from the towns and villages to the moor top and woodlings, we watched the copses going for pit props and railway beds and the rivers getting the bends taken out. There were the pit heaps and brickworks and the canals snaking through the green pastures like hedges do in proper country. And new brick buildings going up by the basin where the

6

canals all met the river and it was all sludge when they had the new locks closed and men were bricking up the culverts and run-offs. And hauling and placing blocks of red sandstone. They dug holes in the ground for coal and clay and sand and they burned lime in stone kilns that smoked and glowed all night.

I can still see the red earth path we walked down to the fair the summer after Big Tom dropped down dead in the stamping rain trying to lever the vardo out of a blackwater ditch with my brothers Tommy and Tass.

When he toppled like a cut tree, white as milk and scratching at his chest, they put up a wailing and bawling and me and Mammy and Benny and Mercy and Charity peered out from under the canvas we was holding over our heads.

The vardo skewed and pitched up at the back, and Cobble the pony was bucking and straining at the halter, scared he was going into the ditch with the cart. Tommy and Tass were clinging on the pole end they had wedged under the front wheels and Big Tom was lying face down with the rain smacking into his back.

I got sight that night in the rain when Big Tom died. I knew he was dead and I knew his soul was hovering on us, and the pony's fear and pulling white-eyed from the pit was like our fear of the pit and all of us pulling white-eyed all our lives.

I got quieter after that, and the quieter I got the more I saw. I learned to hover and float over and see what was what, and drift like down to flutter and spin above the world.

Mammy told me all about pitching by a holly tree, welcoming wrens and robins, itches in your hands and nose, and looking for a white horse in the morning.

That happened in the April, and time we came to the fair in September the leaves on the hawthorn hedges that lined that lane were all greying from their summer green and in places turning red brown and the hawse hung in clusters and were darkening from deep green to deep red and all the sparrows going yampy for them. Linnets' wings were burring in the sun and the last martins were swooping low fore they ventured away into the wide sky.

The oak leaves in the wood above that path were yellowing and brimming with green acorns and Mammy said it meant a hard winter coming, all that acorns and fruit and brambles. I saw the underside of them leaves with morning sunlight glowing through them as I looked up, tugging little bawling Charity by the hand as we all walked behind Mammy to the fair, even though we had no horse to sell nor baskets nor ribbons nor stitching nor nothing.

But looking up at the sun glowing through the leaves, and hearing the scutter of sparrow wings, I saw the underside of everything and I knew I was going somewhere that day like them martins knew they was destined for a journey.

Somewhere to the underside where sun glowed through.

We stopped and ate all the brambles because we were starving by then and Mammy waited, though she took none herself and she was thin except for her big belly where a new babby was growing.

Below the lane in that small valley all along the canalsides lines of barges and craft were moored as far as the eye could see, their chimney pipes were blowing smoke in the bright morning air from stoves where they were boiling the tea, and outside the lockkeeper's lodge above the basin was a stout wench spreading white cloth across a table to sell cakes and buns to the bargeys as they walked to the fair.

There were big Shire cross pulling horses tied in the field next to the canal, each with a rope tethered to a steel stake, and a boy was filling their troughs from a leather bucket dipped in the little stream that ran down from the hill, and the water sparkled in the sun so you had to wince looking at it. It was rising bright, though in the east a sliver of moon still showed, and as we walked on and down we saw all the men gathered and lighting their pipes by a big new rick near the open gate of the field all decked with flags and bunting.

There were brewery men there rolling barrels from the dray and the Clydesdales stamping and snorting, and two boys in white brewery coats unfolding wooden trestles, and a big fat wench in a bright white pinafore overseeing the set-up was calling and cursing at the boys as they scurried to set each table and put out bales for seats.

The field was all fresh cut for hay and there was a rope on iron poles that marked the sale ring and a little stage of new yellow sawn pine for the auctioneer. At the far end there was all the horses and ponies, all kinds and all sizes and all for selling and trading come the day. They were fenced behind wooden pales and hazel hurdles and little stable lads were brushing manes and picking hooves.

I knew horses back then and there were Welsh ponies and cobs, Shires and Clydesdales, Connemaras from Ireland, Dales and Fells, Clevelands and huge honey-hued Suffolk Punches. There were big barge horses and wagon ponies and little riding cobs for the gentry's children and ponies for pits and ponies for ploughing and scraggy old ponies for the knacker men.

And all below us the wide road that ran towards the locks and the basin from the town was filling full with a swelling stream of sellers and pedlars, milk girls and tobacco hawkers, handcarts all stacked with apples and pears, ribbon sellers and potmen, loads of firewood on wagons pulled by teams, a fishman and an iceman moving great blocks wrapped in sack on carts, bright wagons covered in painted castles and flowers and hauled on by tough little ponies, vardos and show wagons with green canvas tops, fancy-ware dealers, a ripe strawberry cart, clowns and puppeteers carrying striped fit-ups and painted poles, a dog cart that trundled heavily weighed by the cider kegs. There were soldiers in bright scarlet coats and white sashes, and cavalrymen with feathers in their helmets, ladies in fine full skirts and farm girls in muslin pinnies. Girls in Sunday best with pretty bonnets and men in tricorns and toppers bobbing in the crowd seething into that meadow. I watched a lady stop and pull out a silver box and sniff fine spices up her nose to stop the stink of it all, the horse shit and sweaty lads and open kegs and steam and smoke and men pissing in the hedges.

And in the dip that ran along the stream a ring was roped for the fisticuff bouts that came after the sales and trading were done. There were tents for the fighters and their men and already there were purses on the stakes where they were betting on the finish of it. Even before it began they were thinking about the ending of it and putting their money out to get odds and terms off the bookmen.

On a flat wagon in the far corner there was a forge, already fired and smoking, and the smithy in his leather apron emptying sacks of coal and working the bellows so clouds of light grey smoke wafted across the meadow and we smelled it even where we were looking down, lined up next to our mammy.

There was Charity, Mercy and me and Tass and Benny and Tommy and my mammy who was called Keziah Loveridge and we were Loveridges after our daddy Big Tom Loveridge and we were Romi and we travelled in a vardo and gorgers called us gypsies and tinkers and piker-men because we lived in a vardo and never stopped and never stayed and we worked on Sundays and weren't allowed in churches nor chapels.

We girls, Charity, Mercy and me, wore no bonnets and the boys wore no caps and each of us walked that dusty lane barefoot. Tass, next down from Tommy, wore only his nightshirt and britches, and Benny next down from him wore the cord britches and canvas jerkin he had slept in the night before. Me and Mercy and Charity wore long grey woollen dresses with aprons tied at the back. We walked in line in order of age behind Mammy, and though she was a widow only five months, in two there would be another babby for her to clothe and feed. Tommy and Tass both carried bundles on their backs with all the goods we had, tied away in the canvas sheets we used to string a shelter between trees at night.

We were all hungry last months, and wandering we were always hungry, crying hungry and swelling-belly hungry and Mercy cried all the nights long. The babby Charity dint cry and that was worse, meant she was sad, sick and fading.

The last food we ate was two days before when a farmer's wife gave us porridge and new apples as we all sat on the verge opposite her gate. It was a big, grand farmhouse of red brick and a slate roof and a garden with a wall at the front where there were apple trees and the apples full and green and sweet. That wife took some pity on us, a line of Loveridges tramping up that road with no horse nor wagon, and, ignoring her husband's rule not to feed any tinkers or pikers, she brought a pot out to us, gave us a fresh bucket of water too, and we all had a new green apple picked that day.

My mammy had got used to beggary and taking food and shelter where it was offered since Big Tom had dropped down dead. And our old pony Cobble dropped down dead too a month later in the rain and wet while we all crammed under the tent and shivered. Poor old Cobble missed Big Tom, Mammy said. He pined away and died of horse fever after Big Tom went and we all pined too and Mammy cried at nights by the fire. We buried Big Tom outside the churchyard in Yaxley because we were not in the Church and we worked Sundays and the young curate said he couldn't be buried in consecrated ground. And we were so hungry we roasted old Cobble on the fire and he was right chewy.

We had a camp in a copse near Yaxley, and me and Mercy got three pennies a day for scaring birds off the peas and barley. Tommy and Tass worked pulling stones out of a field and they got a bob a week, and we stayed there working and living in the camp until one night I knew there was bad coming in on us because I saw a crow as the sun went down, and then men with staves burst into our spinney and drove us all out. Tommy and Tass had their heads splitted by sticks and we left the big kettle and Big Tom's old shiny boots behind and we all ran into the night. That night I floated over like a bird and I sent vile curses down upon them men who stamped and spitted at us as they harried us from their copse.

Then we wandered the lanes. The spring and summer were dry and warm, which was as well, for all the coats and blankets we owned were in the old vardo, rotting away in the ditch where it killed Big Tom. There was no going back for them now. That vardo was cursed sure and certain as the trees changing.

We picked where we could find picking work, and Mammy stitched bags and blankets for fairs, and the boys pulled stones and dug ditches.

But by that September any coins Mammy had in her purse were gone and it would be winter soon enough and a new babby coming. We wandered raggle-taggle and camped and begged where there was water or shade from the sun. And we always stopped by holly or hawthorn.

We had come to this fair every year when Big Tom was alive. Mammy sold her stitched bags and blankets, and we ran around the sweet mowed meadow while Big Tom met men from other camps and talked horses and places where there was work to be had. We traded Cobble at the fair before I was born when Tommy and Tass were babbies and Mammy was carrying Benny. I wasn't even there then. I was the spark in Big Tom's eyeball and the grin on his big lovely face.

Mammy said Big Tom had fought fisticuffs at fairs fore we were born and he had once won a two guineas purse agin a lad from

Walsall who he knocked out cold after they had fought for an hour. He had a bite scar on his forearm like the big crescent moon.

So we had been every year for nine years to that day, and I was eldest girl next up from Mercy and Charity who was the babby then but not for long. I loved them all but I was a right moody mare in them days and I never spoke much and I watched things going on and waited fore I spoke or used my voice. But I could see what was coming for me.

Now we rounded the bend that led down to the basin and Mammy stopped and turned back to us. She held her hands up and we all straggled into a line: Tommy, Tass, Benny, me and Mercy and Charity.

We all stared down towards that colourful and moving mass of people swarming onto the farefield below. Now carriages drawn by horses were coming up the road below, one fine landau with liveried footman riding at the back and gentlemen on horseback following, and their beaver hats were slick in the sun like they'd been oiled.

And now Mammy said, 'We have risen so early and walked this dusty lane so far to this fair, with no horse or baskets or stitching to sell, and I have made sure Annie wore the cleanest and least mended dress and I washed her face this morning and smoothed her hair down. Oh, my little Annie, the quietest and most sombre of all, who sits alone in brooding silence while you others play and shout. And I know you others think she believes she is too high for us and wishes to be a lady. Oh, my Annie, who never smiles or laughs with your dark eyes, all old and knowing . . .'

And then she stopped talking and there were fat tears running down her cheek. She nodded to Tommy and he took my hand and said, 'Come on, girl.'

And he led me down to the fair. And Mammy called after him, 'Five guineas,' and then she looked away.

2

Below the locks in the basin one empty coal barge did not have a smoking chimney and no kettle boiled on the stove. The boat sat high in the water, its load gone the day before and its gaffer pleased with the coins he got for hauling it from Tipton Port. He now sat on the tiller seat grey and sweating from the ale the night before and fumbled in his coat for his pipe. On the side of the boatman's cabin there was no name painted and no roses or castles in bright colours; the whole craft was grimed with coal dust and seemed to absorb the rays of the bright sun climbing above the basin. The Gaffer felt the sun on his face and coughed and knocked his pipe against the boat side and leaned and watched ash and tiny flecks of baccy float down onto the black water.

A boy was running along the towpath, his cap pushed back on his head and his shirt of striped ticking billowing open as he peered at each of the moored barges he passed. He ran past the Gaffer's, then stopped and hopped back, bending and squinting at the filthy coal boat. He ran to the Gaffer's end and said, 'Are you the Gaffer Fogo?'

'I am, my boy, and you are in a powerful hurry,' said the Gaffer, lifting a lucifer to his pipe.

'I'm come from Heaney. Your man is to be in the dip there in the field as soon as the last sale is done. They say it will be soon after noon.'

'My man will be there, do not fear. Although he is presently deep in a slumber that may be broken only by the smell of ale. Here, my lad, take a sixpence to The Cock for me and bring two flagons of the pale ale so as I can wake him with no difficulties . . .' The Gaffer held out a coin.

The boy straightened and looked dubious. 'What would my men say if they knew I was fetching for the opponent? We have Lord Ledbury coming this morning to meet Heaney and talk the fight through. He has put up the purse and he has a wager of fifty pound on our man. What would his lordship say?'

'He would say you were a good Christian lad. The Slasher cannot move without ale, cannot wake without it, and most certainly cannot go a bout without it. There will be a penny change that you shall keep for going.'

The boy thought for a moment, then took the money and ran off towards the end of the basin where there stood red-brick warehouses and keepers' cottages and lines of wooden swing cranes jutting out across the water. The Gaffer stood and watched him go, then leaned over the steps and knocked on the roof of the cabin, three loud bangs as he brought his big hand down flat on the coal-black roof.

'Billy Perry, wake up! There is ale coming for your breakfast. Billy Perry, awake! Awake, my beauty, for today you make your fortune!'

From inside the cabin there was a low animal grunt and then a dull thudding and banging, the grunt lengthening into a long sonorous growl that vibrated low and menacing inside the darkened quarters and the Gaffer went back to his seat by the tiller, flopping down and smiling.

'A lad is coming with the ale, Billy boy . . .'

There was a sharp clack as the door to the cabin was pulled back and Bill Perry stepped out, stooping and doubled over, blinking with a fearsome look of malice at the sunny September morning.

He wearily climbed the three steps to the deck and straightened to his full height. He was shirtless and wore sagging long grey drawers with a button front. He stood six feet four inches and his chest was broad and round as an oak tun, his shoulders like the great limbs of an old tree. His skin was tanned a rich toffee brown except for the old scars across his upper arms and chest which were unnaturally white and shone like small slivers of ivory from the deep hue of his skin.

His huge head could have been hewn from rock, with the colour and texture of a layered sandstone outcrop, and whichever mason worked to form that lumped and blasted countenance, he must've been, as the Gaffer had remarked on many occasions, either blind or dead drunk. The nose was almost the shape of a shepherd's crook, the bone broken and flattened into a smooth curve that began in the heavy brow above his small blue eyes and ran up and round and down as if hastily moulded from clay. It ended in large flared nostrils that bristled with greying hairs. Behind his thin lips the teeth were yellow and black and cracked, some split so they looked as if they had been sharpened, and his smile, when it came, was said to make ladies shriek.

He squinted into the sun then stepped to the boat edge, unbuttoned his drawers and pissed into the water. The Gaffer listened to the plunging sound he made and said, 'There's been a lad from Heaney says we meet after noon. I've sent him for ale.'

Bill turned, buttoning himself up, and grunted again, then nimbly stepped onto the towpath. His lithe rhythmic movement seemed to belie the rocklike bulk of his body, and once on the path he jigged from foot to foot, stretching his scarred arms above his great head and pointing his long thick fingers towards the sky. His hands were huge and flat, like spade heads, pitted with scars like his arms and grimed the colour of iron.

The boy came trotting down the path holding two stone flagons and stopped dead when he saw Bill Perry, bare-chested and stretching his monstrous arms towards the sky. The boy's eyes widened into a horrified gawp as if he had seen something from a nightmare and the Gaffer called, 'Aint pretty, is he?'

Bill held out his hand and grunted at the boy, 'That my ale?'

The boy stepped tremulously forward, holding out a flagon which Bill took, the span of his hand making the half-gallon jar look small as a medicine bottle as he closed his fingers round it. He unstopped it and upended it into his mouth, the ale swilling and gushing in the jar as he drained it. He let out a long satisfied 'aaah', then wiped his mouth and regarded the boy.

'Good lad,' he said. 'So you're come from Heaney?'

'Aye, sir,' the boy said.

'And do you know me, boy?'

'Aye, sir,' the boy said quietly. 'You are the Slasher.'

'Right you are, my lad. I am the Slasher and I could tek off the tip of your fine nose with one jab if I so desired. What do Heaney and his men say of me? I've beat him once, you know, donkey's years ago.'

The boy shrugged and smiled.

'Well, what do they say of me? You'll get no hiding if you tell the truth. What do they say of me of a night as they nurse their ale?'

Bill laid his great slab of a hand on the boy's shoulder and gently but determinedly squeezed, his huge fingers probing the boy's soft thin flesh.

'Well, my boy?' he said.

The boy squirmed as the stone fingers sank into his shoulder like some unstoppable iron vice closing and gripping. He shook then began to go limp as the fingers bored into his muscle, and he spluttered, 'Well, they say . . . they say you are done with the drink and can no longer fight. Lord Ledbury thinks Heaney will win it. He has a wager of fifty pound on him . . .'

Bill Perry began to lift the boy, who wriggled and flopped like a fish on a line and let out a yell as the huge arm levered him up from the path as if it was a crane. He brought the boy steadily up to his face.

'You tell em this, fine lad. I aint done. And I aint finished and that Irish pig will know he's met the Slasher soon enough. And tell his lordship he might as well piss on his fifty pound.'

He opened his fingers and the boy dropped like a coal sack, and Bill said to the Gaffer, 'Gie 'im a tanner.'

The Gaffer said, 'A tanner?'

And Bill said slowly, 'A tanner for his trouble. Go on – gie 'im a tanner.'

The Gaffer fumbled in his pocket, huffing and shaking his head, as the boy stood up then took the small silver coin the Gaffer proffered.

He looked up at the Slasher. 'And it's Jack Broughton Rules. And bindings.'

Bill smiled and showed his broken teeth. He held his fists out to the boy. 'These boys don't need no bindings. Tell Heaney he can bind if he wants to keep his hands pretty but I slash better bare as God made me . . .'

The boy nodded and backed away as Bill unstopped the other flagon and downed it.

The Gaffer said, 'I'll fry some eggs up, Billy.'

Bill climbed back aboard and sat on the tiller seat, staring out across the basin towards the warehouses and cottages. They were building a new wharf on the far side and new houses and store sheds, and men were climbing the scaffold poles carrying hods of red brick. The canal side was shuttered with planks and two navvies were mixing a steel vat of lime and sand ready to pour.

Bill said, 'It's all changing here, Gaffer. All the building and making. Used to be meadows and trees yonder there.'

The Gaffer said, 'Everything changes, Billy. They're making more for unloading. Good, though. They're trying to mek it better than the rail for loads. Straight down to Bristol docks from there . . .'

'Railways. Bloody things, shifting people where they don't belong. Shifting folk where they aren't needed nor wanted. There'll be them here from Birmingham today come on the rails . . .' Bill said, scowling out across the basin where swallows dipped and chirped.

He was forty-two, old for a fighter. Old for a bargeman too, but he was both. He knew he was born in 1796 and his father was a miner in a coal-black town in Staffordshire – a furious little man called Timothy Perry who kept to the old religion and would knock down any man who suggested they go to the Baptist chapel or the Methodist mission, or who told him he was damning his six children to a papist hell. He spat at the preachers and Methodist men who came around the mines waving the Bible as the men climbed from the wooden carts after ten hours underground. Timothy loved the Latin Mass and Bill still said 'Ave Maria' and 'Pater Noster' before a fight and before he laid a bet.

Bill felt old, felt his skin sagging, and his knees and shoulders ached and ground until ale dulled the pain and brought sweats brimming from his brow every morning. This was his last fight: him and the Gaffer came down by barge with a load of coal from Tipton Port, and even leading the horse and pulling the barge in brought a tight flat feeling in his chest. He never told the Gaffer. And win or lose he would make enough to buy an alehouse, which he would call The Champion of England. There was one on Spon

Lane just by the wharf he could get from the widow for ten guineas: ale pumps and looking-glasses and fine oak tables an all. And once he had been the champion of England, and he feared no man, and he dreamed of a quiet life selling ale and telling tales. And he had tales.

Hadn't he as a strapping lad of just sixteen knocked Tass Parker clean out, after nine rounds, when Parker was blinded by the blood from the knuckle cuts on his forehead and he stumbled and lurched into Bill's swinging left that shifted his head, so the crowd let out a booming 'oooh' and Parker was out before he hit the mud? They called in dragoons to quell the riot after that one. The field erupted into fury with men swinging and punching at each other and trying to get their stakes back off the bookies, and the bookies' men swinging sticks and batons and heads cracking and bones breaking. Parker had a crowd of pretty lads with him and they all laid wagers on their man. Nobody had heard of Billy Perry from Tipton and nobody but Tim Perry and two miners of his acquaintance had a penny on young Bill.

Hadn't he once punched a donkey into the canal before a crowd of drunk men for a wager of ten bob and a gallon of ale?

Hadn't he been to London, and once fought for a prize on the frozen River Thames before a crowd of lords and ladies and fine gentlemen on a bed of coal ash as snow tumbled? He fought a Jew called Mendoza and their blood froze pink as a dog rose on the ice.

He had met Jack Broughton, who said he was the finest stylist he had seen and who admired his flicking jab that split skin and his dancing capering gait honed and refined from the day Bill understood the one great truth of fisticuffs, which was that the way to win a fight was not to get hit.

And he rarely got hit. His bowed legs, nimble and bouncy like coach springs, meant he bobbed and bibbled, never still to strike, and his right hand jabbed and flicked, pulled back on contact so it felt like a whip when he got you. Then he had the big slashing left he barrelled around from nowhere that flattened a man, jerking his head over on his spine, shifting the vertebrae in his neck so they ground across each other. He'd broken the necks of two men, that he remembered. As a lad he had learned the slashing left to the side of a man's head when he strong-armed his barge through at locks. Few refused to give way when they saw the big bow-legged lad coming up on them.

He had tales he dreamed of telling before a coal fire with good ale inside him. He thought about getting a wench too. A good working girl to run the alehouse and cook and bake. Like his mother had. She was a black-haired dark-skinned Romi who ran from her people to marry Timothy after he met her standing outside the chapel in Birmingham, crying for not being let in for the Mass. He made her cover her hair and told the priest they were man and wife. She was tall and long-boned and moved with a measured grandeur like she was a queen, and Bill could still feel her slim cool fingers about his face. She died of fever when he was nine and his father got more furious and forced the seven of them to Mass every Sunday, even if it meant walking eight miles.

3

Babbies got offered up at fairs and I had heard Big Tom and
Mammy talking about it but I never thought it would happen to
me when I was part growed, not a proper little un you could tek
and keep and make your own. I was offered for working, scrubbing
and mending and cooking and fetching.

They got offered if there were too many of them and their
people couldn't feed them, or if their daddies were sick or their
mammies were dying or if they had nothing, like us. And it was
mostly our people who took them, but sometimes it was gorgers.
Big Tom told us of a girl offered who got bought by a gorger
lord and teken to a big house and given dresses and taught to
read and got ponies and servants like she was blood to the lord
who got her.

And as I walked down the lane with Tommy holding my hand
I thought that might be me. I might get a lord for a father and I
might be taught reading and get a pony and dresses. Tommy never
looked at me as we walked down. Mammy and the others all sat
on the verge by the gate and begged off the crowd coming in for
the fair, begged bread or coins or whatever they could get for they
were all mad with hunger and Mammy was woozy with it, and
kept flopping asleep in the bright sun.

Mammy said Mercy and Charity were too little for offering and
the boys were boys – so it had to be me.

Tommy was crying then too, big old tears on his cheeks, knowing
what he was going to do. I felt bad for him and I said, 'It's all right,

Tommy, I know why an all. You get five guineas for me and they shall all eat and Mammy shall get a new wagon and a pony.'

I said it but I dint feel it. I felt like I was walking down into a black pit with each step, not to see Mammy or Tass or Benny or Mercy or Charity no more. But you loss and loss in this life and we lost Big Tom and we lost Cobble and we lost the vardo an all. And now I was going to loss them. And if Mammy dint eat bread she'd loss that babby.

Tommy said, 'I'll tek the name an all, and we'll know where you are and we'll stay by there sometimes and see you. You don't worry, my Annie.'

And he put his hand on my head and then he was like my daddy, a big heavy hand on my hair. He was thirteen and a right strapper, big and broad like Big Tom and just grown big long arms and hands. He could safekeep Mammy and look after the others and maybe if he got bigger he could fight fisticuffs for purses like Big Tom did.

We watched the sales and the trading in the crush of all them bodies, legs and skirts and jackets in front of my eyes, while the auctioneer called the sale and farmers paid up with wedges of notes unfolding. I wanted to grab those notes and run away with them and give them to Mammy.

We watched the pony sales and I loved a little dark-brown Welsh pony who skipped and bucked and was scarce broken, and she had big rolling eyes and she pulled and showed the whites to the fat boy leading her. She went for three shillings, and I wished we had that and I could tek her back to Mammy and break her proper and bridle her for a wagon. She could've pulled it too. She had a good wide front and nice and fat in her rump. She could've pulled any vardo we put her to.

But we never got her, and she pulled and bucked at the farmer who got her on a trade for an old knacker pony plus three bob and as he walked her away from the ring he got a long whip out of his carpet bag and started whipping her. Smack-smack-smack on her rump end and she keeled away from him and reared up trying to clout him with her front legs while he held the halter and whipped her and said, 'Ye bastard . . . ye bastard.'

And then I broke away from Tommy and I ran at him and caught the whip as he raised it and I shouted, 'Ye don't whip her, ye bastard.'

Tommy came running over and he grabbed me and he said, 'Sorry, squire, sorry, squire, she's my sister . . . she don't know . . .'

The farmer, in his hairy coat and his big fat belly poking out, said, 'She's a mouthy little wench, aint she? I'll give her some of this,' and he waved the whip at me. I wanted to stick that whip up his arsehole, the miserable gorgy bastard, but Tommy pulled me away and I dint look back at him whipping that pony.

'You never whip a pony,' Big Tom used to say. 'You talk to them and gently push them where you want, and you whisper to them and you tell them what's what – but you never whip them. Only gorgers and demons whip a pony.'

Tommy led me round and we saw all the fair, the stalls and the bread and cakes and fish and sausages they were selling, and we felt sick in our bellies with the hunger.

Then a big bell started clanging and the crowd rushed away from the sale ring and all started to bustle about where the bouts were in the dip by the hedge.

Tommy took me by the hand, and we snaked through the legs and gaiters and boots and sat cross-legged at the front there.

Tommy said, 'There'll be a row here, you watch, if Heaney don't get it.'

All round there were men, some in suits and some just farm men and travelling men, and all waving money at the bookmakers. There were four of them taking the bets and stuffing notes and coins in their pockets and scribbling slips and shouting to the runners on odds and the runners were tearing out through the crowd and the crush and tacking back to their blokes where the rivals were and what they were giving. There were farm girls too, in their Sunday best dresses and rough old wenches off the barges with big red dirty hands. There was even ladies in that crowd, standing back and giggling behind their fans.

I sat and felt the warm cut grass under my bum and smelled the sweat and the breath of the crowd all about me, some singing and chanting and some calling out bets to the bookies and some just waiting quiet for the bout.

There were four iron stakes in a square and a thick rope tied round them, like a horse sale ring, and then a big red-faced man in a coal-black coat and a high black hat walked out into the ring and he blew a shiny brass trumpet loud and everyone shut it and watched.

He walked around the ring and boomed out at the crowd: 'This is a great and remarkable day when you may remark and you may recall that you were in this field and in this great country under our new Queen, may the good Lord bless her and grant her long and vital life, and you were here, and you were watching when they rematched Tom Heaney, the Irish Hurricane, and the old lad, Bill Perry, the Tipton Slasher, and you may recall and you may remember the rainy day down there in Hatfield when these two gentlemen met last and the Slasher took the purse. And there have been many arrangements and assignations and messages and letters run the length of this kingdom to arrange this historic rematch. Now, ladies, do not squirm and do not squeal when these man mountains meet – for there will be blood, there will be cuts and wounds and bruising, but do not forget the nobility of this art of pugilism. The seeming savagery of these men pitted here is underpinned by a noble and honourable art of skill and precision, of cunning and technique, of athletic exertion and martial intelligence, where man pits himself against his fellow in the most primal and ancient of the combative arts. And did not Cicero in Rome of old tell the senators that this was the most noble and graceful pursuit for a man, and for a man to be pretty and full in his manliness, and for him to know the extent and degree of his own soul, he should bind his fists and face another man so bound in pugilare? Did not Euryalus and Epeus stand square and bold before the Greeks at the funeral games for Patroclus, watched and cheered by Achilles himself . . . ?'

Tommy turned to me and said, 'The Slasher is old and he's wrecked with the drink and Heaney is fitter and he's faster. But I want him in this one. Slasher's a didicoy, Daddy said.'

Didicoy means he's got some Romi blood in him. If Big Tom was there he'd have cheered him against a gorger.

I looked over to the big tent on the other side and there was a tall boy in a short blue coat, his hair all tumbled in blond ringlets. He was fine and pretty, and he stood tall, holding out his cane and laughing with three other boys so apparelled, fine coats and curled hair, two of them holding their hats, and a footman holding the pretty lad's hat. They were taking wine in tall glasses.

The fat man in the centre of the ring went on: 'And we owe a debt of the deepest gratitude to the most honourable and noble, young Lord Ledbury for the purse hanging there upon the stake today . . .' He pointed over to the pretty lad, who smiled and bowed, and the crowd clapped. 'Indeed, you will observe not one but TWO purses fixed to the stakes there, for in his generosity and profound sporting sensibilities his lordship has provided a purse for both the fighters in this epic battle – and the genius of this is that these men fight NOT for gold but for honour and proof of their manly prowess, like the Greeks of old . . . and did not Virgil in the Aeneid . . .'

I stared across at the two leather bags hanging on the stake next to the lord and his friends. 'How much is in them, Tommy?' I said.

'There's thirty guineas for the winner and twenty for the loser – it's called a double purser.'

I tried to imagine if I could crawl through all the feet of that crowd on the stubbly grass and creep up and snatch the purses and run back to Mammy and the others with thirty guineas and twenty guineas. That was the most money there had ever been in all the world. We could get a fine pony for five guineas easy and bread and a new kettle and a wagon probably for only five guineas more and there would still be guineas left over. The boys could get boots and we could get dresses and ribbons and cotton for stitching. And I started to brood and feel a black anger in me that all it needed was what was in them two little leather bags to solve all our problems and keep us all together and me not offered up.

Before I could creep over to them purses, the man in the middle stopped shouting out at the crowd and everyone cheered and roared as the fighters came out from the tent and walked into the ring.

One was a giant, like a big old heavy Shire as he walked slow to the centre, staring straight ahead. His hands were not wrapped and he wore only black drawers and black canvas boots. He was the colour of a stone ale jar and his skin was shiny and thick and creased like saddle leather. He held his hands in fists the size of sheep turnips and he just looked out at the crowd and they cheered and shouted, 'Come on, Billy boy! Come on, the Slasher!'

The other was like our Mercy to Tommy agin the Slasher, the top of his head barely come to his shoulder and it was shaved bald and shone like polished copper. He was tree-trunk thick about his body and his hands were bound with coarse white ticking and he held them down there by his sides, not balled just resting.

The crowd put up a barracking for them both while the man in the big hat waved his hands and blew his horn for quiet.

'Ye papist Heaney, ye dirty Mick papist . . . Are you needing some ale, Billy? . . . Are you needing some Dutch courage? . . . Ye big ugly bastard gypo, Slasher . . . I could tek you . . . I could tek the both . . .'

The two of them stared ahead, not looking at each other, as the man called the Jack Broughton Rules they were to fight by.

'These gentlemen will forbear to bite or kick or gouge, they shall not use knees or feet to disadvantage the other and this contest will be decided solely on the blows of their fists . . . a round shall end when either man goes down and a moment shall be allowed for the fallen man to recover his equilibrium safe from the attentions of his opposite. The seconds may bathe and clean wounds between the rounds but the time shall not exceed one minute for this purpose . . . the bout shall end when . . .'

His booming voice and the murmurs of the crowd faded in my head then and I looked at the Slasher. He was all wreathed in blue light in my mind, and I watched him breathing in and out, great and noble like a bridled horse about to run, and no fear in his eyes, no doubt neither, and as they swept that crowd, tiny blue hard jewels, mouth open and sticks of teeth, and they rested on me there in the front, he grinned.

4

In the sixth round Bill Perry dropped his hands and stopped moving.

His chest was tightening, the swirl of sounds around him merging into a high-pitched keening rush that revolved and whirred inside his head like some monstrous engine; he thought it would spin itself apart and send iron bolts and steel washers bursting out, tearing ragged holes in his skull; and the terrible menace of the burgeoning hum was underscored by the flat thud-thud of his own heart in his ears.

And he wanted ale. And twenty guineas was plenty for the alehouse any road. He had earned more and lost more in his time. And now he wanted an end to it.

Heaney loped in under him, forearms crossed against the fearsome sting of the Slasher's jabbing right hand, his bald head streaked with blackening blood as he straightened and curled his broad left fist up and under Bill's great stone chin. Heaney arched his back as he followed through, seeming to lift Bill off his feet as the head snapped back and gobbets of blood shot out either side from the clamped mouth.

The Gaffer ran into the ring as Bill slammed down onto the dusty ground. First time he had ever been knocked out. The man in the top hat began the count, the crowd joining in as the end got nearer, before erupting into cheers and fierce bellows when they reached TEN! and Bill Perry did not stir.

The Gaffer rubbed Bill's face with a wet cloth, then gently

patted his cheek. All around him was the roar and crush of the crowd, men cheering and charging towards the bookies. Boots stamping and coats swirling as the Gaffer whispered into the hot blood and sweat of his ear, 'Billy boy . . . Billy . . . come on, lad.'

The inside of the ring was now crammed with people: men waving slips at bookies, runners and heavy men batting them back, ladies shrieking, and the cries of men tussling and grappling mixed with the dust and pounding of feet around Bill Perry's great head. The pressing weight of his immense body seemed planted into the cracked red earth as if it had grown suddenly overnight like some terrible scarred puffball.

The Gaffer pulled at him and levered him upright by the shoulders and Bill slumped forward into a sitting position, the Gaffer catching and cradling the skull that shifted and lurched like a freed millstone about to spiral away from its wheel.

The Gaffer said, 'I've got your ale, Billy . . .' His voice tightened into a high panic as he fumbled in his satchel and withdrew a flagon, struggling to unstop it with one hand as he held the Slasher's wobbling head up with the other.

Then, as the two of them crouched on the ground, the Gaffer saw a pair of bright patent shoes, buckled in ornate silver at the end of grey silk-stockinged feet. He looked up. Lord Ledbury and two of his dandy boys were looking down at them.

'I am much obliged to you, Perry. You accounted well of yourself for a man of your years. I am much impressed,' he said, looking out over Bill's head at the maelstrom of men and dust behind them. The lord nodded to one of his boys and a leather purse was dropped, chinking faintly as it landed next to Bill.

'We have had our slave money paid, Mr Perry, and we are in fine means this September. Lucky for you. There is an extra five guineas in there. I admire your style and your resolve and perseverance; I would not relish such an encounter with the papist.'

He looked down, a faint sad smile on his lips.

The Gaffer felt the life suddenly shoot back into Bill's head as consciousness flooded back to him. Bill raised it slowly away from the Gaffer's blooded hand and looked up. The clot of blood above his puffed and swollen right eye was blackened, and glistened like wet coal, and tracks of sweat trails showed white across the creases of his face through the grit and filth. Only one eye would open, but the bright blue of it flared as he caught his lordship's look. The young man and his two companions were momentarily transfixed by the vision of the waking giant beneath them.

Bill spat a white and pink dollop out onto the earth, then said, 'And much obliged to you, sir. He's a fine fellow, the Irishman, and you were well to back him.'

Ledbury bowed and turned away with his men into the crowd, which was now thinning. Carriages were trundling towards the field gate. A sudden cool breeze blew over the field, stirring hand-bills and betting slips and raising puffs of dust like smoke from a dying fire. Soon the ring was empty save the two men: Bill sitting square in the middle on the red scuffed earth and the Gaffer kneeling and bathing his wounds with a rag soaked from a bottle of spirit.

'Thought you was a goner for a minute there, Billy,' the Gaffer said, dabbing at the livid cuts about Bill's eyes.

The pugilist's face remained impassive, and he did not wince nor cry out at the sting of the spirit. 'Did you see the dark little wench there at the front?' he mumbled.

'I seen the fine ladies swooning when you caught him with a slasher and moved his head – there was gobs of blood spraying all over,' the Gaffer chuckled.

'Little Romi wench,' Bill said.

31

'Ne'er mind her, Billy. Come on. We are rich and the ale tent's open.'

Bill stood slowly, buttoning the white linen shirt the Gaffer gave him from the satchel he carried. The two men walked across the ring and out towards the tents. The crowd who had watched the bout were now all crammed into the ale tent, lines of men drinking from stone jugs and crowded three deep at the long oak table where women in aprons pumped hissing liquid into jars. A rich smell of sweet malt hung across the scene, the tables outside thronged and sodden with shining puddles of spilled ale.

As Bill and the Gaffer walked into the scene a great cry went up; one small man in tweeds and a farmer's cap rushed towards the big man bearing two foaming stone jars, which he held out to him.

Bill took one in his huge paw and downed it to more cheers, then he cast the jar away and downed the other, raising his right hand to acknowledge the shouts of admiration from the crowd. More ale was set before him as he lowered himself on a bale before a crowded table. The Gaffer whispered into his ear, and Bill nodded and muttered as the other man walked quickly away to a group of big men in black coats drinking near the tent opening.

By the hedge facing the tent a line of hawkers and pedlars was calling and selling from flat hand trays and little wooden tables before them: pies and penny buns, ribbons and trinkets, smoked fish in paper wrappings, hot potatoes and cups of buttermilk.

The boy stood square in the middle of the sellers, holding the girl up. His hand was planted under her behind and she sat, held aloft at the end of his upstretched arm, still and passive as a statue. He was a big lad, in a yellowed shirt and grubby jerkin, and he called to the drinkers at the tent and the stream of people heading towards the field gate. Some stopped at the strange sight of the muscular youth holding the small dark-haired child high and calling: '. . . she is offered for cleaning and cooking, she can tend and serve horses, she can tend children and bake, she can fetch and carry all manner of things, she is skinny but strong and she is of good old Staffordshire blood . . . She speaks little and cries and complains never, though she is fatherless, and her family is in the direst want with another on the way this winter . . . Her father died of a tragic accident and her poor mother is fading for hunger with no pony nor wagon . . . She is of sweet nature, never wilful, never scornful, and brims with Christian gratitude for good treatment and small kindness . . .'

As he spoke he turned her slowly side to side so the golden afternoon sun caught the child's face and made her black hair gleam like jet.

A black-coated reverend, who had stopped to listen, muttered to his small gaunt wife, 'It is the way of these people.'

The woman shuddered under her bonnet and said, 'It is disgraceful.'

They turned and walked on as the boy continued to call: 'She will not eat much, just plain porridge and bread and clean water is all she needs, and she is of strong stock. Her father was Big Tom Loveridge and some of you will have traded with him and drunk ale with him and we ask . . .'

At his table amid the hoots, guffaws and slopping ale of the crowd, Bill stared across at the girl. As she turned slowly in the sun before him, the noise all around dropped away and there, framed in his one good eye, she sat, ethereal and shining in the amber beams. Her huge dark eyes met his and they locked together – and this time *she* grinned.

5

They let me lead the mare. She was a grey Welsh Cob cross Shire and she knew the path and the towing, and dipped her head under the bridges and went steady. They had her blinkered but she dint need them. She looked on and pulled just right. Walking by her and the smell of her, I felt calm and clear about it all on the first night after Bill Perry got me for six guineas. He bid up on a farmer and Tommy was all smiles it was the Slasher got me. Same blood as us, he said, and a fighting man – Big Tom would be smiling in Heaven. Bill told Tommy I would be with him at Tipton Port and they could come and visit and he laid his big hot hand on my head and breathed out beer. And I never cried when Tommy went off with the money in his purse, running back to Mammy and the others through the crowd and dust.

Bill held me up and I looked in his big ugly face. Nobody but a mother could love that face and I dint either. But there was something in his eye, hard and blue and twinkly, that I saw and I knew it was right: some knowing I had about him and me and where we were going to go. Maybe I could hear Big Tom telling me from Heaven or I could see them babbies full of bread and Mammy leading a new vardo and pony.

The crowd in the beer tent cheered and called when he held me up and shouted, 'Here she is, the daughter, the Slasher's Daughter.'

The Gaffer was kind and careful with me, and he held my hand going back to the barge and told me about the mare and the port we were going back to. 'We'll learn you the barging and Billy's a kind lad – he has a good big heart in him. We'll learn you to love him.'

I liked they had the mare and they put me to tending her, and they made a little straw bed for me in the coal hull at the stove end where it was warm. They got me to fetch sticks for the stove and draw water for the mare, and then the Gaffer showed me how to loop a rope round a post with one flick.

Bill was smiling and happy, sitting at the back by the tiller sipping a jar of ale, and he grinned at me when I went past him fetching stuff. He was filthy and all streaked with blood so I boiled up the kettle and cleaned him down his face and arms and chest with a steaming rag and he smiled all the time, like a big old farm dog baring his pointy teeth. There were stabs and slits and dents on his knuckles and I wrung out the rag time after time trying to get the grit and black out from his hands. Then he put on a shirt and a jerkin and sang a song about a bargey girl who loved a soldier and he died in a war so the girl filled her pinny with stones and drownded herself in the canal.

He was like Big Tom. But Big Tom was handsomer and younger and he had more teeth, and less scars and bumps on him. But he was like Big Tom. Or I felt he was like Big Tom.

The Gaffer brought a pot of faggots from the alehouse and bread off a baker wagon and I ate proper, all the gravy and onions and peas. I wolfed it, and Bill Perry laughed, but I weren't bothered, just happy feeling it all going down into my aching belly.

Bill said, 'We'll get you a dress, little wench. We'll get you ribbons and a Birmingham silver brush for your hair. And some good leather boots.' And he laughed and clapped his hands looking at me. He was so big he blocked all the light from the sun going down.

I reached over for the spoon for more gravy and the last faggot, and the Gaffer said, 'She has grand long arms, Billy. She'd have a good reach for jabbing.'

And Bill laughed and said, 'We shall teach her jabbing and slashing too. She shall be a fury for us.' They were both looking at me like children with a new toy.

On the first night we went north for an hour till the sun started going. And I did a lock with the Gaffer. A lock is a wonder. A pure wonder – the way the rush of water lifts you up level all slow and gentle like a mammy's arm lifting her babby. The way the gates can only shut one way and are held fast by nothing more than water pressing. Then the lovely slow drift of them opening when the level is right. The pony pulls and you float out the same height as the land around. Whoever thought of a lock for lifting a barge was cleverer than a barrel of foxes.

We pulled north for another mile or two till all the sun was gone and the moonshine turned the cut water silver and the Gaffer banged a stake on the path and tied us up. I knocked out a bale of straw for the mare and she lay down in it on the towpath. My legs felt hard and stampy when I jumped off the barge onto the hard ground. Inside the boat they had the stove going and lamps, but I said I was going to stop with the mare on the bankside and Bill said, 'As you will, child.'

I got my blanket and curled up next to the mare's belly where it was warm and she lifted her head and looked down at me like I was her foal.

We come into Tipton Port the next afternoon, me leading and the Gaffer tilling and Bill asleep in the bunk. There were a row of locks up to it and then we come round under two bridges into a big wharf all packed out with boats and on the sides horses and wagons and cartmen. There were wood cranes dangling and sprawling all over the blackwater from storehouses and tents, and gangs of black coalmen lifting baskets and emptying them from a huge tumbling pile that pumped out dust in clouds. On the far side there were lines of nailers banging out glowing nails on anvils, making a clack-clack-clack that echoed over all the shouting and calling; as you got nearer you could hear the tinkle of the steaming nails falling into the baskets. There was an alehouse right there on the towpath, and men and women all sat out on the benches with jars. There were children ragged as me all running and begging. A cobbler stand was selling boots and he was beating nails into a boot on the last. There were two little boys shovelling up the horse dung and building a big old pile up agin the side wall of the alehouse. All was dust and smells and clanging in the black air, and behind there were factory chimneys, round and red brick, piling grey smoke into the sky.

And this was a town. I hant never seen a town fore this look I was having, holding the mare on the pathside while the Gaffer poled the barge round. I weren't sure I wanted to see much more of it neither.

The Gaffer shouted to me and pointed to the start of the cut up to Liverpool and the start of the cut down to Birmingham and then he banged on the roof and called for Bill to waken. 'Tipton Port, Billy. The boozer's open,' he said. He shouted over at me, 'Tek her round the livery over the bridge there, get her fed and bedded. Tell the boy we'll settle with him tomorra.'

I walked the mare over the bridge and took a lane between two high brick walls and then down into the wharf. Going through the crowd there, leading the mare, she was calm and quiet because she knew the place, and then she stamped and pulled over towards a yard that ran out from the wharf where there were stalls. I let her take me in there and the boy looked at me like I was there to rob him.

'Whose is this, gypo? We don't have no gypo ponies in here,' he said.

'She knows she's bedded here, ya cheeky bleeder,' I said. 'She's Bill Perry's mare and she wants feeding. Ye'll get your money tomorra.'

When I said Bill's name he looked at me hard and then took her bridle. He was about twelve and skin and bone with straw-coloured hair and a snotty nose. He said 'gypo' agin fore he led her off.

The Gaffer had the barge tied up by the alehouse and Bill was climbing off, and the crowd were calling to him, some cheering, some cursing, some as had lost money on him waving slips. He walked over towards the alehouse and he was a head high above any bloke there, slow and glaring at them as was cursing him and they soon shut it.

The Gaffer rubbed my head and said, 'Go and sweep the boat out. There's a besom on the side there. Then you shall have some bread and sausage.'

Him and Bill were sat outside the alehouse on the benches and people were coming up to them and talking and giving them jars.

There were no trinkets in the barge, no china or knick-knacks or fancies on the shelfs and black coal dust on everything. In the cursed vardo we had lace and stitched pictures on the shelfs and some blue-and-white china plates and cups that never got used and come across the sea on ships and Big Tom had given them to Mammy when he married her. Me and Mammy were always scrubbing out the vardo and she said gorgers lived filthy in their houses and never polished nor dusted.

The barge was cold and dank and filthy inside and wanted scrubbing, so I set to. I shook the blankets and sheets out, for they were grey and grimed. I got the pail and heated the kettle and found a bar of soap in the cupboard and I put them all in to soak. The hot water made the black and grease lift out of them and float on the top. Then I swept all through the galley and turned the straw mattress out and laid it on top to air. I cleaned the two portholes with vinegar and then I washed down the floor and scrubbed the slate tops and the hearthstone. I cleaned all the dust off the shelfs and found the copper pans and a copper vase all stacked under the bunk. And I scoured them with vinegar and salt. By the alehouse there was a bank where there was still cornflowers and poppies and I ran over and picked three bunches and knocked the coal dust off them, then I scoured off the top of the table and the benches in the galley and then ran to the alehouse.

Gaffer and Bill were fine and smiling with the ale and Bill took me onto his lap and shouted to everyone I was his daughter. 'This here is Annie Perry, my Annie. And great woe will betide any man that wrongs her or treats her bad.' And they all cheered. I asked for pennies for beeswax and linen, and Bill frowned at me and then fished in his pocket and gave me a tanner. So then I knew when he was all warm with ale was the best time to ask him for money.

I ran out the wharf to the market stalls by the huge black church in the little square where there were Romis and pedlars selling lace and stitching and I got four slips of lovely white lace and a block of beeswax. I bought bread and fat and a small side of bacon too.

There was all sorts from all over, and on the stalls and in the lane to the wharf and by the barges you heard all manner of words and talking and voices. You heard Romi and Black Country, and the red-haired Irish talking Irish and scores of big blond Dutch unloading timber and linen bolts and talking in their tongue that sounded like they were hockling up their phlegm, and there was soldier sergeants barking orders and two African black men loading hides onto a flat barge with a steam engine in it puffing out smoke, blathering in their words and shouting and singing. The nail wenches were singing while they clacked out the nails and the coalmen chanting while they shouldered sacks, and from the livery the horses whinnying and stamping, pigs in the slaughter yard screaming like babbies with colic and dogs barking and black crows on the muckpiles cawing. From the alehouse there was a fiddle and pipes and a big Irishman singing like a growling bear. I stood stock-still in the middle of the wharf yard and heard it all going in me and round in my head so I thought I would never hear no peace and quiet again.

At the barge I waxed the table and the benches till they shone and I waxed the cupboard doors and rails that ran along the galley. There was brass sconces for candles on the walls over the table and I cleaned them with vinegar and salt and they shone too; I even cleaned the brass hinges on the door through and the brass lamp. I set a rope line across to a post on the bank, rinsed the sheets and blankets and put them to dry. I laid the clean copper vase full of flowers on the table and I put more flowers in a stone cup on the shelf. Cornflower and poppy drive out sorrow and tears in a vardo or a barge, and I set the lace slips on the shelfs where they glowed white and reminded me of our vardo fore Big Tom died.

And I weren't doing all that just for kindness, but because I had to live on that barge and I wanted it nice and I dint forget the six guineas Bill paid for me and I thought it was fair dos to him to get his money's worth now Mammy would have her new vardo and pony. I thought of her and Tommy when I looked on the flowers there, smiling in the gloom of that barge.

Then I heard a row over from the alehouse. I climbed out the barge and watched, sitting up on the roof of the galley. Bill was up on his feet before a crowd of men, some big fellas and some little weasely men, all in leather jerkins and shouting and pointing, and one of them was laid out flat on the cobbles with a great crack in his head where he'd been slashed.

Bill was shouting, 'Curse and damn you, clamming Irish . . . curse and damn you all.'

The Gaffer was trying to hold him back from behind and other men were crowding behind him, and two women were squaring up too, one pulling her shawl off and nodding at the other woman, who was a big fat bride, shouting and cursing the other. The land-lord was stood in the middle of them all in his apron and bowler hat shouting, 'Call the constable! Call the constable!'

I just sat there watching it all like it was a show. One man had grabbed Bill now and the Gaffer and the men behind had got hold of him and then more men from the Irish were fastened onto them and they were all rolling and boiling like a ball of rats round a carcass, lurching this way and that, and tables and benches going over and ale jugs shattering. The big fat wench was swinging at the other woman, who had stripped to her stays and shift and was stood like a proper fighter, chin in and left out and right tucked up over her face, and she was bobbing. The fat wench was just swinging at her, not looking where her fists were going and her chin was out and up proud. The smaller woman jab-jabbed her twice with her left and caught her above the eye and it split and the fat wench shook her head away, standing flat and not moving, so the small wench stepped in and had her right under the chin with her right fist. Her head cracked back and she went down with a slap onto the cobbles.

I'd never seen a woman fight. Big Tom told me they did it in London but fisticuffs was for men and no good wench would strip to her bloomers and go a bout. He said women who fought were the roughest old gorgers and whores an all.

But he never saw the wench outside that alehouse and her face so full of joy when she decked the big girl. She had her hands up like a fighter, and the men not scrapping in a pile with Bill and the Gaffer all clapped her, and she was beaming and bowing. She was a young un too. And pretty an all, glowing in her white shift, and her limbs were long and strong and lithe as a proper-bred filly. She was fair-haired and had good white teeth – you saw them for she was laughing and dancing – and I liked the look of her.

The constables came tearing in with staves and started knocking everyone about and pushing the Irish crowd down away from the alehouse, and in all the fury and flummel of arms and legs and men rolling about in the dust I saw Bill Perry stand up straight in the middle of it all and down a jug he somehow hadn't spilled, and he handed off a constable who come up to him and held the lad by his head while he finished his ale and then he roared, 'I'm the champion of England and no man can gainsay that . . .' Then a constable clouted him hard on the back of his head with a stave and he went down.

I stayed right there, sitting on the barge top. The landlord was righting the tables and cursing and Bill and the Gaffer came crawling out of the crowd with Bill's head streaming blood, but he was laughing and singing and he still had a jar in his hand. There was boys scrabbling in around the tables for dropped pennies and someone dragged the fat woman away and slapped her back awake.

Bill now had his arm round the fair wench's shoulder and he was whispering in her ear and she was screaming with laughter and the Gaffer was paying coins over to the landlord, probably for all the busted jugs and tables and benches and also for Bill's ale.

Bill saw me then, perched up on the barge, and he waved and called and came over with his big arm still about the fair wench.

He was all clarted up with dust and blood and ale, filthy as a runt piglet.

He held out his arms and said, 'Annie, my Annie – did you see yer Bill? Did you see me tek em all? This here is Janey Mee, the best fighting nail wench in Tipton, aint she a beauty? See the little Romi, Janey? She's me daughter, me only daughter who I love, aint she a dazzler?'

I said, 'I've scrubbed this barge, Bill Perry, and you'll not come on here till you're proper washed. You'll not bleed all over or bring your dust and filth in here now . . .'

For a moment he was stunned, and then he let out a huge whoop and the fair wench clapped her hands and hollered, 'She's got you, Bill Perry, she's got you!'

And Bill was laughing too and going, 'Oh, right you are, madam, right you are!'

The Gaffer come over then and I told him the same and he nodded and said, 'The wench has cleaned it all for you, Bill. Come to the pump and wash.'

Janey Mee stepped up to the barge and leaned on it and grinned at me. She said, 'There's only me and you in Tipton not scared of him.'

Oh, she was a fair beauty close up; she had eyes as blue as an April sky and under the dust on her skin she was fair and white smooth. She was still smiling, and over by the pump I could see Bill stripped to his waist getting a bucket flung over him by the Gaffer.

Janey said, 'Can I come on, little Annie?'

And I said she could and we went down into the galley and I put the kettle on the stove for tea.

6

There was three forges just up from us, and across the cut the ironworks where they rolled sheets and steam-hammered square lengths all night long. The furnace in there made the sky orange all night and fat sparks danced up in the steam and curled and fell like they was the shed leaves of a white-hot iron tree. There was no peace never and no clean air; it was always black with smuts and filth and billowing iron steam. The foundries pouring and boiling the iron night and day, and white lines glowing from the moulds and the casts and men calling and screaming. There was no dawn and no night there, and no birds sang when the red sun rose each day as blurred and hazy as a flame through muslin.

Most wenches worked the mine, and little uns too; and though the law was none under ten could go underground, I knew plenty that did. And plenty loading barges with coal and barrowing spoil.

The nailers kept it up clacking all night if they were on an order and had to fill baskets for the foggers who gave the orders and paid them. The nailmasters sent the foggers round the nail shops with rods for making nails and the foggers said how many they wanted and what they were paying for a load.

And God help the fogger who had to tell Janey Mee and Hammer Jack they was getting less a load when he come to count. Janey and Hammer run their forge together like a man and a wife but they weren't married and they had no babbies. Plenty younger than me worked in all the forges, some hammering and shaping and some fetching iron into the fire with tongs or hauling nail baskets to the barges in twos.

I told Bill I weren't never going in a forge and I weren't never going in a mine and he said, 'And you never shall, my angel, my sweet Romi princess.'

He said the alehouse would give us a living and he'd be the guvnor and I'd be the lady of the house and serve ale and make faggots and bread. The Gaffer had three barges on the cut by us and he lodged with us when he wasn't taking a load up to Liverpool or down to Bristol or over to Birmingham to load trains going to London and then onto ships bound for all the wide Empire and India too.

The Gaffer said the ships in Liverpool took nails and iron to America where there was thousands of African slaves and the rich men lived in white stone houses bigger than the ironworks, and where if you went west from New York the land and woods and big wide rivers never ended. He brung me a globe from Liverpool, the most beautiful thing I had ever seen, and said he traded it from an Irishman off a steamship. It was bigger than my head and it spun slow and all the countries were different colours and the seas were pale blue and the mountains were brown. The Gaffer said it come from Austria and he could read a bit too so he found the word for Austria, and it was a big island coloured pink at the bottom of the globe.

I wished I could read then. I wanted to read the names of the countries where they were written in thin black letters that curled like the black hairs on Bill's arms.

Bill called the alehouse The Champion of England and he paid three guineas for a sign with the words in gold and a painting of him in his britches stanced ready for a row. It hung up over the door into the parlour where there was a big oak bar and proper seats and fancy cut-glass panels. There was brass lamps I had to polish and clean and the floor was flagged with grey stone that dint show all the dirt, and there was a lot of dirt, so I just swept that out and I scrubbed the step once a week. There was a caskroom where we kept the ale and a scullery at the back where we had a sink and a tap with clean water that run from a main pipe in the road. We had a stove in the scullery, a nice big black iron one where I boiled the water and made stew and faggots. There was a lavvy out the back in the shed that always had men trooping in and out all night when the boozer was open, although some of them just pissed in the canal.

I had a little room upstairs with a proper box bed and a dresser with a mirror, and I kept my globe in it and the hairbrush Bill give me at Christmas and three dresses, two for working and a white pinny dress for best. I kept a sack over the pinny for everything in that place got grey with smuts and burnings; you never opened a window even in summer for the drift of black dust from the foundries and the forges.

And I had boots an all, nice soft leather ones the Gaffer brung from Birmingham, where they have shops selling shoes and dresses and silver wares and crockery. I only wore the boots for special days like going to the fair on Tipton Heath or if there was a bout fought in the yard at the back and everyone from all over came.

At night when I lay in my bed and listened to the clang and wallop from the foundries and watched that never-setting orange sun glowing I thought about Mammy and Big Tom and the other Loveridges. I wondered if they would come like they said and fetch me away. But the days passed one after another and they never. At the start, I was sad and longing for them and the road and hedges. There was no spring campion nor May blossom in Tipton. There was no still nights of foxes coughing and owls shrieking, no skylark watery warbling like a happy spirit on hot summer noons. No morning song from the tits and thrushes or chatter from sparrows nor yellowhammers calling for bread and no butter.

But the days passed and months went by and soon a year and then another, and days and nights vanished where all around was coal and dust and clanging.

Me and Bill rowed all the time and I mostly won. I could floor him with a glowering look and if I frowned long enough he'd give in and if I refused to kiss him for sorry he even cried. He was a big babby man was Bill, and I was never feared of him and he never raised his hand to me in all the years I was his daughter. Sometimes I'd give him a gypsy-curse look and he shuddered and yelped and crossed himself. If I came in the bar room where he was gathered with all his mates downing their ale they'd all shout, 'Look lively, Billy, here comes the guvnor!'

And having Bill Perry as my daddy started me with fisticuffs. As I come up past twelve I got long and supple like a pure-bred yearling.

And then, the summer I was thirteen, I got set upon by five slogger lads under the bridges on the way to the market with a basket.

They were idling there under the new bridges for the trainway where the sun never got and the walls were green and dripping. And as I come along on that sunny Saturday morning they were smoking their pipes and scuffing stones into the canal with their caps pushed back and their thumbs hooked down by their fancy brass belt buckles. They wore sailor's trousers with wide bottoms and nailed boots.

And as I come up and saw them and they saw me I thought about climbing up the bank and going along the road between the forges and not going on down there into the dark dip where they were. Five of them turning their heads to look up and the big lad nodding and grinning.

But then I thought about Big Tom and I thought about the knowing I had about where things are going. There was a smut-blacked gull circling over and it screed out into the air and somewhere I was hearing this was a lesson I was going to learn. My legs felt wobbly and I wanted to piss. Some voice out of somewhere was telling me to stop and turn to them and learn something I needed to know in the sharp shadows under them bridges.

The big lad, he was about fifteen, spat and shouted up at me, 'You're not coming this way, ya dirty Rumney, this is our path and our patch.'

Then another one, a long skinny thing, pulled out a barber's strop from his belt and started slapping it on his hand, then they all started walking up fast towards me.

'You come here, you filthy little gypo bitch. Your mother was a bitch and yer father was a scabby rob dog,' the big lad called, looking like the Devil with his cap pushed back and his black teeth grinning.

The little mouthy one, who had a stripy shirt and red braces, started screaming, 'Come on, diddy, diddy, didicoy, black didicoy!'

I froze then, with terror, and a slow voice in my head was saying *don't run*, same time as my heart and my legs and my skin was bursting to turn tail and leg it. Then they were on me.

'Strop the gypo!' the little one screamed, and I saw the blur of the strop and the grey skin of the skinny bastard's arm and a swoosh and a great clattering smack to my jaw and a burning sting like a hundred jaspers, and the big one's hands on my shoulder and the little bastard hauling on my hair and trying to pull me over. And I stumbled and slid on the grit, and fell back rasping and gagging and flailing, casting the basket away, going down on the stones and ripping the skin off my thigh – and then the boots come.

Black nail boots whacking and white flashes with each black clout.

So here is what I learned then.

The world slows down when you taste your own hot blood and feel the daylight bursting in behind your eyes inside the dark of your head. The thoughts slow down and you lift away and look down and see the tops of their heads, the crown buttons in their caps, the puffs of dust as their feet swing at your head and your belly. And you see yourself shudder and bend like a raggy doll. And their voices sound like echoes down a tunnel. And you feel jolts but no pain. No stinging or burning. You feel calm and you remember their faces, the colour and check of their caps, the names they are shouting. The skinny one's braces were purple like loose-strife and he had a scar on the back of his neck.

'Do her, Tanner . . . Mikey, stamp the little bitch . . . oh yes, oh yes, there's her arse . . . do the Romi whore, Turner . . .'

Then you come back down and the heat and the wet of sweat and blood and piss and snot gushes over you.

And I was screaming and there was fire and poison inside me. The big one stepped back and then bent and held a leather knife in front of my eyes. His fingers were black and his nails were split and scaffed on the handle.

'Next time you'll get this, see, wench? You'll get this in your belly and up your cocktrap, got it?'

The others laughed and the skinny one was pulling the pennies out of my pinny pocket and he said, 'Ha! Cocktrap! Cocktrap! . . . Good one, Billy Sticks!'

The basket was in the canal, floating and twirling in the sunshine. The big lad stood back and I remembered his face proper, his small

49

puffy eyes and his rat nose and fluffy 'tache. Billy Sticks. And Turner and Mikey and the skinny one was Tanner and the little one with all the cantin was Jackboy.

And I never told Bill about the sloggers but I told Janey Mee. If I told Bill he would have started a war worse than Napoleon. He would have gone down the lane and round the backyards and front steps till he found them and clobbered down every door in Tipton and then knocked their heads off for them. And Bill caused enough trouble and brought enough strife into our alehouse without battling sloggers all over Tipton.

And I dint want Bill doing it. So I covered the bruises and I kept out of Bill's way for a day or two. I had enough of the knowing now to know it was all meant any road.

There were five of them like the points on a star and they come from under a bridge, a crossing of water, and the night after it I started my monthlies. So I knew this was a calling from Big Tom in Heaven, and if you can't learn to fight you can't learn to live.

Janey was beautiful, and her arms were shapely with beating nails out in her forge with Hammer Jack. She was taller than Jack and she ruled him rotten. Janey could drink ale with the men, she'd clout anyone who grabbed her behind which was round and stuck out, and her bosom was full – and I thought she was the most beautiful woman on God's green earth though I never saw her in a pretty dress nor lace nor a bonnet with flowers in it. The Gaffer said she was more beautiful than Helen of Troy but I dint know who she was neither.

I told her about them sloggers and the monthlies and knowing it was all a sign from Big Tom in Heaven and she said, 'I'll learn you fisty and then we'll go and get em. A wench is only safe in this life if she takes her revenge and everybody knows it.'

So Janey started the training in the backyard of the boozer while

Hammer Jack and Bill and the Gaffer and the lads from the forges and the wenches from the mines drank ale and sang and cursed inside.

We were out there night after night, and Sunday afternoons when everyone else was snoozing off the ale from dinnertime. Janey said she got learned by the Slasher and now she would learn me.

First she taught me how to stand, side on, chin in, then she showed me how to push off me foot when I swung, how to twist from the waist on some shots and roll from the shoulder on others. How to jab and snap back to split the skin and how to bend and defend with two fists.

'Fisty is all side on,' she said, bouncing in front of me, her gold hair pulsing out from her lovely face like the leaves of a willow fore a rainstorm. 'Ask Bill and he'll tell you the way you win is don't get hit and fool em when you hit em . . .' She made her shoulder drop on the left so as you thought she was throwing, then she jabbed with the right and you never saw it coming.

She only clipped me when we were training, open hands, and I had to dodge and step back and hold and fake so as she never touched me. She taught me to watch the space either side of her waist so as to see if her elbow was going to go straight: if it was she was throwing, if it stayed bent she was faking.

Fighting is all about watching and reading and knowing where they are gonna go next. It's about seeing where the space is before they fill it: the size of the space tells you how they are gonna fill it up with a shot. It is about hearing their breathing: in when they pull back, out when they let go.

Janey got me hitting a sack stuffed with oakum she propped up on the back wall and she had me skip round with a rope while she jabbed at me. She had me moving and she made me parry and low block and high block and slip. She learned me how to duck both ways and come back out with an uppercut, how to step in and push back, how to punch through and snap back.

But most of all she taught me how to read a move and see where it was going to lead.

I got clouted proper about once a night by her and I learned how to tek it. I got hit when I read wrong. When I dint cover my side when she stepped side and swung round I got one in the kidney and it stung like buggery.

We was out there while they were all drinking. The summer was hot and the nights were short and the air got thick and brown with smuts and vapours from the works; you had the tang of coke and burned oil in your throat. That summer I got long and strong. I wore my hair up under a cap and wore britches and flat pumps when I was doing fisty with Janey. She puffed us out every night, skipping with a clothes line and squatting and jumping up till I ached and cracked. She threw water buckets over us when I was steaming to get me used to shocks and not lose concentration on moving and reading. She showed me how to punch in notes, like little tunes of music and how to sing them as I did them: one-two-three, two-two-one, one-two-one, three-one-three-one . . .

She sang a song called 'The Barge Girl's Dandy' and clapped the one-one-one-two-two-two rhythm while I punched the bag.

I learned fisty with Janey Mee all that year, and one night Bill and the Gaffer come out and watched us. He had three Chartist men up from Wales with him. They were touring and lecturing and talking about strikes and votes for working men.

He just stood there with his ale watching. We had a lantern out with us for it was November and he was shadowed in the gloom by the back wall there with the Gaffer and the Chartists all smiling.

Bill said, 'See yer learning, Annie. Trying to be like old Bill, are ye?'

52

The Gaffer said, 'This is not a sport for wenches, Annie. It's not for wenches to learn. Have a care for the child, Janey, learnin her fisty . . .'

I showed some blows to them, a one-two-two-two-one and finished with an uppercut and Bill laughed, 'What are you peggin, girly? You shall niver fight in a ring long as I'm your father.'

Janey was sat on a bale by the yard gate and she called over to Bill, 'She could clip you, Bill. She's faster and sharper 'n any man in there.'

'She'd not clip me if she tried, Janey Mee, ya cheeky baggage. But she would not try for I would never stand square to a woman nor raise me hand to one, as you well know, though your mouth would well warrant it sometimes.'

The Chartist men were laughing, and a stout one with a huge black beard stepped forward and said, 'We need fit, strong young women for the cause, Mr Perry – young women who are not afraid to show their bloomers for our cause.'

The men all laughed, and Bill caught his arm around me and pulled me in and gave me a big hug like he did when he was full of ale. And then he took the beardy bloke by both his lapels and held him high up with one arm. And he said, 'This one is not showing her bloomers to no man, Mr Peak, cause or not.' Then he dropped him.

In the winter the nailers went on strike because the orders fell off and them as they got were two pennies less. The nailers were starving and begging bread all over Tipton, and the Chartists and radicals were calling for strikes. They wanted the mines out too and the foundrymen to all march to the iron-master's house and demand work and fair pay. The radicals were all over in those weeks when the weather turned bitter and the canals froze up, handing out bills and leaflets with writing on and standing up outside the works hall in town and calling for strikes and marches.

The night all the nailers and forgemen gathered to march up the hill to the ironmaster's house, Janey come and got me. She said, 'Come on with us, Annie. Them sloggers are in that crowd thieving and robbing pockets. We'll go and give em what for.'

Bill stayed at the Champion with the Gaffer, and me and Janey walked down to the square where the men was all gathering up outside the new Railway Hotel. There were hundreds and hundreds, some holding pitch torches, and some nailers had their hammers and tongs and they waved them and shouted for more pay. Mr Peak the Chartist was stood on a box calling out to all. There were nail wenches and women from the mines all stood arm in arm in long lines chanting and kicking. Some of the miners fired off charges of powder from muskets, and cones of orange sparks were shooting up over the crowd and sweet smoke puffs billowed across to me and Janey, stood at the back close into the gates of the livery yard.

And then I seen him. Billy Sticks, bigger and brawnier than that Saturday by the cut, hanging back behind the crowd, slouching in the alley mouth next to the King's Head, and the only big oil lamp in the square showing him all lit up and orange. He was hunched over agin the cold, sneaking glares and no-good looks over the backs of the women. His checked cap was the same one he had when he stropped us, but it looked smaller on his bigger head and he wore a full white kerchief round his neck.

Next thing I knew, Janey was by me and I said, 'That's him.' And she nodded.

The crowd roared and shook their torches up and down, and there was much trampling and dampling as they all turned and spilled out towards the Wolverhampton Road, chanting and singing and waving hammers and tongs into the frigid air.

7

Bill Perry said nothing about the clouds that began to fog his vision in the winter of '42. He felt he was peering through steam some days, and when he shook his head tiny white lights bloomed in front of his eyes.

But he said nothing. He carried on pouring ale and sweeping out the bar and listening to the blather of the men who crowded in most nights. During the strike he let each man have four jugs on tick, but he never wrote their names down and most had a few more than that at his expense. A working man needs his ale.

By seven most evenings he felt warm and loose and comfortable the way only a bellyful of strong Staffordshire ale could make you feel and he never fretted on the dwindling funds in the lockbox where he kept the takings. And he swore his vision cleared and got sharper after seven or so jugs of the warm sharp ale he pumped from the brewery barrels. But each day, as the strike went on and the bitter weather worsened and the cut froze, his sight was fogging and shifting. There was often a bleaching of the colour from any scene he looked on, even on a cold, sharp, brilliant morning when white hoar frost frilled the brick walls and dark cobbles of the port.

There were many lads, and some wenches too, who would care to challenge Bill Perry if they knew he was blinded and weakened. As it was, foggy eyes or not, he still belted someone at least once a week, them as were mouthing and disrespecting, them that spoke wrong or looked with lust on his beloved Annie, them that said they had no fear of the Slasher and the Champion of England. There were always them that needed a straight hiding.

He had fines too, eating into the pile of notes and coins in his lockbox. Constables and magistrates served summonses on him for assault and disorderly conduct, for raising riot in a public place, for serving ale outside hours.

The ironmasters and the pit bosses took on lads from Bilston workhouse, signed them in as apprentices and set them to working full man's hours while the strikers starved and gathered outside the Railway Hotel to listen to the radicals from Wales.

And while it was going on the Champion was taking less and less; some days they sold nothing, only gave away bread and ale to starving miners and nailers.

The nailmasters and foggers wouldn't budge on the pay for a load. One fogger who came in the Champion told Bill there were nails and iron rods coming in from Belgium for half the price they were charging. 'They are gonna get nowt if they stay out, only starving and the workhouse,' he said.

Bill thought he was a hard bastard, with his full, fat belly and his bowler hat. While he was stood at the bar downing his ale, no other man or woman would stand with the fogger no matter how many ales he offered to buy. But he paid in good hard coin and that night it was the only proper money Bill took.

The fogger's name was Arthur Tinsley, and he worked for a nailmaster in Bromsgrove, buying and shipping the nails and selling the iron rods to the nailers. The women hated him. They said he offered free rods for a feel up their bloomers.

Somehow they limped on that winter while little Annie trained out the back with Janey Mee. And Bill dint mind the little wench learning a bit of fisty – she'd never fight proper nor challenge for a title these days. He remembered women fighting in London when he was a young un, great lumps of things they were, stripped to their petticoats and hair flying. In one alehouse he saw the famous Jack and Dina McGinley do a show bout against each other while the fine gentlemen watched and cheered and wagered. And them as bet on Jack lost. Billy had his money on first blood, and it was Jack, big lad as he was, who caught a sharp cutting right from his missus that opened up a fine weeping wound across his brow.

He was glad he was not a working man like his angry crook-backed father. He had got everything he had with his fists and his wits, and he swore his Annie would never hit an anvil nor go underground so long as he was her father.

As she grew he loved her more and more. She bloomed from the moody dark-haired child, giving curse looks and muttering gypsy spells, into a fine long woman, her black hair pulled back with a simple black ribbon, and slender limbs that moved with a grace and elegance that made tears spring into Bill's foggy eyes. Her skin was the colour of honey and her black eyes drove men into silence.

The night the Chartists came to the port during the strike they led a march to the houses of the Batch brothers of Batch Brothers Foundry and then on to Ardleigh where Sir Andrew Wilson-Mackenzie, MP and mine owner, lived.

And somewhere outside the barred gates of Ardleigh on that damp foggy night the Riot Act of 1714 was read by the captain of a regiment of dragoons before the hundreds of miners and nailers and foundrymen were charged. The horses tore through the crowd and the dragoons slashed with their sabres. Men and women fell and were trampled; amid the screams and fury many climbed the walls of the lane and fled across the fields. After the first charge the regiment regrouped and cantered back through the decimated crowd, cutting down those fleeing and sabering the floundering wounded.

Sir Andrew watched from his horse, safe behind the gates of Ardleigh.

There were many casualties, and groups of miners ran back to the port to fetch stretchers and boards to fetch those unable to walk. The rest of the crowd scattered, fearing another charge.

Two men lay motionless on the road as the sound of the hooves of the dragoons faded away into the dark and the captain reported to Sir Andrew through the iron gates of Ardleigh.

One was a Welsh Chartist named Owen Hewson and the other was Hammer Jack, who lay spread-eagled in the centre of the road, his long-handled forge hammer still in his grip and a gaping split in the back of his head where the white of his broken skull shone.

8

In the alley Janey hauled him back away from the crowd and he stumbled and I went, 'All right, Billy Sticks – remember me?'

He was not so skinny now, and his teeth were nearly all gone black. His head knocked back on the red brick and he said, 'What the bleedin hell?'

It was gentlemanly and all for decorum to wait till he was ready and his fists up and him stanced proper, but I saw his hand going down to his waist for his knife and I never said no more. I just give him the left hard and straight into his jaw, and then a nasty sharp jab at his forehead, and it split and blood shot out back onto my hand. I had no bindings and it was just bare fist and I had them held just off, tight clenched like Janey showed me, to take the blow and not shatter my hand bone, but I punched through and his head went wobbly as an hour-old foal.

It is a fine feeling, that. To feel the sudden flare of a blow landing and the man's head give like a wall stone dislodging.

He doubled over with a 'fucking bitch', and I stood over him to hit down into his head, but just then I saw Janey shake her head: hitting when he was doubled was like hitting when he was down and she wouldn't have that.

I'd have had that. Mind, he was a big lad and I skipped back from him a pace as he straightened himself up, and he was nearly a head over me and he got his fists up, one holding his crook knife, and he stared in my eyes and went, 'You're Bill Perry's little gypo bitch, aint ye?'

I was all tensed and brimming with fizz and I went 'yep' and stepped to the side of him and got him in the low gut with another right and then uppercut him with the left as he doubled down on it. I was watching and reading the whole time. He still had that knife and he started moving away from the wall. His mouth was open and I could smell his rotten teeth as he lurched onto me, pushing at me with his big shoulders. I knew he was trying to get us with the knife and I managed to push him out from me and duck under and he skittered away across the alley. Turning, I got him again on the back of his head and I felt my knuckles smack into his hair and hard skull bone.

He was too big and steady to knock over with a blow. He pushed back off the wall, grinning and slashing out behind him and in front of him with the knife.

Janey shouted, 'Watch him, Annie!' She was stood back against the wall and she'd got her clay pipe out and was tamping her baccy into the white bowl. She said quietly, 'Watch the knife, Annie. The fucker's trying to stab you.'

I felt good though. I felt light and skippy, like an invisible hand was lifting me and guiding me along, around and about him. My first proper bout and him with a knife an all and me skipping and floating out around him and waiting till he slashed so hard he turned his head away from me and then I got him, a one and two to the side of his big ugly head. Drips of blood were flecking all over.

And I liked the blood and the force of him ebbing out the holes I knocked in him. I hopped and glided about him, like a crow pecking at the eyes of a new lamb.

And this was my first proper fisty and agin a lad an all. I wished Bill had been there to see it.

Billy Sticks suddenly pushed himself out from the wall again and come at me both hands out. He dropped the knife and it clattered away down the drain in the cobbles. And with that sound, I must've looked down and dropped my fists for a second, and then he had me by the throat agin the wall, squeezing his bony black thumbs into my windpipe, going, 'You bitch . . . fucking die . . .'

Things was going black and shafts of popping yellow lights were bursting in my head and his stinking breath was filling my mouth. His face was going white and I felt the blood erupt from out my nose and his squeezing and grunting. And his pushing and pushing, in and in and in, and my arms were limp at my side like dead, hung hens.

And I seen all of it then. I seen all of it – the throttling and the gagging as I was – in a gold light gilding the black edges as I fell.

I seen my Big Tom toppling over in the rain and my mammy waving me off and saying 'five guineas' and Bill supping the stew on the boat and the Gaffer and the globe and the sparks and glow of the forges and my Birmingham silver hairbrush.

And I seen my Tommy running, clattering on cobbles shining silver, wet from rain, and two men behind him, shoving and pushing through a crowd, and him holding a little black pistol. Mammy weeping and holding little Mercy in a child shroud.

And then, just as I was about to go down into a sweet silver sleep, there was a good big thunk!

A smack and a crunch like the sound of a spade rasping into gravel, and Billy Sticks dropped before my eyes. A great fountain of blood shot out from the back of his head where Janey was prising away the cobble she had in both bloody hands. He fell like a full coal sack and lay still and heavy as a shot horse.

'Oh, holy Jesus,' Janey said. But she was smiling and she put her hand out and held my cheek. 'You did him good, little Annie.'

She always called us little Annie, though by then I was taller than her.

We ran and left Billy Sticks in the alley twixt the alehouse and the stable yard. We ran back through the wet streets all strewn with handbills where the crowd had been, lighted torches smouldering and horse shit everywhere, but the street was quiet and nobody saw us running down past the livery and ironworks back along the cut to the Champion.

I never thought nor worried about Billy Sticks nor if Janey had killed him. I dint care and I dint fear no demons after me for a murderer, only I had in my mind the pictures of Mammy and Big Tom and Tommy and the babbies I seen when I was woozing in and out of that gold and white light when Billy Sticks was strangling me.

9

Many miners ended up in the new Bilston workhouse. Families unable to pay rent during the strike were declared on the parish and began the sad walk away from the port to the new red brick building on the Wolverhampton Road that stood in wide lawns and whose buildings were laid out in the shape of a cross.

Annie watched scores of ragged children trudging up the long hill, strung out behind their parents. She was reminded of her wanderings with Mammy and the little uns in the days after Big Tom died. She had heard nothing of them in the years she had been with Bill at the alehouse.

The Gaffer said, 'Bloody marvellous,' when the strikers finally went back. Beaten and demoralised, they returned to the nail shops, mines and foundries with neither the pay rise nor the cut in hours they had demanded. The Gaffer started moving loads of nails, coal and iron on his barge once again.

Bill Perry was paid two shillings and sixpence for the use of his yard to store the bodies of Owen Hewson and Hammer Jack until the inquest, then another seven and six for the use of The Champion of England when the coroners called the hearing that took place over two days. The witnesses at the inquest were paid two shillings each for their testimony. The doctor who examined the bodies and pronounced their deaths due to extensive and deep head wounds caused by sabre or sword blows was paid five shillings.

The coroner sat without a jury, but with two magistrates to

hear the evidence. One of the magistrates was Sir Andrew Wilson-Mackenzie.

The court recorded a verdict of lawful killing under the terms of the 1714 Riot Act and noted that both the deceased were in active contravention of the act at the time of their demise. The findings were sent to the King's Bench in Birmingham to be kept on record.

When not hauling nails to Liverpool the Gaffer said he would teach Annie how to read, and on one trip back he brought a book for her called *The Eclectic First Child's Reading Primer*; it had an engraving of a tiny curly-haired child in a pinafore sitting under an apple tree on the front.

The Gaffer told her he got it in Manchester and it cost him ninepence. Annie spent hours copying and sounding the letters at a small table in the corner of the Champion. First she traced each letter with her finger and uttered the sound the Gaffer told her it made. Then she started to copy them onto a slate with chalk and say the sound.

Bill laughed at Annie as she sat reading in the corner; he'd call to the men drinking ale about him, 'Reading now . . . if you please . . . there's a rare sight for your eyes, gentlemen – a gypsy wench book-reading.'

One man said, 'Well, she's prettier 'n you, Billy, and now she's gonna be cleverer an all.'

Another man said, 'Wouldn't take much.'

And Annie kept on; in only a few days she could recite the entire alphabet.

The lads apprenticed to the mines and the foundry from the workhouse were not welcome in the Champion, and Bill would turf them out if they came in wanting ale. They were mostly babbies anyway and had broken the strike at the mine when grown men lost their jobs and were put on the parish. Bill also barred the Chartists and radicals who still flocked into Tipton looking to organise strikes and marches, and he would knock down any man he heard showing disrespect to the Queen. He paid two guineas for an engraving of the young Queen, which he hung over the fireplace in the front bar and used as an excuse to start a ruction if he heard foul language anywhere near it. Many was the nailer hurled bodily through the front door for using salty language before the Queen.

The one person whose foul language and radical views were tolerated was Janey Mee. Janey was at the alehouse a lot. In the days after Hammer Jack got killed by the dragoons she sat at the bar beneath the big brass oil lamp drinking ale and crying. Bill cuddled her and they sometimes sang songs about broken hearts and faded roses and shrouds. He grew more and more attached to Janey in the months after Hammer Jack's death. She was still the only person in Tipton who was not frightened of him, and the two of them drank and sang and fought together most nights. Janey, for all her foul mouth and burn-scarred hands, was a lady as far as Bill was concerned and she was devoted to Annie, who she still coached and trained in the backyard on summer evenings.

In October, after the nights began to turn short, the fogger Arthur Tinsley was robbed and shot as he made his way on his horse away from the port. Whoever rolled him got away with the satchel of coins he had taken from the nailers for the iron rods he supplied. The robber, who Tinsley said was a dark lad in a black cape, took his pony too and galloped away up the hill through the woods towards Bilston. The wounded fogger staggered into the Champion clutching his blast-blackened shoulder, shouting, 'I've been rolled and shot! He's had all the chink and me nag!'

They settled him on a seat and brought him ale while a lad ran to fetch the doctor and the constable.

When the constables came Tinsley bellowed for a hue and cry to apprehend the robber. 'He was a young lad, a dark lad, dark like a Rumney, and he come straight out of the wood and shot us!' The robber would not be far away. But the assembled drinkers in the bar felt no need to run down the man who had taken the nailmaster's money and the hated fogger's pony.

The two constables walked back up the road towards the woods and saw the hoof prints of the pony leading away from the scene and the patch of blood in the dust where Tinsley had fallen bleeding from his mount.

Bill and Janey boiled salted water and bathed and dressed the angry wound on the fogger's shoulder. Annie sat watching from her table in the corner and spelled and sounded out the word 'shot' on her slate.

Nothing much was done to find the robber but two weeks later another fogger was robbed in the early morning coming through the woods. The robbery was much the same. The man was shot from his horse by a man who burst from the trees in a billowing black cape and tricorn hat pulled low over his face. Again the fogger was shot in the shoulder and the purse of coins and notes that hung from his saddle was snatched. The robber said nothing, only kicked the wounded man down into the roadside ditch before mounting his horse and riding away.

The stolen purse carried the weekly wages and payments for the nailers who worked for a Harold Stout, a nailmaster in Birmingham who sent his fogger weekly to count the loads and make payments.

This time a hue and cry did go up when the nailers found there was no coin to pay them for the week. A dozen men and women took to the road, banging tongs and hammers, with the constables shouting and calling, and went past the spot in the trees where the fogger was shot and up onto the heath where they scattered along the pathways looking for hoof prints. They found the pony unsaddled and bridled on the far side of the heath, gently clipping at the long, dry grass. Whoever had abandoned him had vanished into the trees and scrub that ran down towards Bilston where the factories and forges were already pumping steam and smoke and sparks into the autumn morning air.

The hunt for whoever had robbed the two foggers was scaled down. On a freezing night just before Christmas, as the puddles in the road began to ice over, Sir Andrew Wilson-Mackenzie and his wife Lady Agnes were returning to Ardleigh when a man bearing two pistols sprang from the hedges on the Wolverhampton Road and shot the standing footman from the back of the two-horse hackney.

The robber, this time wearing a kerchief across his face, caught the horse's reins and pointed a cocked pistol into the driver's face saying, 'Stay calm, my lad – it's a robbery.' He ordered the driver down from his post and to lie flat on the ground then opened the carriage door and said, 'Good evening and a happy Christmas to your lordship and ladyship. Now kindly hand me your purses and your ladyship's jewels.'

In the dim light of the carriage lamps Sir Andrew could see the man was young with dark eyes, and he recognised the accent as pure Black Country. Lady Agnes burst into tears and called, 'Do not kill us, sir!'

Sir Andrew too was terrified as the man stretched his open hand into the carriage to receive the purses and the fine diamond necklace Lady Agnes was hastily removing from beneath her cape. The man's hands were long with slim womanly fingers, and a bracelet of red ribbon encircled his wrist. In his other hand he held the fearsome pistol whose gaping muzzle seemed to Sir Andrew to be the very entrance to the mouth of Hell.

Sir Andrew called to the footman, 'Donald, are you killed?'

The robber, backing away from the carriage door, whispered, ''Tis a small ball scratch to his shoulder, your lordship. Your miners suffer worse from coal shards every day.'

The footman, who lay prone on the icy road, cried out, 'I am hurt, sir, I am hurt!'

The robber took both lamps from the carriage and ran into the wood, leaving the carriage in pitch darkness. Sir Andrew shouted to the driver, 'Follow him, man! He has the lamps!'

But the terrified driver remained on the ground, thinking, he has a charged pistol he has not yet discharged, and replied, 'I am hurt too, sir. My ankle is twisted beneath me.'

From the carriage window Lady Agnes watched the bobbing yellow glow of the lamps grow smaller and dimmer as the robber escaped into the woods, those last few acres around Ardleigh that had not been felled for pit props.

Sir Andrew sat in the cold dark of the carriage, muttering, 'He shall hang . . . He shall hang for this . . .'

Within days handbills and posters appeared around Tipton Port, proclaiming the robber to be 'a most heinous and violent fellow' and calling for witnesses and those of suspicious mind to come forward and inform the magistrates. The bills contained a sketch of a broad-shouldered man wearing a short black cloak and old-fashioned tricorn, and described him as 'swarthy, beardless and no older than thirty years'.

Around the port the robber became known as the Black Cloak.

10

Learning reading is like learning fisty. You've to see what something means, and one thing don't always mean the same twice, nor three times. Like a dropped left shoulder don't always mean that a right is coming and when a man steps back shaking his head it don't always mean he's hurt. But Janey weren't no help with learning reading; it was the Gaffer showed us the sounds and the letters and what letters made what sound.

We never talked about Billy Sticks after that night in the yard when Janey clocked him with a cobble, and we never heard from nowhere they found him dead. His father never come in the Champion asking about what happened to him. His father looked like a corpse himself, coughing and spluttering his lungs out all over from the hot steam in the foundries.

But whatever happened to Billy Sticks, them other sloggers left us be after. I seen Tanner and Mikey on a corner by the Railway Hotel and they gave us a good wide berth and never called me out for a gypsy or a whore again.

Once I got the book off the Gaffer I got mad on reading. I loved the way I could work out a word from sounding the letters, but I never knew if I was saying them right. It only took me three weeks to learn the names of all the countries on my globe. The Gaffer sat with us while I did it and he went, 'Yes . . . yes . . . good . . .' But when I asked him to say 'Mauritius' he dint know how you said 'ius' – he thought it was 'ee-us', but he dint sound so sure.

While I was reading the Champion was filling up and everyone drinking ale. Bill lost loads of his money in the strike giving away ale and bread, and then he had the fines for fighting and disorder and the magistrates sending letters saying they would take his licence away if there was any more trouble from him.

I tried reading one of them when it come with a proper red seal on it. Bill skipped about the bar saying, 'Never mind it. Never mind what them bastards say about me.'

In the end me and the Gaffer got it read between us. The Gaffer said Bill wanted to watch it or they'd take away his livelihood and Bill said, 'Bugger them down dead,' and pulled himself another jug.

But he was getting slower, and he hobbled when he walked, and he squinted and peered like his eyes were bad. Janey was at the Champion all the time too, and they both drank ale and sang, and she walked after him and sometimes she even told him what he was looking at, like she was his eyes. Fore long she was stopping the night in Bill's bed and I was right pleased because it was almost like having a mammy and a daddy, except they were drunk all the time and they never made no food nor cleaned. I did that.

When Bill was really grogged he made everyone salute his picture of the Queen and sing 'God Save Her'. He said it was a way to see if there was radicals and Chartermen in the place; if they would not stand he'd belt them where they sat.

Then, one Friday afternoon in August while I was scrubbing the front windows, trying to polish the smut and smoke from them, and getting the piss stains out of the brick with a stiff brush and caustic, two fine ladies and a gentleman come walking up Spon Lane.

They were knocking the doors and talking to the men and women who were in and giving them handbills, and they talked to the little uns too, them as were out playing in the lane. Most folk were working at that time and staying on later too, for Friday was payday at most of the foundries and mines. I watched them, thinking fine-looking as they may be, they was far up a dark lane at night handing out them bills and none of the folk as took em could read far as I knew.

The gentleman was tall and wore the black frock coat and white tie kerchief of a choker; he had bacca-pipe whiskers going grey and he carried a stick. The two ladies were young and both wore plain grey linen dresses and neat white bonnets, and I thought they was chancing it with all the sparks and smuts floating about in the air.

They saw me outside the Champion and walked up. Closer in, the ladies were lovely pieces, both slim and white-skinned and red-lipped, with strawberry-blonde tresses tucked under their bonnets. And they was the very same, two peas in a pod, both carrying a small black leather-bound book with fine gold edging to the pages that shone in their delicate hands.

As they walked towards me, both with the same sweet smiling face, I felt big and lumpy and rude and rough as sawed timber. I hid my big broad hands all scarred from the fisty and scrubbing under my apron.

The Reverend removed his hat and bowed, and for a minute I thought he was quiffing us, but the ladies give little bows too, and their smiles were so pure and pretty.

The Reverend said, 'Good afternoon, my girl. Is your father at home?'

I dint want to say he was full up to the knocker sleeping it off with Janey Mee, so I said, 'He is not, sir. Besides, I am the mistress of this house, sir. My name's Annie Perry.'

He smiled. 'I gather this is the home of the famous pugilist, the Tipton Slasher?'

'You are correct in that, sir, but Mr Perry is away at Birmingham this afternoon,' I lied.

The Reverend held out a handbill and said, 'Do you read, child?'

'I do, sir. I taught myself with a book from Manchester and a slate off our roof.'

I thought to myself, he's gonna see my racket here if he asks us to read this out.

But one of the twin ladies stepped forward and said, 'We are the Misses Warren, Annie, and this is our father, the Reverend Elijah Warren. We are newly come to the port with the new church up on the hill towards Hazely, where the houses are being built.'

We all knew that manor: fine mansions like Scotch castles for the ironmasters and nailmasters and pit managers going up along a proper road, high up over the port where no one could smell it though they'd see the glow of the foundries at night.

Some men from the port went up there at night blagging timber for their fires, and two as were caught by the peelers who patrolled it at night were boated off to Australia at the Assizes in Wolverhampton.

I said, 'Very good, Miss. My father is not a Church man, mind. And if he was I doubt you'd want him in there on a Sunday. His looks would scare the Devil and the words as come from out his mouth would choke the angels . . .'

The two Miss Warrens laughed and their eyes sparkled, and the second said, 'Would you like to go to school, Annie? To learn to read the Bible? To learn to spell and use correct grammar? To learn about our Empire and history?'

The Reverend said, 'How old are you, child?'

I said, 'I am just sixteen, sir.'

The first Miss Warren said, 'My name is Esther, and this is my sister Judith . . .'

And she held her pretty hand out to me and I just welled with tears; they come out brimming and hot with the thought of touching her hand and the thought of going to school and learning.

The Reverend said, 'There, child . . . are you quite well?'

The two Miss Warrens clustered in on me and Judith said, 'Father, leave us to talk to Annie. We can calm the child. You run and give the bills across the road there . . . We shall attend to Annie.'

The Reverend hesitated for a second. Miss Judith's eyes flashed and she said, 'Go, Father . . . We are quite capable.'

Even with my eyes stinging with helpless tears I thought it a fine thing that they could boss their father like I could Bill.

I settled to sit on the window sill and Miss Esther said, 'We are to begin a poor school, Annie. The parish has provided a building at the bottom of the lane and there is room for you to come and learn. My sister and I shall be the teachers and the Reverend will conduct religious services for all the poor children.'

Miss Judith said, 'Annie, you are a clever girl. You taught yourself to read. Imagine the life of learning and reading you could have.'

Miss Esther grasped my left hand. It looked like a leg of raw mutton in her tiny paw. 'Imagine, Annie . . . learning is the gateway to a new life in our Lord Jesus. That is why all poor children must come and hear the Word and learn to read it.'

I said, 'Most of em are working, Miss. Most'll not be allowed out the mines and nail shops for learning.'

'But the law is to be changed soon, Annie. The Parliament in London is to decree that all children must have schooling and stop having to work in the mines and nail shops.'

I said, 'How will that sit for their families, Miss?'

Miss Judith said, 'Annie, this port is lost in a sea of ignorance and vice at present. We must change the conditions for poor people. Our father is a committed reformer.'

'Does that mean he is a radical, Miss? For he'll cop a nose-ender off Bill Perry if he is, Reverend or not.'

The two Miss Warrens laughed.

Miss Judith said, 'Annie, you are a delight! Say you will come . . .'

I said, 'I cried because I know I can never, and because you are both so pure and pretty as cornflowers and I can never be . . .'

And I set to crying again.

Why I told them this I do not know. But they made me want to tell them all the dark things that were bobbing about inside me. The getting sold for six guineas and the beating from the sloggers, learning fisty and fighting and hearing cursing every day, and leaving Billy Sticks a-bleeding in the alley. And all the boozing and shouting and fists flying at the Champion. Ragged starving children walking off to the workhouse.

They made me see bright green and meadows of flowers like I did when I was a babby, when we wandered free with Big Tom leading Cobble. Before I come to this port with its black air and blood-slicked cobbles and the gaping cut running through her like a river to Hell.

For all my seeing I never saw this coming neither: this chance on a road in May, outside the place I was thinking was my home. A father and two daughters, him in black and them in grey with white bonnets getting flecked with the filth floating about. It all meant something, I knew it, and I needed to walk and think on it.

The Miss Warrens both bent and hugged me, and implored me to ask my father and come to the poor school on Friday next to register as a pupil.

The Reverend was walking back towards us and they turned towards him. Miss Judith said, 'I think we have another pupil, sir.'

He placed his hand on my head and smiled and said, 'You are clearly a good child, Annie, and you shall see more light in the darkness of our little school room than in a hundred taverns and lusheries, no matter how clean their windows.'

I I

The heath on the high ground that ran between Tipton and Bilston had never been enclosed. It remained common land, unfenced and free for villagers to graze cattle and horses, even as plots of land all around the towns were enclosed and taken control of by landowners, ironmasters and factory owners. Even as the Inclosure Act was enforced, and strips and parcels of good grassland and vegetable gardens at lower levels were wrested away from the poor and bundled into the land holdings of the rich, the heath and its scores of snaking animal paths and yawning black bogs remained untouched.

Perhaps it was that there was no easily felled timber on it – it was covered only with stunted pine, goat willow, hawthorn and small, twisted oak trees. What grazing there was, was poor. In times of hunger in the coal and iron towns below, people came to find wood blewits and puffballs after rain, but little else that could be foraged for food grew there.

Engineers from Sir Andrew Wilson-Mackenzie's mines had drilled and tested the sandy heather- and fern-covered land at various sites over the years but found nothing that indicated there was coal to be had. Nor was there lime, iron ore or saltpetre beneath the acres of gorse and dry feeble soil. Had they found it, the Act would've allowed Sir Andrew and his business partners to fence and claim the land as they had with so much else of their holdings. It was too high and too far from the canal, roadway and new railways to be of any use for a factory site and, save the bogs, there was no water on the bone-dry heath to run millwheels.

It stayed wild, and few took the dusty path that ran across it. In winter its height and northerly aspect made it grey and bleak; it was battered by winds and frigid with ghostly frosts and mist, and December snow often stayed in its shady hollows until past May.

In summer, those who walked or rode across it were met by its brief blooming of vibrant life and colour: the yellow gorse and purple heather, harebells and trefoil in spring and orchids and violet lousewort in summer. Vivid blue butterflies sprang from the flowers and the song of woodlark and warbler filled the air. Lizards and adders sunned themselves on the sandstone rocks, and at night the bracken whirred with the sound of nightjars.

Only once in the year did the heath become populated, when scores of boots, carriage wheels and unshod feet tramped up the long hill lanes from the towns on either side.

Since before anyone could remember, the heath had been the site of the late summer fair. Lammastide saw the one day a year apart from Christmas when the nailers, foundrymen and miners could take a day's holiday. It was a celebration older than the churches in either town. Older than the faith they professed. And each year as the populations of the towns swelled, the numbers thronging to the Lammas Fair grew.

So few of the crowds who came now worked on the land that the meaning of the festival was all but lost. It was no longer a celebration and thanksgiving for harvest. In recent years it had become a favourite of the travelling show people, and the dusty flat plot where ferns and heather were tramped down saw tent upon tent of games, shies, curiosities, entertainments and amusements.

The councils of the two towns vied with each other every year to book more and more extravagant shows and spectacles. To the borough council of Tipton it was rightly named Tipton Fair, to those of Bilston it was the Bilston Fair. To the nailers and miners who crammed the lanes over the three days it ran in the last week of August, it was simply called the Heath Fair, and excited children dreamed of their yearly visit while struggling fathers and mothers scrimped their pennies year-long to spend at it.

The year Annie turned sixteen the fair played host to Mr Astley's Illuminated Circus; the inside of the vast tent was lit by gas and oil lamps which threw great washes of coloured light across the ring. There was trick riding, rope walking and trapeze shows throughout the day of the fair and people thronged the tent to see the famous clown, Charlie Keith.

The theatre tent hosted Jerry Smith's New And Original Grotesque Pantomime in which a hapless tramp was chased, bludg-eoned and thrown about by a succession of spurned lovers, angry fathers, furious employers and a troupe of bellowing fishwives belting him with herrings. From inside the tent the bursts of delighted laughter echoed across the crowds queuing to get into the next performance.

In the booths and smaller tents that ran like rows of terraced houses down the field there was a chance to see other attractions. Samuel Taylor, the Ilkeston Giant, towered eight feet and six inches above the crowd. In the next booth the Extraordinary Iron Man invited those parting with a penny to hit him across the stomach with iron bars, and in his final performance of each day he allowed a man to shoot him in the belly with a pistol ball – all apparently to no ill effect or suffering, and to which he did not flinch nor cry out, but remained statue-like with his arms raised and a look of stoic determination on his face.

In one tent the Melodramatic Society of Great Britain and Her Empire presented 'The Sorrowful Maid of Fallen Repute – Her Doleful and Finally Most Tragic History'. The sorrowful maid's anguished cries and sudden hysterical sobbing could be heard vying with the growls and lascivious mutterings of the villainous Frenchman, le Comte de Malplaisir – the cause of her most tragic downfall.

Tiny Terence and his Mysterious Mice performed from another striped fit-up, where the midget performed a series of astonishing tricks with a group of five white mice housed in a miniature castle.

In the games tent miners were merrily fleeced of their pennies by card sharpers and sleight of hand cup-and-ball men; there was bingo and roulette, card games, backgammon and chequers, and money was wagered and lost all day long.

At both ends were huge ale shops where alongside beer and strong spirits, fairgoers could eat cakes, faggots, pasties, pigs' trotters and whisky-laced homity pie. A whole sheep was roasted and sliced over a fire pit, and hot potatoes with cream and onions were served with the meat.

In the year 1845 there were boxing booths too; three challenged passers-by to go up against a professional pugilist. Each offered a cash prize for any man who could last one full round. The biggest prize on offer was at the booth run by a local lad, Jem Mason, the Bilston Bruiser.

So confident was the big lad, who was not yet nineteen, that he offered the astonishing sum of ten pound for any man who could floor him, knock him out or otherwise stop him according to Jack Broughton Rules in the space of a five-minute round. He stood a full six foot two and was broad across the shoulder and slim in the waist, with long powerful arms and short wide fingers that curled into fearsome fists.

The truth was that Jem did not have ten pound to pay out to a winner. Neither did Paddy Tacker, the fast-talking little Irishman who acted as his agent and manager. But in two years and five proper paid fights he had never lost, and he was young and full of fizz enough to take the risk he never would. And in the three days of the Heath Fair he could earn close to ten pound taking a shilling a time from the challengers.

He had avoided ever being hit full in the face, so his nose was straight, smooth and aquiline, his large blue eyes unscarred and his full lips unbroken by another man's fists. His hair was a short and tightly curled blond and he wore no beard.

The stable lasses at the livery yard where he apprenticed as a farrier called him Apollo and Mrs Fryer, the yard boss's young wife, was prone to lean on the doorway of the forge and regard the sweating youth – near naked but for his leather apron – and remark, 'By the heavens, you are a beauty, Jem Mason,' whenever her husband was away.

It was the second year Jem had done the booth. Paddy set him up and took a tenth of his earnings across the three days. With the money he earned this year he was going to buy his own wagon and horse and travel the fairs across the country. He wanted to go to London to try his fists there, where a man could make twenty guineas a fight, and Paddy said that was where they would go as soon as they had the necessary.

Booth fighting was easy. Most of the men came in the afternoon after they'd been supping in the ale tent for hours and Jem lost count of the number of staggering coves he'd simply walked round and clocked flat in the first few seconds. Sometimes the big fellows from the foundries fancied their chances. They were strong useful boys too, steel-armed from years of tonging white-hot crucibles, but they weren't trained. They had no rhythm, no movement, no discipline, and they couldn't see what he was going to do. Jem could always spot a move in the ring.

Paddy said, 'You have to have the instinct, Jem. Most lads, even big strong fellas, don't have the instinct, but you have it, my beautiful lad. You have the instinct.'

Jem sometimes wondered if working with horses, as he had since he was eight years old, gave him the instinct. Some sixth sense of what was going to happen. Some unseen change in the glow that came off them that told you. With a horse he always knew. He knew if it was tired, if it was ropey or colicky, if it was fired up by mares and ready to buck and kick at him, or if it just wanted a cuddle and a cooch – and many did. He could just feel it by being near the beast, as if the animal soundlessly whispered its needs and intent to him. He could see a good horse as soon as it moved its head and he could see a bad un too.

He had been apprenticed to the livery at the port after his father died of a fever to the chest, made worse by the years he spent in the billowing steam of the foundries. Jem's mother got him taken for nothing at the age of eight, and he worked endless days and nights ostling brushing and watering, oiling and cleaning saddlery, and forking muck, paid only his board and food. He slept in the stables at night with the clink and stamp of the horses the only lullaby he knew.

After his mother died suddenly of winter sickness when he was ten, he was alone but for the horses until old Mr Fryer spotted him and his way with them, and bought him as an apprentice farrier. In the following years he grew into a strong lad with powerful arms honed from hammering hot metal and working the bellows.

Paddy had stopped by for shoes for his old mare as he touted for talent in the Black Country towns when Jem had just turned sixteen. The chattering Irishman spotted Jem's muscled arms and rippling shoulders, and his gentle precise way of moving as he bent and clasped the mare's hoof between his knees.

You can always trust a fellow who has a way with horses, thought

80

Paddy, especially when they looked like the farrier lad. There is no guile in a horse. And the boy could read and calm a horse like none he had ever seen. And the lad took no training; he had the instinct from the first time he showed Paddy his big swinging right hand. Hammering metal or hammering men in the alehouse back-yards, the big laddie was made for both, and he and Paddy began to make shillings on the summer Saturday afternoons in organised bouts.

The men he persuaded Jem to take on in the ring could be as guileless as horses too. They brimmed out their next move without saying or moving, and if they were faking either way, that was the easiest. And they never knew their best moves neither, even a quick long-limbed lad who could've stung and jabbed and broken Jem down would always want to swing a slasher like Bill Perry and he'd leave himself wide open. Jem knew what the boy was going to do before he did.

And Jem knew of Bill Perry from his days in the livery yard at Tipton Port before he came to the Bilston yard. And he knew what was said of him now. Paddy said he was old and broken with drink but, 'I still wouldn't put meself on his wrong side if I didn't need to. Bill Perry was the best of all the old pugilists. But I hear he is a sorry sight these days.'

And so that day as the sun beat down on the fair Jem was surprised to look up and see the Slasher himself stood before his booth. A crowd was already gathering as Bill Perry hobbled forward, leaning hard on a stick and peering at Jem. Next to him was a woman, a rough old nailer wench by the look of her, and behind them stood a tall dark Romi girl, dressed in boy's britches and her black hair pulled back.

Jem's eyes met hers and he knew like he knew with a horse and he felt for a second like he had been hit with a flaming bellowser.

His head went giddy and full of popping lights and his chest tightened round his thumping heart.

Bill peered at him again, holding out his handful of pennies: 'I'm here to learn ya, me handsome. I'm here to tek yer ten smackers, lad. You're a hobbledehoy but I'll soon learn yer a man's game.'

The crowd, now bunching in to see the Slasher and the Bilston Bruiser go at it, roared.

12

I aint never seen anything like him.

I aint never seen a god.

And there he was stripped to his britches and glowing gold in the sun, eyes pale blue as forget-me-not. Long black lashes. And him made so fine and like a marble statue, smooth and clean and the curves of his muscle shining polished pine.

I felt it, just like I knew he did an all, in that minute we come eye to eye while Bill bellowed and ordered like the drunken Admiral of the Red he was.

I smelt him an all. And he was warm hay and charred oak and spices and hot summer turned earth.

I wanted to get a hold of him and touch his honey-gold skin and his glowing face. I wanted to run my fingers in the gilt shining hair and feel them tight curls on my skin. I went shaky and dizzy with it. I felt like I'd been walloped one.

Then, all of a sudden I was above myself again looking down on it all like a skylark burbling in the heavens. The sight of him all aglow there on that stage. I knew him too from somewhere. And I knew we were to go along together. I floated over it all and felt the wind might blow us together where it would, and longed to dip and fall and settle on him gently and call him away to me.

But Bill was roistering and galloping at him to tek the bout, after his three hours in the ale tent going jug for jug with Janey, while I wandered the fair and saw the colours and smelled the smells and got warned off stalls for a gypo looking to cop.

And Bill had stood there in the tent saying, 'We shall have a beano, so we shall,' to the crowd gathered about him. It was one of them that named Jem Mason as the new bruiser in the parish and called on Bill to challenge him.

The walk-up there was bad that morning. We rowed and had cross words the whole way up, as Bill hobbled on his stick and Janey led him, seeing where his eyes wouldn't. The subject of the rollock was me going into school and learning with them Miss Warrens, who I'd been dreaming of, in a pleasant parlour where I sat in a modest frock reading the Bible and taking tea with other ladies.

All Bill's giving and fighting and getting fines had come home to roost for the Champion. We owed money to the brewers for ale and they had sent a note – I read it to him – to say they would supply no more barrels from the end of the month till the outstanding account of six pound twenty-three shillings was paid. The magistrate's men came almost every day to demand the vigour on the fines he had, the butcher wanted two pound nine for meat, and the baker said he'd be charging a tanner a loaf till Bill paid him the two quid he owed. We was lucky he owned the Champion and so far had not put it up on a loan. I dint know nothing of money and coin and cash and investments, but I knew when you was in a bad hole you had to stop digging it.

And there were ironmasters who wanted our plot there on the canal and they sent foggers to offer loans to Bill. Me and Janey stopped him, though he would've signed the whole lot over to them for the twenty quid he needed. And if he got the money they offered him, it would not be long before he crunched a back payment and they would be in for the lot: the alehouse, the plot, the pumps and fine wood bar, and us all on the parish. They done it to others whose bit they wanted.

So we stopped him on that one. But he started on about the money every day. How we needed it. He raged at us for wanting schooling, raged that I couldn't swan off for learning.

As we walked up to the fair that morning he went, 'You're a sold gypo child and you are mine and, like it or not, lady, you owe us. You owe us yer board and yer safety and yer good fine figure. That was me, that was, my graft and my blood and sweet sweat to mek you a house and home. And you won't leave us. You won't leave us, or you'll be back to the broken starving fields you come from. And that's no error, my fine lady, with yer put-on airs trying to lessen an honest working man in the esteem of those about him.'

So I dint say Bill had not done a proper day's work in all his years of having the Champion where I scrubbed and cleaned and cooked while he languished away his mornings the wrong side of his ale and his afternoons and evenings getting himself back over on the right side. I loved him, mind, the big stupid old bastard that he was, but he would not dictate to me where my life was to go.

That day, and ever since I met the Miss Warrens, I felt some of the pull of where it might be going. I knew the warp and weft of it and could see how it was wove. I was starting to hear the call of it, the sweet songs rippling ahead and above me like the unbodied burble of a skylark floating on a high summer breeze.

We left it when we got to the fair, with Bill saying, 'You will not disobey your father. You would not be so disobedient as to disobey your father, and that, we all know, is right and proper. It's even in the Good Book, put there by God himself, for the instruction of wayward wenches like you, my fine Annie!'

Him and Janey went in the ale tent and gathered a crowd like they always did. But I knew and Janey knew he was not up to nothing if he started for a row. His legs were slow and twisted and his wits were scranched, probably for all the blows they took in the rings and bouts. He could hardly see now though he claimed he could. And for all his word I knew it that he weren't my father. I loved him but he weren't my father no matter what he said.

And boozed as he was, he heard the crowd of wasters and stone washers dare him on to a bout. He looked over at me when I got back in that tent, all hot grey dust in the afternoon sun, and he saw us and said, 'I will not contravene the will of my own dear Annie.' But he was far and wide into his cups with his big ugly head jerking back and forth.

He stood, and the tables around him turned and scattered. One man called, 'Fuck a duck on him . . . he's a proper monster . . .'

And he was. He loomed unsteady and flying his big fists about at everyone, and even the Gaffer, who walked up to the fair with us all, who had come along for most of his exploits, said, 'Not now, Billy. You're not fighting no bout today.'

Bill said, 'I needs the ten pound from that lad. I needs the money if my daughter is to leave us and go for schooling, aint that right, lady?' He looked at me standing there in the crowd watching the show. 'I needs it, I needs it, gentlemen. For there shall be no more ale in the Champion if I don't get them smackers. No more ale! They mean to ruin me, gentlemen.'

All the crowd booed when he said about no more ale, and then he got to and began to stagger and bounce out the door of the ale tent with Janey at him going, 'No, Billy . . .'

We all followed him as he stepped through the fair, banging into people and hollering that he was the Champion of England.

We got to the Jem Mason boxing booth and watched him put a young miner down in a few short combinations; the lad was up-ended in about thirty seconds of stepping in and waving down to his muckers, all grins and giving it the fists. He dint last long. Jem Mason was fast and clever and moved lovely.

After he done the miner Bill stepped forward, holding out his pennies.

Then the boy looked at me.

There was a crowd at the back of us shouting and calling for a bout. You could see that Jem Mason weren't keen, the state of the Slasher an all.

I said to Janey, 'We'll have to stop him.'

She said, 'I wish you well with that, Annie. Besides, he does need that money. Less you got ten nicker he can pay everyone off with. He'll be all right. Once he's in a ring he wakes up.'

Bill was climbing up through the ropes. A little Irishman in the ring, with a red face and a scarlet jacket and topper, took the pennies out of Bill's hand and saluted down to him. Then, rubbing his hands, he called down to the crowd. 'Now we shall see a proper go, ladies and gentlemen! What about this then? The Tipton Slasher agin the Bilston Bruiser! You can say you were here to see this moment. Crowd in, crowd in, folks – do not miss this one!'

Jem Mason danced back into the corner. The crowd was getting bigger, people running over from the tents when they heard the Slasher was fighting the Bruiser.

I had a bad, bad feeling in me. I could see black and wreaths and funeral carriages and I knew this would be Bill's last fight for good if I let him get in that ring. Then my calling come again, a sense of Big Tom up there smiling at me, a sense that the clamour and chanting of the crowd could be for me and this was a way to steer my boat there in the dust of the farefield. I watched and read the whole scene around me and saw the meaning in it like I was reading words. And I was looking at Jem Mason and reckoning my chances too. Leastways the chances of putting my hands on him.

I pushed through the crowd and got to the ring, and just as Bill was pulling himself up I grabbed him by the shoulder and hauled him back so he toppled down into the crowd, and I nipped up onto the boards of the ring. I stood up straight and held my fists up. I pulled off my coat so I was just in a white chemise.

There was a big cheer then from the crowd, although some booed an all. But some shouted, 'Go on, Annie! Go on, Annie!'

The little Irishman come up on me. 'Get out of here, girl. He's not fighting no girl. No girls in this ring . . .'

I clipped the end of his nose with a little jab and he backed off, holding it, blood bursting out his fingers, going, 'Yow, ye wee bitch!'

I said loud so as the crowd heard, 'It don't say no girls. I can read, ya cheeky bleeder. It don't say no girls and we've paid our shilling. I am Annie Perry, the Slasher's Daughter. I can tek any man here, and I'll have no bother with this pretty lad.'

The crowd went mad with that, all of them cheering now; a big gang of nail wenches were at the front there calling, 'Go on, Annie! Go on, Annie!' Bill was being pulled back by the crowd and he was shouting up at us, 'You do not have my blessing for this, wench! You do not have my blessing! Obey your father, obey your father . . .'

Never mind what I said and tried to show, my heart was hammering, and I was hopping foot to foot – in part to stop my knees from shaking.

Janey had come to the front and waved up to me. I bent down and she said, 'Watch his right, and he likes combinations, and he is fast . . . God help you, Annie.'

I turned, and Jem Mason was being pushed out of his corner by the little fella who was going, 'Go on there, Jem. Teach the wee bitch a lesson.'

I danced and boxed over to him. He just stood still in front of me with his hands at his sides and shook his head. He had to shout over the crowd noise: 'I aint hitting no girl. Sorry, my love, but I aint. Paddy'll gie ya yer bob back. I aint fighting you.'

I had a good look at him. He was about five inches taller than me, but his arms were stocky and he dint have my reach. His legs were a fine pair of drumsticks, like oak limbs at the top and lovely-shaped round his calves. His belly was flat, plumped with little ridged muscles, and he was broad as a roof beam: big round shoulders, his right was the biggest. He had a slim neck for a fighter and his face was so unmarked it was hard to believe he'd ever been in a ring. His bindings still had spots of blood on em from the miner. And I could smell him too and it made us jump and dance about him.

The crowd were hollering and booing now, and Jem turned to them and held his hands out and shouted, 'I aint hitting no woman.'

Some were calling back. ''Bout time you did, boy!' 'Best way to learn em, Jem!' 'Go on and thump her!' And the nail girls were chanting, 'Ann-ie . . . Ann-ie . . . Ann-ie . . .'

Looking at his face, I got the memory of him. He was the cheeky bleeder at the Tipton livery who called me a gypo when I first come to the port with Bill and the Gaffer.

I danced away, him still shaking his head and about to turn away, with the crowd booing and shouting him for a chicken, then I skipped to the side of him and shot a fast jab at his face. It snapped against his cheek and cut him, and he turned, eyes flashing.

'There's a scar for your pretty face, ya cheeky beggar,' I went.

He faced me, still not stanced, still his fists at the sides, and went, 'I know you.' And he grinned. Blood was coming out his cheek and he put his fingers up to it and looked at it.

'I aint hitting no girl. I'll kiss ya but I'll not hit ya,' he said, still grinning at me.

'Well, I aint kissing you,' I said, and I got two more jabs in, and then come under with a right to his belly. That doubled him and the crowd bellowed.

'You bin trained, aint ya?' he called as he came back up puffing.

89

And he moved back stancing, and his fists went up across to guard. 'I still aint hitting ya,' he said.

'Well, I'm hitting you,' I said and a right-left hit his forearms. I could feel his hot skin through my fists as they landed, and they were good shots an all, and they must've bruised him but he dint wince nor show it.

He danced back away from me, his guard up, and I watched him move, looking to see if he dropped or feinted or nodded. I came in with my eyes locked on his, trying to find a gap to jab at, and his guard went down for a second and the cheeky bugger was still grinning at me.

I pushed off my right foot and threw a long left over the top of his guard, and as I come forward he pivoted to the side and I stumbled though the space where he had been. The crowd oohed, and Jem turned and held up his fist. They thought I was going over but I dint. I got my feet back under me and did my own pivot so as I was swinging round onto him with my left. A proper slasher it was, and him with his hand up, head turned towards the crowd. It caught him square on the side of his jaw and I heard a crunch and I dint know if it was my hand or his jaw. His head moved up and to the side and his body stayed where it was.

With a horrified 'ooh' from the crowd Jem Mason went down: his legs gave and he fell flat smack on the boards. The little Irishman shouted, 'Holy Jesus!'

With the sound of his body hitting the deck the whole crowd went quiet for a second. Then it burst into a fury with screams and shouts and bellows like cattle at the slaughter. I could see Janey and the nail wenches all hugging each other, and men waving their hats. At the back I saw Bill's big ugly head and he was nodding at me and smiling. Constables were wading in now, pushing their way into the ring.

In all that commotion I looked down at Jem who was still out. His eyes closed and still the stupid grin on his lips, he looked like a happy babby at his mother's breast except for the jab cut opened on his cheek.

And I stood over Jem and said, 'You owe us ten quid.'

Fists were flying in the crowd as the constables tried to break it all up; it was billowing and breaking and re-forming like a starling roost.

The little Irishman patted Jem's unbroken cheek going, 'Come on now, Jem.'

Then Jem's eyes snapped open. And he seen me and he grinned and said, 'The Slasher trained you right, Annie Perry.'

I said, 'I'm a gypo, Jem. We can all fight – and tek money off ya.'

He said, 'Am I getting that kiss now then?'

I said, 'Aye, all right, once I've got me tenner.'

The crowd was chanting my name and the constables were flapping at them with their batons to get them out of the road. Janey was shouting at me to come over, but the little Irishman said, 'We'll go in the back – come on, girly.'

There was another cheer when Jem stood up straight and shook his fists, and men were shouting, 'Beat by a wench! Shame on you, Jem,' but he just laughed.

Inside the tent, Jem wiped himself and pulled on a shirt and said, 'You better gie 'er what we got, Paddy.'

And Paddy, unlocking the strongbox, said, 'You're not giving it all, Jem. I don't think we've a tenner here anyway. And she's a girl. And it was a cheat. You weren't fighting. It's a scamble, Jem – she's a gypo, she's twisting us.'

But Jem smiled and said, 'Fair's fair, Paddy. That left was a cracker.'

He turned to me. 'Nobody ever done that before, Annie Perry, and a little forget-me-not on my cheek.' He touched the clotty scar.

I said, 'I'll kiss that better for ya,' and he laughed. Our eyes was locked together then and he put his arms round me and I took the back of his head and pulled him into us and we kissed. And it was better than winning a thousand bouts an all.

Paddy shouted, 'Go on now with your spooning, the two of youse!'

I said to Jem, 'You can keep the money, boy.'

And Paddy said, 'Good lass. Christian lassie. Fair play to her.'

Jem said, 'You won it fair, Annie.'

'You weren't fighting us, Jem. I know. But I've knocked you cold so don't you forget that if you wanna see us agin.'

'I'll come to the Champion,' he said.

Then he hugged me hard like Big Tom used to when I was a babby. And though it sounds queer he put me in mind of Big Tom. Long strong arms round us. He looked us right in the eye and said, 'We have a way to go together, you and me, Annie Perry.'

Then there was a fracas outside the tent and I heard Bill's voice. 'She is my daughter and I must ensure her best treatment by those gentlemen!' he was shouting, and Janey was going, 'Leave her be, Billy. She's getting your money.'

We come out and there were two peelers trying to stop Bill climbing up into the ring again. The crowd was breaking up and wandering away in the scorching afternoon sun.

Little Paddy skipped down next to him and said, 'It is all grand here, constables – this gentleman is a friend.'

Bill said, 'Where's my Annie?'

'I'm here, Bill,' I said.

He was squinting and peering again, and all could see his sight was going. He reached out with his fingers and found my face. His big rough muttons dabbed at my face and he said, 'I'm blinded by this sun, Annie, but I seen ya. I seen ya gie 'im a slasher.'

Paddy took Bill by the shoulder and said, 'Mr Perry, I am Patrick Tacker, agent and manager of sporting men. Will I buy you an ale and we'll have a wee discussion regarding a business proposal I have for ya?'

Janey came over to me and said, 'Did you get his money?'

I said, 'No, Janey. He's keeping it.'

She said, 'Annie, we are in a hole without it.'

I said, 'I just met the man I shall wed, Janey.'

The crowd was all but cleared now, some to the shows, some back to the ale tent, and Janey went with Bill and Paddy and the Gaffer. Jem come out and sat with us on the boards out front in the afternoon sun.

He was all gazy and soft then, holding my hand and going, 'You are the most lovely thing on this green earth, Annie . . .' And I liked that, and I liked the little tick of a scar on his cheek I give him.

I told him I was learning reading and going to school and he told me he was going to get a proper wagon made up and two strong ponies to tour the shows with my ten quid. He was a farrier an all and that is a proper good trade.

The fair was quiet now, the acts and shows starting to pack up for this was the last day. I sat there happy and warm with my hand in Jem's, feeling like I was lucky and clever and beautiful.

Then, far away at the end of the field, out the corner of my eye I seen a figure stood by the scrubby willow twixt two tents, and he was looking down towards us, across the dusty trampled ground. Soon as I caught sight of him I knew he was staring at us. He wore a black cloak and an old-fashioned tricorn.

13

The poor school was housed in a stone block that had formerly been a grain merchant's offices. For the previous two months workmen had been cleaning the exterior and altering the inside of the building, putting in a fine pitch-pine doorway and desks and a blackboard in the biggest room. Conveniences were installed in a small brick block at the rear and connected to the new drains that had recently been dug for the houses on the hill above Tipton Port.

The work had been overseen by the Warren sisters, alongside their father, who had raised the money for the rental and conversion and a small stipend for the two new schoolmistresses after a long round of visits to the most wealthy men in the vicinity. Each had raised a small subscription which, combined with the money invested by the parish council and the church itself, had been enough to begin the school.

The Reverend Warren had even persuaded Sir Andrew Wilson-Mackenzie and Jeremiah and Josiah Batch that their best interests lay in educating the children of the poor. He argued that the recent strikes and unrest in the town were a result of the ignorance and blindness of the poor to the Word of God. Those living in want would be forever prey to the seditious views of the radicals so long as they dwelt in the vacuum of darkness created by the separation from His Word. And so long as they could not read, they would forever dwell in that darkness. And the best place to start was with the children. His correspondence with the Bishop in London had convinced him that restrictions on the hours a child could work in the mines and nail shops were likely to become more stringent. He had spent many afternoons in the previous months taking tea in the houses of ironmasters and making the point he felt so passionately about: that proper Christian provision for the poor was the key to avoiding revolution. 'They must learn their place in God's order,' he said. 'We must render unto Caesar. And render unto God.'

It was the ladies, he believed, who were most moved by his arguments and accounts of the poverty and vice that festered in the streets and alleyways of the town, less than two miles from the elegant porticos of their newly built properties. Lady Wilson-Mackenzie of Ardleigh Hall was most moved, shaken as she was by her recent experience of highway robbery and possessed of a clear conviction that her husband had a Christian duty to provide for the poor of the parish.

The Reverend Warren also observed that in other parts of the region Nonconformists, Quakers and Methodists were already building housing and schools for workers, and offering shorter hours and better pay. Even the Roman Catholics in Birmingham ran Sunday schools and evening Bible classes for the poor.

The Batch brothers themselves were Baptists, but agreed to contribute, Jeremiah of the opinion that a knowledge of arithmetic needed for new processes in the iron industry would require men who could 'reckon and figure' in the near future. Their own father had been a foundry worker who had bettered himself because his mother had taught him to read. He went quickly from nailmaster to foundry owner and ironmaster, and had built a fine house two miles east of the port that overlooked the works now bearing his sons' names.

Sir Andrew was less forthcoming in his enthusiasm for a regular contribution to the new school, but under pressure from his wife he agreed to pay the monthly stipends for the Reverend's charming daughters.

Now, on the first Friday of September, as driving rain fell on the town, the Reverend Warren, the Misses Warren, Sir Andrew and Lady Wilson-Mackenzie, Jeremiah and Josiah Batch, Mr Thomas from the parish council, Mr John Pottage also from the parish council, Mr Chalmers (a reporter from the *Birmingham Journal*) and a group of ladies and gentlemen from the congregation at the newly consecrated St Michael's on the Hill stood arrayed in the new school room beneath a banner which read: *Welcome Children*. They awaited the arrival of the first pupils to register for lessons which would run in the early evenings during the week and all day on Saturdays. Above the small raised platform at the end of the room, beneath a high window now flecked with raindrops, hung a dark wood carving of Christ Crucified – recently moved from the new church on the hill.

The fine French bronze clock which the Misses Warren had purchased to stand on the mantelpiece above the fire approached the appointed hour. It struck four and the chimes filled the room for a moment as the assembled dignitaries stood in silence.

And nobody appeared.

Miss Esther, sitting at the desk behind an open registration book, looked up at her father. He gave a weak smile. Miss Judith stood in the doorway, glancing to and fro along the roadway as heavy rain spattered the cobbles. In the line of carriages outside, the drivers and footmen huddled, grumbling, under oilcloth cloaks, and the horses stamped and snorted.

At five past the hour, the Reverend Warren finally turned to the group. 'Perhaps a prayer . . . ?'

Sir Andrew thumped his stick on the ground and blurted, 'Well, it had better be a good one, Reverend, for your handbills and imploring from the pulpit do not seem to have had much effect. Where are the hordes of poor ignorant wretches my money is being used to better?'

The Reverend was nonplussed by the outburst and Josiah Batch stepped forward to say, 'Well, with respect, Sir Andrew, shifts don't finish till six, and it's pay day Friday for a lot of them.'

'Then I expect that rather than enjoying the liberation of the Gospels here, they will be enjoying the libations on offer at The Champion of England,' said Sir Andrew.

The Reverend held his hand up. 'Please, Sir Andrew . . .'

The others in the gathering shifted uncomfortably. Mr Thomas of the parish council said, 'If I may, gentlemen . . .' But Sir Andrew cut in: 'No, you may not, sir . . . I have been made a fool of.'

There was rattling from the doorway which led to the kitchen and outhouses. The door opened and Jessie, the Reverend's doughty housekeeper, wheeled in a rather unsteady butler's trolley. The assembly watched as she pushed the trolley laden with teapot, teacups, saucers and milk jug into the centre of the room and came to a stop. The jangling of spoons and china fell away as she looked up at the faces turned towards her.

'Are you wanting your tea now, sir?' she said hesitantly.

Sir Andrew let out a snort. 'I shall wave the carriage over.' He turned to go, ignoring his wife's imploring look.

And at that moment Miss Judith turned from the door and called, 'A pupil! A pupil is coming!'

Those in the school room shuffled to arrange themselves in a welcoming arc beneath the banner as Jessie pushed her trolley to the side. Miss Esther remained seated at the wide oak desk at the heart of the welcoming group, and Sir Andrew, reluctantly and with some huffs, took his place at the far end.

And through the door, dripping and red-faced from running through the driving rain, came Annie Perry.

14

In the wagon on the way down to Hallow Heath I tried to read the words and sound the letters, and I tried to read the Bible Genesis – the Creation of the Earth. It was the Bible Miss Judith gave me for my own to keep on my first time in her school. She said I was to try to read it every day starting with Genesis. I done near two weeks of lessons and two full Saturdays in the school room and my reading was getting lovely, said Miss Judith.

It was seven years and a bit since I had been at Hallow Heath Fair. Seven years since I'd seen my mammy and the babbies and Tommy. And now here I was coming back with a wagon, all painted up the side proper: on the one side, *Jem Mason – The Bilston Bruiser*, and on the other, *Annie Perry – The Slasher's Daughter*. It was all bright colours and stars, and at the bottom it said: *Paddy Tacker's Famous Boxing Booth – Celebrated Throughout the Empire*.

I could read all that by the time we left – me and Jem and Paddy at the reins, and two good strong cobs pulling. Jem had bought the wagon and Paddy had it painted by a signwriter in Brum, and then we packed the ring and the stage in it and all set off for the last horse fair of the summer.

Paddy told Bill that, together, me and Jem could make twenty pound easy with the draw that we were and the oddity of a wench to challenge the wenches. He said, 'And she is a beauty, Bill, a rare beauty, and men will throw shillings to see her stripped to chemise and bloomers.'

Bill had him by the throat for that, and Paddy spluttered that whatever I wore would be respectable and he would guarantee everything was proper. In the end Bill said yes. The Champion was closed for we had no ale to serve and no money to pay the brewers we owed. The Gaffer was buying bread and cheese for us by the end of August.

Miss Esther said the Bible was the Word of God and that all wisdom and learning and knowledge in the world was in it, so if I read it I would know everything there was to know and never want nor be in darkness.

First day in the school was a shocker. Just me and all them fine folk and me dripping puddles over the floor. No others from the port come that day for it was a Friday and pay day. Them fine folk all looked at me like I was a dirty dish clout. Only Miss Esther and Miss Judith smiled. Miss Esther said, 'Annie! Oh, bless you, dear,' and led me to the table to see the book where you had to register your name and your house and who was your father.

A tall man in a fine coat, a right rude and blustery case, said, 'This girl is no child, Reverend Warren. She is old enough to be a mother herself.'

Reverend Warren said, 'She is the child of Bill Perry the pugilist. She lives in a slew of vice and ignorance there in an alehouse, a low den of frightful sin, Sir Andrew. The girl is just sixteen. She is clever . . . why, she has already taught herself the alphabet.'

Sir Andrew stepped over and had a good look at me, like I was a pony he was buying. He said, 'She has Romi looks. Are you to trust this wretch in the company of your daughters?' He stared hard into my eyes and I give him the look of a foul curse with them. I looked him hard and straight till he seen the curse, and then he looked away and I knew I had him. I was itching to clip him one and I weren't a bit feared of him as everyone else seemed to be.

He walked towards the door. 'Perhaps your daughters can teach her some humility in the presence of her betters. The child is impudent and defiant. But can we expect any more? Her father is by all accounts a veritable savage.' He puffed out hard and shook his head. 'Come, Agnes,' he said.

They all relaxed once he was gone. Miss Judith took my hand and said, 'Dearest Annie, please do not be put off this endeavour by Sir Andrew,' and Miss Esther took my other and said, 'He is a man of the most dogmatic and unforgiving temperament, but we shall prove him wrong.'

He's not as unforgiving as I am, I thought, and I resolved to tell Billy what had been said of him and to remember Sir Andrew in all my nightly curses.

I was the only one there that Friday, but on the Saturday following there was twelve of us, and me the oldest by four years and towering over the lot of em. Miss Esther and Miss Judith skipped about, fizzing with joy on that morning when we all come, and the first thing we all had to do was go and wash in the outhouse where there was sinks and privies, and there was a little Scotch woman in there who ruled us rotten and scrubbed all the little uns' faces with wet sackcloth till they cried.

Then we had prayers with the Reverend, standing with our heads bowed, and then we all sat on the benches, which were nice smooth oak, and each of us got given a slate and a chalk and we did letters starting with *A*.

And I knew all mine so I chalked the words I liked best. I chalked *Jem*, and I chalked *Love*, and I chalked the word *Slasher*. I liked that word best. I liked the *shush* of it and the *aaa* of it and the way it sounded like it was cutting. I chalked *Bible* and *God* and I chalked *Miss Judith* and *Miss Esther*.

I was thinking on why words meaned what they meaned. Why three little letters in a row said a thing and it was the thing, but why was they a thing? Why was *c-a-t* a cat? Why did *w-o-r-d* mean word? A word. A word. A word. A word. It made my head ache.

Then a little bleeder sitting next to me put his hand up and went, 'Please, Miss Judith, this Romi wench is not doing her letters. She's a-scribbling.'

Miss Esther come and got me out and took me to the back of the room where there was a desk. She said, 'Annie, you are far more advanced than the other children. We shall instruct you separately for your reading is beyond theirs.'

And then I had the joy of all great joys. On every evening for the next two weeks and all day on the Saturdays I sat at that big oak table with Miss Esther and we read the Bible. I read out the Book of Genesis to her and she corrected me when I got a word wrong and I spelled and sounded each word and strung em like fisty combos so as I could belt through a sentence. And how glad I was that God had created this green earth out of the chaos and let there be light.

And we talked too. I told her about my mammy and Big Tom and how I come to Tipton with Bill Perry. I told her how I had learned fisty and she held her hands over her pretty mouth and let out a great sigh and said, 'Oh, Annie . . .' I never told her about going out to the fairs. I never told her about Jem Mason neither, for she blushed when Adam was naked and hid himself in Genesis 3:10 and explained that before they ate the apple they were clothed in righteousness but once Eve had had a nibble they saw their nakedness and had to have clothes made of hide.

I never told her I had seen Jem Mason when he was most assuredly not clothed in righteousness on a warm night in the long grass up the back of the Champion.

I knew she was from another world to me. She had never lived in a vardo with all the smells and fighting of brothers and sisters or heard the slapping flesh of her daddy heaving himself on her mammy in the chill of a December night. She told me about her mother who died when she and her twin were both eleven. I couldn't see her father heaving himself on anyone, for he was a dry twisty man with thin lips and bony hands. The beauty in those girls must've all come from the mother. The Reverend peered down as me and Miss Judith read together, and when he smiled his lips pulled back from his teeth so it looked like he was snarling at us.

It took the best part of a day to come to Hallow Heath, and when we pulled up there to stop the night before it started, it was as big and spread as far as I remembered it from being just a babby with Big Tom.

While Jem and Paddy set the ring and the stage and pitched our tents for the night, I walked round the field on the cut stubble, now in soft boots where fore I had bin barefoot. I seen the gate where Mammy sat with Benny, Tass, Mercy and Charity and her swollen belly while Tommy took me to get sold. I seen the long red earth lane we walked down on that morning feeling our bellies swelling with hunger.

I wondered where that new babby was now, where they all was and why they never come to Tipton to find us. Tommy said they would but they never did, not once. I dint have no real hard sorrow in me about it, mind. I couldn't get any feeling about them and where they all was, even standing there on the spot where I last saw them. Perhaps because I was so full with love for Jem, so warm and filled with it, and when I saw him I felt a sparkle in me. Perhaps because I was learning to read an all, and learning to fight and make money for us. Sometimes two joys can push one sorrow from your heart like an old nail knocked out by a new un.

It was still warm and the air felt hazy and soft. Men were staking out the ring for the sales, and the ale tent was pitching and a big wagon of barrels was being rolled out. The ponies and sale horses were all in the big far paddock, some tethered and some penned. Far over where our wagon was, I could see Jem in his white shirt and cap stood talking to the farrier.

I sat on the spot where Mammy and the babbies last sat. There were campion and cornflowers gone over to seed in the verge; the campion pods rattled in the light breeze and the blown cornflower heads nodded along, shedding their seed onto the ground. Meadowsweet were floating their fluffy little flowers over the verge and the bees were bumping and buzzing. I felt all of a sudden that I dint want to go back to the black and smut of Tipton. I knew I missed seeing little summer flowers going over in September. In the hedge the brambles were fat and soft and I remembered when they was all we had to eat.

Miss Esther said to me when we were sitting at the table meant to be learning the Bible, 'You have suffered greatly in your life, Annie.'

And I said, 'So have you, Miss Esther. Your mammy died, mine just sold us.'

She smiled sadly and said, 'I think that women must always bear the pain in this life. Perhaps it is God's revenge for Eve's temptation. I would it was not so, but I fear it is.'

I loved her voice and the way she said words. I wanted to get shot of my Black Country Romi voice and sound like her. Her lips were small and neat and they moved from word to word, precise and measured like the second hand of a good clock.

I said, 'Janey Mee says a woman has to learn to fight in this life or she'll be knocked down and stamped on by all the men.'

'I do not approve of Janey Mee's chosen way of fighting, Annie, but I have some sympathy with her attitude.' She flushed when she said it and glanced upward as if she thought someone was watching her. She went on: 'I have many books you can read, Annie, once you are fully able. Wonderful books. Books which open the world.'

I said, 'Isn't the only book I need the Bible then, Miss Esther?'

She glanced about again, and I knew she was thrilling in herself when she said, 'The Bible is important, Annie. But it is not the only book. And it is not the only book that is important. And you will be my dearest friend if you do not repeat that to the Reverend . . .'

Paddy and Jem were calling over to me sat there dreaming and remembering. Paddy was waving a loaf of bread and a big round of cheese. I felt hungry and I walked back over. They had the ponies fed and watered and tethered, and there was a fine little tent next to the wagon. Jem had a nice fire going with sticks. The stage was up with striped stakes at each corner of the ring and thick white ropes. In front of the ring there was a big painted sign board:

PADDY TACKER – BOXING PROMOTIONS and
SPORTING ENTERTAINMENTS of QUALITY
Come Gentlemen . . . Come Ladies TOO. Come all Challengers!
Gentlemen Shall Challenge
Jem Mason – The Bilston Bruiser
Ladies shall challenge
Annie Perry – The Slasher's Daughter
One shilling to last one round.
JACK BROUGHTON RULES.
Prize for a full round, legal counted knock down or knockout
£10 Sterling.
NO KICKING NO BITING NO GOUGING NO
LEATHER GLOVES
NO HEADBUTTING NO SPITTING
The Decision of the Judge is FINAL.

I sat by the fire and Paddy give us a big mug of tea and plate of nice soft bread and strong cheese. Jem come and sat by me.

Paddy said, 'So we are set now. It'll be a good big crowd tomorrow. We shall rake it in. I want you to do a little exhibition show to start off. Shadowing and clipping, you know. It'll get the crowd going.'

Jem said, 'I still aint hitting her, Paddy.'

'Well, you don't have to hit her. Ye fake it, man – just bob about there. The crowd needs to see the two of youse. Annie, you wear britches and a buttoned white chemise, and we'll put a scarlet kerchief on ye.'

Jem said, 'If someone gets hold of it they'll strangle her, Paddy . . .'

'No, no, it'll not be knotted. It'll be tucked round. It'll look grand, y'know. You gotta give em a show, Jemmy. You give em a show, they'll part with their money.'

I said, 'I'm only fighting the wenches then?'

Paddy said, 'You are.'

'I never hit a woman neither, only Janey,' I said.

'Well, you can start tomorrow,' said Paddy. 'Now, Annie, did Janey show you how you bind yourself? You know, here?' He put his hand on his chest and he looked right awkward.

'Oh, my tits?' I said. 'Aye, she did, Paddy.'

He went bright red and Jem laughed. Paddy said, 'We shall have no coarse words here, girly. You're not in your alehouse now.'

I slept in the wagon and Paddy and Jem shared the tent for Paddy said it was his promise to Bill there would be decorum and respectable arrangements.

The fair filled quick in the morning. Crowds and carriages and gentlemen and fine ladies, and crowds of bargeys and farmer lads and drovers. There were Romis dealing horses and Irish and Dutchmen. There were crowds of soldiers come from the barracks in their red coats and gangs of navvies and labourers from the canals and railways.

There was no fisty bouts in the afternoon and we were the only boxing booth. And Paddy got me dressed up in a clean white buttoned chemise and he tucked a red spotted kerchief in round my neck and I tied my hair up with a broad scarlet ribbon.

Jem wore white britches and was stripped waist up, and many girls – and even ladies – give him the eye as they passed. I bound my hands with tacking strips to save my knuckles.

Paddy did a big call out when we started to pull in the crowd, and me and Jem stood next to each other and held our fists up when he said our names. Then we done a little mock skipping bout, with open hands and little taps and flicks, and Jem got a big cheer when he stepped past me and slapped my arse. And I got a bigger one when I swerved him coming in and done the same back. We always kept our eyes on each other and Jem was always smiling at me. He pulled queer faces at me too and made me laugh.

All the time Paddy was calling, 'Observe, ladies and gentlemen, observe and wonder at the athletic beauty of youth, at the fine and elegant movement, at the grace of their forms in combat . . . Ask yourself: do you have their speed? Their light-footed bravado? Their honed and refined martial instinct? . . . Ask yourself . . .'

Jem moved lovely but he was flatter and slower than me; he had to plant himself to throw a proper blow, and he sometimes laboured when he went back. We'd have to work on that.

After the show bit was over a big blunt-headed farm lad came out of the crowd, waving a bob and saying he'd have Jem's teeth out. He lurched and lumbered at him and kept trying to get him in a clinch and pound at his kidneys. But he dint last long, for Jem got him close in with an uppercut and sat him down hard on his arse.

Then another big lad who looked Romi to me pulled off his waistcoat and climbed up. Him and Jem stanced and went on Paddy's bell, but the big lad dint think nor reckon what he was about. He just give a blood-curdling yell and came tearing and charging in like the cavalry and he ran straight onto Jem's big right and he was flattened cold.

Nobody come to challenge me till later in the afternoon when a big gaggle of dairy girls who had been in the ale tent all day showed up. The biggest was a fair girl about twenty-five and she was a big bride an all. Plenty of cream and butter she'd had. And she was flush-faced and shouting she wanted to spend her shilling, getting egged on by the others all squealing and cackling like a coven.

Because this was gonna be the first wenches' fisty bout Paddy did a big call out and he got a fair old crowd gathered. The big girl lumbered up onto the boards and her girls were cheering her. Paddy asked her name and she said, 'I'm Bella from the dairy.'

And Paddy bellowed, 'Ladies and gentlemen, the manly art is to be graced by two ladies! This is a rare entertainment, folks, a rare show of the noble art. Gather in . . . gather in . . .'

I stood next to Jem at the back and had a good look at her prancing and swinging her big fat arms in front of her crowd. Two bookmen had turned up, and they stood off at the back of the crowd with their heavies and their ledgers and leather purses, taking wagers. Jem and me watched them and he said, 'Will I have a couple of bob on you, Annie? First blood and a knockout?'

I said, 'You'd not lose your money if you did, Jem.'

He said, 'Watch her, Annie. She's strong although she's heavy as a carthorse. She'll be a job to get over. You watch her, my Annie. I'll stop it if she gets on top or hurts ya, don't worry.'

'You'll have no need,' I said, and I kissed him.

Bella had pulled off her skirt and was in a white petticoat and a saggy old blouse so you could see her big old udders swinging about when she moved and the lads in the crowd all started a call for her to show em. She was near staggering drunk, I could see, and she was howling and laughing back at the throng beneath her.

Paddy called us into the centre and I stood proper, side on stanced, and she swayed about grinning at us. Paddy took a bulging red purse from his belt and chinked it out to the crowd and crossed to the poles and hung it like a proper stake and called, 'This here is the purse of ten pound to go to the winning lassie. To last a round of five minutes, a knockdown count or a knockout . . .'

The crowd all cheered again and Paddy nipped back and whispered in my ear, 'It's only pebbles in there, girl. You'll have to flatten her quick.'

When the bell went, Bella looked round like she was lost, then she swivelled her head and saw the faces of the crowd and she grinned and looked back at us and her eyes went dark and savage. I knew she was going to charge us and I hopped back a pace as she lolloped forward with her big claws out for my eyes. I dint want to hurt the girl, so I stepped smart to the side and I clipped the back of her head with a jab as she crashed through at me. She stumbled but stopped herself and got her feet back, and I moved in while her hands were down, jabbed her twice in the snitch and it bust. She screamed at the blood and her hands flew up to her nose and she went, 'You little bitch!'

I said, 'Give it over now, wench, or you'll get hurt.'

She swung her big right arm over at me and I ducked and come up under her chin with my right and then snapped two more jabs into her throat as she went, head back, stumbling away from me. But Jem was right: she was a bugger to get over.

All the crowd was screaming now, some going, 'Finish her, Annie!' and some going, 'Bust her head, Bella! Get her down and stamp her!'

I said, 'I don't want to hurt you, girl. Give it over and climb down.'

She shook her head and then pushed back off her left leg to come in at me again and she was snarling like a vixen. From the corner Paddy with his watch called, 'One minute gone!' She never got to me. I sidestepped her again and this time I give her a good hard one to the back of her head and it bucked forward and she followed it down. Her face slammed hard and she lay still in the blood soaking into the boards from her nose.

Another eruption come from the crowd as Paddy hopped in and started counting. The dairy girls were all cursing and spitting at me and the boys run to have it out with the bookies and the big lads with staves they come with.

Jem come over with a towel for us and said, 'Good going, Annie. It's easy, innit?'

I said, 'Hope they're all as drunk and clueless as her.'

The dairy lass was out for the full ten count and Paddy declared it a knockout. Jem nipped down to get his wager off the bookmen and we got Bella sat up and slapped awake. Soon as she saw me there with a flagon of water for her, she burst into snotty tears.

And that was about as noble as it got for all the afternoon and the next day. I fought twenty-one rounds in all. After the crowd for Bella, Paddy put the price up to two bob for a go with me, and there was plenty of takers.

Like Jem said, most were too soused to know what was going on.

Most of them stumbled or fell, or I flattened them. Some of them wenches sobered up quick and thought better of it once they got into the ring and hopped out sharp once I was stanced and the bell went.

Five of the bouts was called foul for trying to trip me or bite me or kicking out at me privates, and the crowd chanted, 'Shame . . . shame,' and the men they was with tried to muscle Paddy for their stake back. But none of them wanted a row with Jem so we kept the shillings, and over the days the purse for me and Jem got fatter and heavier.

I only had trouble with two of em.

One was the stout wench who was a cook over at the ale tent. She stood a shade taller than me and her arms were long and nice-shaped from all the stirring and heaving cauldrons. She was calm and she never got angry even when I stung her with jabs, and she dint seem a bit boozed. She stayed on her feet for four minutes thirty seconds and she hit some good gut shots that winded us. But in the end I was too quick for her and I put her down with a slasher that rocked her head sideways.

The other was a Romi.

She kept her long patterned skirt and beaded jacket on for the bout, her hair tied up in bright silks, and proper gold earrings and clanging charm necklaces. She was tall and graceful, with a thin elegant neck and slim wrists that jangled with bangles and bead wristlets. She chimed like a china cabinet when she moved, weighed with all her finery and dressed up proper for the fair. And she left it all on when she got in with us.

The crowd of dealers from her family took it serious and argued out terms with Paddy and finally wagered four pound against his ten on their wench.

And fore she got in with me, the men and boys stood round her all jabbering in Romane at her, and her red lips smiling and her jet-haired head nodding.

Paddy made her tek all her rings off, mind, and she bound her hands in scarlet silk.

I had a bad feeling about her even as we squared up.

She moved very slow and stately like a dancer, and her black eyes never left mine. And as we stood waiting for the bell she lifted her hand to my face and held my cheek gentle and said slow and chanty like a spell, 'I know you, Annie Loveridge. I know you was offered up and sold for a pony and vardo by your mammy, and I knows where your mammy is now . . .'

Then the bell clanged and she hit me square in the face with her other hand fore I could even get back and stanced. It come from nowhere and I went back gagging with it.

She stepped away and went circling like a cat stalking an injured sparrow.

Jem was calling, 'Watch her, Annie! Watch her!'

And she'd stung us. I felt my head go back and the blood bubbling in my nose, and tears sprung up. My head was rattled with it and what she said about my mammy.

And now she was moving round me slow, rolling her fists over each other and humming a spell to herself. I shook myself back with my guard up, and the blue lights in my head popped, and I got moving and bobbing and got my eyes back to her. She was smiling and nodding and humming at me and she was half crouched and sliding around us like a sail boat, chinking from her gold and her charms. The crowd had gone silent but for the other Romis whispering at her.

Janey had told me this was how Romis fought, slow and circling and not making any move for ages. They called it 'charming' and they were looking to mesmerise you like they did with snakes in India. They wanted you to watch their eyes and get pulled and not notice a move they were going to try.

I knew I needed to get on the side of her and use a combination. I stopped looking in her big black eyes and started looking hard at her shoulders and feet. She started doing little hop-dance steps, one foot to the other, and now her hum was sounding like a hiss, like 'isss-ya-ya-isss-yay-aa', and her fists rolling over and over and her head nodding and charms clinking.

But she'd squared and opened herself up a bit, and I spotted her shift her weight onto her left foot and I whipped into her with a fast low one and two and one.

She had no guard and they got her low in her gut, one near lifting her, and she stumbled back and I followed with three more. I got the top of her arm as she turned and I knew it had stung her cause I felt her muscle squidge flat like a butter pat. Her left dropped and she spat a curse and drew back, coiling herself in behind her right.

Once you've hurt someone and you know you can, it gives you a right lift, and now I feinted a left, twisted as if I was throwing it, and when she crossed her right to guard, I came in at her with the right, fast.

She tried to spin away from us and toppled over towards the ropes and I give her three more quick jabs in her belly and then caught her lovely with a right as she bounced back at us off the ropes. Now she was doubled and the Romis by the stage were shouting and cursing up at me. Paddy was shouting, 'Finish her now then, Annie!'

I got in alongside her and grabbed her hair with my right. She was gasping for breath and I had a second to steady her, and then I punched down hard into her head with my left and there was a right jagged crack.

She was down and flat, and I stood over her and said, 'You know us now, don't ya? What you say about my mammy, ya bitch?'

Then the Romis and others in the crowd all jumped up onto the boards and there was merry chaos. Paddy was batting em back with his stick and Jem wading through to grab me and pull me clear. I heard a whistle and then the stage was full of peelers too, clouting and pushing with their staves and folk toppling off through the ropes back into the crowd. Jem dragged me round to the back booth fore there was a proper riot, and we heard the constables hollering they'd read the Riot Act and have dragoons in if it dint all calm down.

Paddy bundled in from the front, clutching the purse and grinning. He had a proper shiner on his right eye but he was fizzing.

'My beauty, didn't you do her like your father, eh? I think her bloody spine snapped with that last one – forgive my French. They're carting her off to the doctor. She thought she was a sorceress, that one, but you broke her spell, my Annie.'

The crowd cleared off slowly, most to the ale tent, as the second day was coming to an end and all the horse sales were done.

A constable come to the backstage and warned Paddy off any more bouts that day. He said we were causing a public nuisance and precipitating riotous assembly and he'd have a magistrate down and have us in the gaol if there was any more of it.

Paddy dint mind none. Me and Jem washed from a barrel and then went out the front to clear and sweep and start taking down the ring and stage, and Paddy sat at his table counting the money into his strongbox.

Jem went and fetched ale for me and him, and we sat on the stage together watching the sun get low on the fair.

Jem give me the looking-glass and I saw my nose was crook and swelled up red. I knew I'd have a bender like Bill Perry after that Romi wench clocked us. Jem said, 'Ye're still me beauty, Annie. Paddy knows a surgeon in Brum can straighten that . . .'

Just then a big fine carriage came pulling up across the scuffed stubble of the field and when it stopped and the footman opened the door, a young red-faced gentleman stepped down. He wore a wig and a long pale blue coat embroidered with roses and turning leaves, and at his neck a white linen collar and lace ruff.

Me and Jem sat there open-gobbed at the sight of him as he crossed to us, holding out his silver-topped cane and spreading out his small white hand, he bowed low as if we was a prince and a princess. Behind him two other young fellows from the coach, both as elegant and dandy as he, also bowed to us, and I wanted to laugh at the sight of them bowing so to a farrier and a broken-nosed gypsy.

Before the three gentlemen straightened I heard Paddy's voice shouting, 'Get down from there, the two of you, and greet your betters proper!'

He come bustling over and bowing. 'Forgive them, your lordship. They are ruffians from Tipton and they know no proper manners.'

His lordship held out his hand for Paddy to shake, saying, 'My dear Mr Tacker, it has been some time, has it not? Do not trouble these young people for I imagine they both deserve to sit so, after their exertions.'

Me and Jem climbed down from the stage, and Jem shook the gentleman's hand, and I tried to bob like a curtsey, but I dint know how and thought I'd get Miss Judith to teach us once we got back.

Paddy said, 'Jem, Annie, this is his lordship, lord Ledbury – a sporting man, a lover of the noble art and a true and fine gentleman. This here is Jem Mason, your lordship. He's me best since Tass Parker . . . fact he's bigger an' faster than anyone about now. And this is my Annie Perry. She is the child of Bill Perry who your lordship knows well.'

Lord Ledbury smiled as he peered at me. 'I saw you fight, child. You are a most impressive young woman. It had not previously been to my taste to see ladies in the ring, but today I found it . . . most diverting . . .' He looked back at the two behind him and they laughed. And I dint like the sound of that laugh. His lordship continued: 'I know your father, Miss Annie. I have seen him fight many times. He is a fine sporting man and I trust he is well.'

I dint know what I was meant to say so I said, 'He's going a bit blind these days, sir. He thinks he can still fight though.'

Lord Ledbury paused and regarded me further, tipping his head to the side. He said, 'Charming . . . you are charming, Annie.'

He turned to Jem and looked him up and down and glanced

back at his fellows before nodding towards Jem. 'Is he not magnificent, gentlemen? Is he not both an Adonis and an Achilles?'

Jem come a full head and shoulders over him, but he stepped to him and placed his hand in the centre of Jem's bare chest. 'How do you stay so perfect, Mr Mason, so unmarked?'

One of the fellows behind said, 'Perhaps he was dipped in the Styx, Percy? I hear the canal in Tipton is just as filthy.'

The other said, 'And after today's show he will undoubtedly be well heeled.'

The three gentlemen laughed, though what was funny, I do not know.

I could see Jem weren't comfortable with the lord touching him and I put my hand over to his and squeezed, and he looked down at me and shrugged like he was saying, 'What's their game?'

Lord Ledbury turned to us again and put his hand up and touched the top of my head. 'And here our own Athena?'

The other called, 'Surely she is Adrastea, who may not be escaped after the belt she gave the Romi woman. Did the woman die?'

The third said, 'No, no, she is Bellona, and the big fellow her bridegroom.'

Rich fine people know they can just touch yer when they want, because, to him, me and Jem were just like horses or dogs. And the three of them chuckled so at their fancy saying, though I had not one clue what they were on about. All I knew was somehow they was belittling me and Jem like we was babbies. The radicals in Tipton said the rich own everything and they think they own the common man too – and these three specimens did so.

Paddy stepped in. He was blustery and embarrassed, and he shooed me and Jem over the road and said, 'Now, I believe your lordship wants to discuss some business with me?'

Lord Ledbury smiled but kept his gaze on my face when he

said, 'Yes, we do, Mr Tacker. Pray, escort me to your office while these fellows amuse themselves hereabouts.'

Paddy said, 'Get back to the packing up, you two,' to me and Jem, and then he walked round to the back booth with his lordship.

The two others stood gawping at us, leaning on their sticks. The taller said, 'They would whelp fine pups, these two, if they were to breed, would they not, William?'

And Jem understood that one. He stepped forward and said, 'Are you looking to get clocked, guvnor?'

Seeing him looming up towards them, they both turned white and scarpered fast, the little un calling back, 'We shall take a turn round the fair. Inform his lordship, won't you?' as he hobbled off quick in his fine leather shoes.

We took thirty-eight pound twenty shillings in all at the Hallow Heath, with what me and Jem charged for the bouts and then the side bets Jem and Paddy done on me. My cut was sixteen and six after Paddy took his commission and expenses, and I rode the wagon back to Tipton with the coin safe in a black velvet bag I kept between my knees.

On the road we saw the Romis' vardos and string of ponies. They were the troupe we'd fought at the fair, and as our little wagon come alongside them on the wide road out of Worcester I seen the wench I beat bundled up in the front, a wide thick bandage around her neck and both her eyes black as crow feathers.

Her head was hanging out the side, and she spied me sat next to Paddy as we come up by and her face creased in fury and she spat, 'You want to know where yer mangy bitch mammy is? She died in the Bilston workhouse and all the little cockroaches she took in with her . . . all of 'em . . . burned and melted with the typhus . . .'

15

The Misses Warren stood together in the window of the vicarage, watching as the rain fell in steely grey sheets. There were still wooden scaffold poles crossing the high arched window where not one hour earlier men in canvas aprons chipped and chiselled at the elaborate scrolled window surrounds, carving images of saints in the arch apex in the new medieval style in which both the vicarage and Saint Saviour's were constructed from pink sandstone and shiny new red brick. Their view out across the walled front garden and down the hill that led to Tipton Port was similarly obscured by pine and steel scaffolds and walls of sodden canvas sheeting which surrounded the other houses being built. The church and the vicarage had been the first to be completed, save for several minor cosmetic additions, and now two new rows of large houses, with solidly walled gardens and rounded turrets like Scotch castles, were slowly growing along the wide roadway that had yet to be fully cobbled. It curved majestically away from the looming red edifice of Saint Saviour's, and would soon be a pleasant tree-lined avenue where the ironmasters, merchants, coal dealers and timber traders would house their families, above and deliberately up-wind of the port and its fetid canal, foul chimneys, flaring furnaces and shuttered hovels.

Today, as the sisters looked down, there was no sign of the port and its blackened earth and brick; it was shrouded by the grey smutty clouds which spat driving rain and made rivulets and streams run in the crushed rock of the roadway.

But driving up and through the rain came a carriage, splashing through the puddles and drawn by two grey rain-slicked cobs. It rounded the corner, and the driver, crammed beneath an oilskin, pulled up sharply in front of the vicarage. He braked the cab, wriggled out from beneath the sodden cover, and hopped down to open the door, bowing and apologising as the Reverend Elijah Warren stepped gingerly into the teeming roadway.

The Misses Warren and their father had been in the new vicarage for six months. Despite its recent consecration the pews in Saint Saviour's had still not been completed and carpenters filled the church every day, planing and fixing pitch-pine planks and rounding the mouldings and carved-end woods of each pew. The whole building smelled of sweet varnish.

Now the Reverend ran in a strange jiggling and unsure gait, hopping and swerving between puddles, his long black cloak slapping wetly at his back when he stopped suddenly, unsure which route to take as he traversed the path to the house, water pouring in torrents from the wide brim of his black hat.

On catching the gaze of the young women peering through the stained-glass window, he waved and grinned madly as if desperate to attract their attention.

The action, so out of character from their dour and stately father, threw the girls into a burst of giggles, and they rocked and bent away from the window, Judith shouting through her laughter, 'Call Jessie for warm towels for the poor man!'

Esther ran through the room and into the booming new wood of the hall to open the door. Judith fell laughing into the chaise before the warmth of the coal fire, saying, 'Noah . . . in his naked-ness . . .'

As the door was opened on the soaking clergyman, Jessie the maid launched herself mad-eyed upon him, wreathing and folding him in sumptuous white towelling sheets, saying, 'You will catch a death, sir . . . you will catch a death . . .'

There was a tumble and turmoil of maid and daughter and wet black-coated father, and vigorous rubbing and cries of 'Mercy!' as they bundled him down the hall, removing his hat and peeling off his soaking frock coat as small puddles formed upon the floorboards. The Reverend straightened before the fire, which made steam rise from the back of his damp clinging white shirt. And his twin daughters sat before him on the couch, smiling and suppressing giggles at the sight of him.

At fifty, he was a man who strove to maintain the sedate, disapproving and learned manner he affected in public in the face of his daughters. It was not always easy. He pursed his thin lips and held his face neutral, though his eyes began to spark with the rising desire to laugh at his own foolishness and sodden dignity.

His wife had been dead eleven years. He had fallen, in the months of mourning following his Emily's death, into a bleak and stateless melancholy where he felt as if his mind and its long-riven set of certainties were being stretched on a great creaking rack like some martyr of old, scourged and pulled into muscle-popping agony as he attempted to reconcile a loving Creator who knew and ordained everything and whose ultimate goal was the liberation of all mankind through the knowledge of his love with the terror and stench of his dying wife who bucked and cursed and profaned God as she was ripped from this life before his horrified eyes at the age of thirty-six.

In a locked drawer in his writing desk he kept the stained and partly shredded cotton nightdress she died in. The stains were bleached and faded now, and the rest of the poor broken thing, though laundered and starched on his own instructions, was faint and flaccid to the touch as he opened the drawer and caressed it every day.

She was still the livid scarce-healed gash in his heart that he did not speak of, and even today he refused to say her name lest that wound burst and torch him inside with the bright coruscating poison he had fought so hard to push down. A dull ache lived permanently in the centre of his chest, and so now, with the twins before him, he welcomed their giggles and bright quick eyes. Their identical vivid faces seemed to quicken in him a sense that he must heal and progress from the floating darkness on which he felt he had hovered since Emily's death. Perhaps it was permitted to smile, perhaps even to smile at his own indignity and punctured self-image.

Esther was the oldest by fifteen minutes, and for all the verisimilitude of their faces the girls had grown into two quite distinct characters. With each day of their young adulthood the twins grew to look quite alarmingly like their mother: long slim necks and red-blonde curls tamed and smoothed into tight bobbed buns and twisted plaits. They moved with their mother's grace and assurance, had her pale marble skin. Both possessed Emily's keen and piercing green eyes that seemed to shine with an uncanny ability to see the truth of a situation and judge the character of a person.

Judith was serious and practical; she loved to plan and to organise. It was she who had managed most of the household bills, and she who had corresponded most often with parish committees, the Bishop's secretaries, wealthy donors and even Sir Andrew Wilson-Mackenzie in the planning and execution of the poor school. The distinction between the twins showed earliest in Judith. Within a year of her mother's death she had begun to order and read a range of newspapers and periodicals and books of practical advice. At thirteen she had taught herself to speak and read French, to the horror of her governess, Miss Shelby, whose father was killed at Waterloo and who considered all things French to be seditious.

Judith was the daughter who had begun in recent years to challenge her father's authority most openly, and as her confidence grew, her father's acquiescence to her grew also. He would perhaps have asserted his primacy in the household more had Judith not grown to look so like her mother, so that the only portrait he had of his wife aged twenty-five was frequently mistaken by visitors for a contemporaneous portrait of one of his twin daughters.

Esther had none of her sister's practicality and easy grasp of organising and running a house. She was of a more emotional nature and had a gentle and compassionate understanding of suffering in all things. As a child she had nursed and cherished fallen thrush hatchlings and injured sparrows and wept fully and bitterly when, as they always did, they died, which prompted elaborate funerals with crosses made of sticks and earnest orisons to the Creator to guard and keep the soul of the thrush or starling or mouse. Esther was the child who remained dreamily wandering in the garden on summer evenings when her sister came into the house to prepare for bed, and the child who ran delightedly into the snow in winter chasing snowflakes and lying down on her back to make snow angels in its newly fallen depth, while Judith shivered inside and called warnings of chilblains and sniffles through the French windows.

Esther read poetry and, prompted by her absorption in the various periodicals which were delivered to their former vicarage in Gloucestershire, had ordered tracts by both Thomas Paine and Mrs Wollstonecraft from a radical Bristol book supplier. She had read *Rights of Man* and *A Vindication of the Rights of Women* by the time she was sixteen.

'Tell us news from Sir Andrew, Father,' said Judith, her giggling now subsided, as she straightened herself on the chaise to sit in the rigid manner of a respectable young lady.

Esther rose and held her hand to her father's cheek. 'You are still chilled, sir,' she said.

'I am well, child,' he said, holding her warm hand against his cheek for a moment and smiling. 'Sir Andrew, I am pleased to inform you, has withdrawn his threat to cancel his subscription. It was, in fact, Lady Agnes who persuaded him. She was impressed by the numbers now attending the school. However, I fear that Sir Andrew still believes that teaching the poor to read will open the door to revolution.'

Esther clapped her hands and said, 'He is a monstrous man, Father. His land and riches are all wrenched from the poor who labour in his infernal mines . . . It is the least he owes them to educate their children.'

Jessie the maid bundled into the parlour with a jug of cordial. On seeing the Reverend she let out a gasp and hurried to him. 'You are not quite well, sir. It is the chilling, I swear . . . A blanket . . . some brandy, sir . . . ?'

As the Reverend settled into his high-backed chair Esther said, 'Do not fuss so, Jessie, the Reverend is fine.'

And Jessie said, 'He is chilled, Miss Esther! The man is fair chilled with running about in the rain! Here now, sir, take some brandy . . . take a drop of brandy . . .'

Judith, amused at Jessie's frantic ministrations, said, 'Jessie believes all the illnesses visited upon mankind are caused by the chilling, do you not, Jessie? Not for her the agency of bacilli in human ill health.'

Jessie said, 'You might smirk, Miss, but I have seen bairns die from chills.'

Judith smiled at her father and said, 'Are you a bairn, Father?'

The Reverend said, 'Thank you, Jessie. I am quite recovered.' He frowned at Judith, who pouted like a scolded child.

Jessie poured cordial for the daughters, who now sat on the chaise together opposite their father, and as she left the room said, 'Supper in twenty minutes. I shall ring the bell.'

The Reverend turned to Judith. 'It does not become you to mock Jessie. She is a good kind woman who loves you and your sister like you are her own. No matter our station, we are all God's children and are all worthy of his compassion . . .' He then slapped his hand to his forehead. 'Heavens! I forgot! Esther, kindly run and tell Jessie we shall have a guest for supper.'

Esther rose and left the room, and Judith said, 'Who is to be our guest, Father?'

'The young engineer who lodges with Mrs Barnet, the Scottish fellow, Mr McLean. I ran into him at the port this afternoon. He is overseeing the installation of some vast rolling machine at the mill on Spon Lane.'

Judith flushed. 'Father, if the invitation is for my benefit, I do not care to see that young man again.'

The Reverend smiled and said, 'He is a fine respectable young man and his services are highly sought-after hereabouts, and he has no family here. Spending every evening with Mrs Barnet must be very dull for him—'

Judith cut in. 'Father, he is the most terrible bore, and his hands are grimy and rough from pulling about at pig iron and steel or whatever it is he does all day. And he is a Presbyterian . . .'

'He is a very interesting fellow, Judith, and a first-rate mathematician. He is to be company for *me*, my dear girl. I do sometimes feel the need for a little communion with gentlemen, living as I do in the midst of ladies.'

'Then let him bore you with his talk of pistons and differential ratios, Father. I shall simply ignore him.'

The Reverend chuckled and sipped his brandy.

Esther returned to the room and was informed of their visitor. She said, 'He is tall and does have a rather fine speaking voice, although his pronunciation is a little queer. I shall sit next to him and amuse him, Father.'

'I am sure you will, my child,' said the Reverend, standing.

Judith said, 'Father, while we are talking of guests, Esther and I should like to invite young Annie Perry here for tea one afternoon. She is a most remarkable child and has learned at an astonishing rate these past months. But she is in want of . . . refinement. She needs to see and experience the manners of polite society. Esther and I believe she will benefit from contact with a different class of person.'

Esther said, 'She dwells in a most sordid world, Father. She was sold as a child to Bill Perry, and her world is full of drink and violence and squalor.'

The Reverend said, 'To what end, though? What purpose will be served by it? What good can it do the girl to expose her to a society of which she can never be a part and which will—'

'What is the point then of educating her at all, Father?' interjected Judith hotly.

'We are forever rooted in the earth from which we sprang, Judith.'

'Then there is no point or purpose in helping a child better herself?' Esther said.

The Reverend knew by the determined eyes of his daughters that he was to be hounded, cornered and finally trapped. He moved towards the door. 'We shall discuss this further, after this evening's expected guest has left us.'

He walked from the room to his chambers to change for dinner, and Esther and Judith sat before the fire. They were silent for some moments before Esther said, 'Do you think Mr McLean handsome, Judith?'

Judith thought for a moment. 'I am rather afraid I do think him handsome. If only he wouldn't speak. He is well made, I grant you. His hands are very big . . .'

Esther giggled. 'And grimy with coal and iron like a nailer. And he trills his Rs like an excited sparrow. *Would ye pass me the butterrrr, Miss Estherrrrr?*'

The bell rang, and from the parlour Judith and Esther listened as Jessie answered and escorted the guest through. The door opened and Jessie showed Mr McLean into the room.

He was indeed tall and well made, with broad shoulders and a head of thick light-brown hair swept back from his fine-featured face. The beard was trimmed short on his strong jaw. He stood awkwardly before the two seated sisters.

Esther said, 'Father will be down shortly, Mr McLean. And I trust the rain did not inconvenience you?'

'No, indeed it did not, Miss Esther. I took a covered cart from the works. Your father was kind enough to invite me when we saw each other at the port this afternoon.' On his final word, there was a slight rolling on the R, and Judith smiled broadly at the young man, eyes sparkling with suppressed laughter.

Esther rose and said, 'Please sit, Mr McLean. Father says you are installing some infernal machine at the works.'

'A roller, Miss Esther. A sheet roller.' He settled himself on the wing chair next to the fire as Esther seated herself again.

'How very fascinating,' said Judith. 'My father says he is impressed by your skills as a mathematician, Mr McLean.'

'He is very kind, Miss Judith. There is a good deal of calculus involved in my work. And a good deal of formulae to be used to configure plates for points of stress in the rolling process. We are investigating a new process for producing sheet steel for the ship-yards in Liverpool and Glasgow . . .' He stopped, aware that the two young women were both smiling broadly at him.

Esther stood. 'Mr McLean, you shall sit next to me at supper and explain the rolling of steel sheets. My sister's interest in steel production is feigned from a sense of polite discourse, but I should like to hear about engineering. I believe you studied in Glasgow?' She held out her hand, and the young man rose awkwardly and took it before following her from the room.

Judith sat for a moment, thinking, that young woman is bolder than she ought to be.

16

I sent a letter to the Bilston workhouse: wrote it myself on new paper I got from the new stores in Tipton and put it in the Penny Post. I got Miss Esther to read it and asked if it was all correct and appropriately phrased and Miss Esther smiled and said, 'Annie, it's perfect.'

Here is what it said:

To the Director
Bilston Workhouse

Dear Sir,
I have by some curious circumstances become privy to informa-
tion concerning the fate of my family, the Loveridge Family: it
is comprising my mother Keziah Loveridge, my brother
Thomas Loveridge, my next brother Tass Loveridge, my next
brother Benjamin Loveridge, and my sisters Charity Loveridge
and Mercy Loveridge, also a young baby, also my brother or
sister, whose name I do not know.

Information I have been told is that they were sent to the
Bilston Workhouse most likely in the year 1839. They could
have come to that place in a later year too.

My name is Annie Perry, of The Champion of England
Alehouse in Tipton Port. Though I was adopted at the age of 9
by Mr William Perry the famous pugilist and raised as his
daughter, I was born Annie Loveridge to my mother Keziah

and my father Thomas in the year of 1829 in the county of Staffordshire. My people are gypsy folk who travel and after the sad death of my father by a broken wagon my mother put me for adoption for she could not feed me along with all them others and with a new baby on the way and so I went to Mr Perry who has been a good and kind loving father to me these years.

I got told in recent times that my mother and the other children all come to be in the Bilston Workhouse and that they also all died there of the typhus in the year I do not know.

I respectfully request that you can find the names of my mother and my brothers and sisters in your book there and kindly tell of their fate. I will be very grateful to you, Sir, if you may do this for me, although to find that they are all gone to Heaven will be most distressing for me.

I am schooled at the Poor School at Tipton Port by Miss Esther and Miss Judith Warren and by the Reverend Warren.

Please, should you have any information for me about my people would you be so good as to write to me at The Champion of England, in Spon Lane.

Very respectfully, Sir,

Miss Annie Perry

I had been practising and practising my hand, and it was quick going from being big and like the print on a handbill to being proper looped and joined. I used the punctuation of the words that Miss Esther taught me and I tried to use some uncommon words which was quite refined to us.

Saying 'Miss Annie Perry' made us feel like I was a lady and that the director of the workhouse might even think I was if I hadn't told him I was gypsy and lived in an alehouse an all. I was right proud of that letter and all the writing it took. I was learning new words every day and also I learned some arithmetic and every day I read the Bible. I had a little leather Bible I read in the Champion too between serving ale, cleaning and making stew and faggots and keeping Bill Perry from causing too much bother.

Bill cried when I come home from the fair with my bag of shillings and pounds. He said I was an angel of mercy and I would save us all. His minding of a wench doing fisty in a ring soon went when he saw the money, but I wouldn't give it him because we had fines and bills an all to pay and if I give it him he'd spend it giving away free ale and wagering on fights out the backyard. He'd give it to any poor soul who told him they was starving and he'd buy more prints of the Queen to salute.

So I kept it, and when the men from the brewers came to get their payments for our ale I paid the bill full and ordered more barrels up front. Bill stamped about complaining I was usurping him.

He stood before the full alehouse one Friday night after they had all bin paid and we had barrels in and he said, 'Honour thy father, it says in yer Good Book, Annie. A child must obey her father.'

And I said, 'And in the Book of Exodus it says, thou shalt not steal. It is the Eighth Commandment God give to Moses and if you tek this money it is stealing for it is mine earned with me own fists and me own blood. Nor shall you bear false witness, Bill: that is the Ninth Commandment give to Moses that means you have to tell the truth. And if you don't do all that you'll go to Hell . . .'

We always had these set-tos in the Champion with everyone all flushed up with their ale and cheering and chipping in their tuppenceworth.

Someone shouted, 'Mind, he is halfway there already, Annie!'

And another went, 'Thou shalt not covet thy neighbour's ale, Billy!'

Bill, swaying about in front of his print of the Queen, said, 'God save me from a disobedient daughter. God save me from all this book-learning she's doing. She's too many words in her head now and she is intent on saying them all to me.'

A nail wench watching our little show called out, 'I've a few words in my head an all, Billy!'

The nailer she was with shouted, 'Let's hear a few of em, wench – nice and dirty ones, mind!'

And they all went on like that, especially on Fridays. Bill stood centre in a fog of baccy smoke, calling and raging and swinging his ale pot about, and I sat at the table in the corner doing my reading and my writing after I come back from the schooling.

Janey and me got the bills paid with the prize money, and we paid Bill's fines too, so as we were right with everyone and had no fear of ruin and the workhouse.

Miss Esther lent me books from her library at home. She told me about poetry and about periodicals she had delivered from Bristol. She said there was all beauty and truth about our lives and who we are in poetry. And in periodicals there were many interesting and improving writings, on history, geography, politics and world affairs. In some newspapers there was writing about the Empire and the doings of Her Majesty the Queen, and about prices for wheat and coal and iron rising and falling in the stock exchanges. She told me about volcanoes in the Indies and mountains and deserts in Africa, and wars fought in New Zealand between the Maori tribesmen and the British settlers. There was news about crimes and terrible acts from all parts of the kingdom.

And here is what I read in that year after the Hallow Heath Fair.

I read the poetry of Mr Keats and Mr Wordsworth, and I read a devilish and dark poem, 'The Raven' by an American poet, Mr

Edgar Allan Poe, which scared me somewhat. I read *Poems, Chiefly in the Scottish Dialect* by Mr Rabbie Burns, writ in the queer speech of Scotchmen. Miss Esther said they were songs you sung and there was some lovely words in them, words I tried to remember to say to Jem when he come over from the farrier's and we took walks up to the heath.

Mr Burns had a broken heart by some Scotch lassie and he ached all the while and I loved the words: 'Ye'll break my heart, ye warbling birds, That wanton through the flowering thorn.' And I thought that this was the most saddest and lovely thing, that there was flowering thorn in our lives and flowering thorn on the heath. A flower and a thorn together is what we know in life and in love too.

I loved Mr Wordsworth's long poem called 'Ode: Intimations of Immortality from Recollections of Early Childhood' where he recalls so sadly being a babby and how all the world is lovely and 'apparelled in celestial light' and then he sees that it is all gone, that world that he loved: the meadows and the streams and groves.

The words 'things which I have seen I now can see no more' made us want to cry and put me in mind of my dear Big Tom and the shimmering meadows of sweet flowers and the whispering oak leaves where we stopped and camped – all long gone and lost, and most probably a railway or a works built on them now.

And I learnt what a wonder there is in words. That these little lines and marks upon a page can make me cry or get angry or want to grab Jem Mason and kiss him and run my hands over his hard muscles. Just marks on a page can do that and marks on a page can make you feel that all your mind is opening up and bursting in celestial lights. Mr Wordsworth said we are born and come from God, trailing clouds of glory, and we are in Heaven when we are born and then it all goes away. He is a most regret-filled and sad fellow in his poem. And so are all the poets I read the works of, and I wondered if you can write a poem and not make it sad and sweet like they do. Poems is all sad and sweet in the same words: it is all two things in one thing like the flowering and the thorns. There is always thorn behind May blossom.

My lessons was soon me reading the books and periodicals I got from Miss Esther, and then we would just talk on them for hours while Miss Judith instructed the little ones. This was how I learned more and more words and more and more about this world, about kings and queens and savages and sages and about seas and forests and sailing ships and Scotch mountains and castles and Welsh mines and the starving of the Irish for want of potatoes – which come from America.

I loved to walk with Jem on the Sundays he come over on his pony from Bilston. He got more handsome and lovely to me, and we never said much, just walked up and around the heath holding hands and giving little kisses. We walked to the heath to pick eyebright for a poultice made with crushed apples that I had Bill put on his eyes. Eyebright is the most beautiful flower in a meadow and it grew in the dry grass on the heath.

Sometimes Jem's feller come up hard and poking out his britches when he held me and I laughed at his poor yearning face. Mind, I wanted it an all, but I knowed that was the way babbies was made and I told him no. So sometimes I rubbed it for him like you do with a stallion and his seed come spilling out and he went 'aaah' like it was hurting him. And this was so funny and also beautiful to me, us grappling about in the bushes up the heath of an autumn Sunday afternoon.

Jem said we should wed, and he made me a very fine and thin ring of beaten bronze that felt warm and heavy on my finger. Inside the ring he engraved *My love, Annie*. It was fine engraving too; he got his landlady to write the words down for him and then he worked and worked with a steel stylus to copy them onto the inside of the ring. For a lad with big hands, it was delicate and pretty the way he done them words with little scrolls between them.

I thought I would burst with happiness when he give it me. We were standing by the canal, and it was a sunset in November and the air was cold and sharp and the red of the sun and the glow of the foundries turned all the brick in Tipton the soft pink of honey-suckle. He pulled the ring from his waistcoat and held it out to me. He said, 'It aint gold, Annie, but you shall have gold, and you shall have everything the world has in it from me . . . Will you be my wife?'

It would be easy to get bellowed away with that, wouldn't it? The pink and the sharp air and him stood there with a ring he made us.

But I tried to see where it was all going. And I tried to read the signs and the augurs all around. I said we would wed, indeed we would, but first I had to sort out Bill, whose sight was getting worse by the day, and the alehouse. I needed to get us money – and a good big bit of it too – so as we were not teetering over a gaping cavern all the while and also to find out what had become of my mammy.

So me and Jem talked and got a note to Paddy Tacker, and he come to the Champion one night and said he thought he could arrange for another Bruiser and Slasher's Daughter bout. He said we could have it on the scrap of field at the back of the alehouse, and if he give out handbills and pasted posters we could surely get a good crowd over for it. Bill agreed to it an all, and him and Janey began spreading the word. Paddy said it would not be a challengers' go; it would be a proper match. There was a farmer from Leicestershire called Ingleby Jackson who would challenge Jem, but Paddy was stumped as to where to find a wench willing to challenge me. But before he left he said, 'Have no fear, we shall arrange things. I think I know who can put up the purse – leave it to Paddy.'

We decided the match would be the day after Christmas, the day some called Boxing Day, and Paddy clapped his hands and said, 'Perfect! Boxing on Boxing Day!'

Just before that Christmas the Miss Warrens said they wanted me to show how good my writing and reading was by writing a letter to the Bishop in Birmingham, who gave money from the church to run our little school and who was desirous of knowing what good was being done in the parish for the poor. A bishop is like a lord or a king in the Church and he is a very important and stately man. Miss Esther said it would be very good for the repute of our school if a child who had been without any reading or writing just six months on could pen a letter using good words and greetings to him. Miss Esther said her father would be pleased too because the Bishop was his guvnor. She dint say guvnor, she said 'authority', but it means the same thing.

So then I had a right good think about what I was to say in the letter and over a week or so, as I was running the alehouse, I wrote this:

To His Lordship The Bishop of Birmingham

Your Lordship Bishop,
I respectfully request your attention to this letter written by me Miss Annie Perry of Tipton Port.
I am a pupil in the Poor School in this parish which is over-seen by the Reverend Elijah Warren of Saint Saviour's on the Hill, the new church hereabouts. The teaching of the children

in this school is undertaken by the two daughters of the Reverend, Miss Esther and Miss Judith, who are so very intelligent and able in their teaching of the poor children of this parish.

Just only six months from writing to you this letter I was unable to read or to write and I had never read or even seen the Bible nor heard of the Holy Word of God that is contained therein. I was dwelling in darkness and in ignorance of His Glory. With the teaching of reading and writing I have had at the school I can now read the Bible and I do so every day. I am instructed in the meanings of the verses, chapters and books by the two Miss Warrens. I am most truly awakened in my understanding of the Holy Word of Our Lord.

Also Miss Esther has instructed me in news from The Empire and the doings of Her Majesty the Queen. Miss Esther has brought many interesting and informing newspapers and periodicals for me to read and talk about with her on many subjects of interest such as wars and politics and I have also been informed about the rising and falling of the prices of iron, steel, coal and wheat in this Kingdom which is most important knowledge for me and for people living here in Tipton where iron is made and coal is dug.

My heart has been most moved and affected by the poetry which Miss Esther has shown me to read. I have read works by Mr Keats, Mr Wordsworth and Mr Robert Burns and they have all moved and lifted my heart with their sweetness and beauty and I do believe that poetry is the part of reading I do love best of all.

My Lordship Bishop, I would like to express my humblest gratitude to your church for making it possible for a poor child like me to have the gift of reading and writing which has opened my eyes to the glories of God in this world where there is so much wickedness and want.

I am an orphan and I was raised and cared for by Mr William Perry the landlord of The Champion of England alehouse in Spon Lane. He is a most kind and loving father and I have been blessed in that I can now read and explain letters to him that he gets from Magistrates and Constabularies about fines he has had for fighting and causing disorder when drunk, as he often is.

I wish your Lordship Bishop a most peaceful and happy Christmas and thank you for reading my letter.

Miss Annie Perry

I was pleased by the letter and I think I wrote good things to the Bishop in praise of Miss Judith and Miss Esther. I lied a bit about some things, like reading the Bible *every* day but I read it most days, and I said I was an orphan although I weren't sure then if my mammy was dead, but my daddy was so I was half an orphan any road.

Miss Esther and Miss Judith asked me to show them the letter I was going to send, but when I finished I thought it was good and I was proud of it, so I walked to the post and addressed it to *The Bishop of Birmingham, Birmingham, Warwickshire.* The post mistress said that would reach him and I sent it.

17

The Gaffer thought it a queer thing indeed that he had been taken on to move four vast iron corner braces for the Manchester and Birmingham Railway Company. He had heard that once this last bridge was done the line to Manchester would be open and goods wagons would move the bulk of the coal, iron and nails north from Tipton Port. It had already happened in the south. He no longer hauled loads down to Bristol as he had for years; the new railway line took everything.

As he stood at the tiller of the coal barge carrying the great L-shaped pieces north, he could see the grim irony of it. He was helping to put himself out of a job.

He had even had a steam engine installed on this boat, and it chugged away noisily, belching smoke and steam in extravagant clouds across the quiet canal. It had sped him up, no doubt, but he missed the quiet clopping and creaking rope of the horse. The constant rattle and hum of the engine put his nerves on edge for the whole trip. And he had had to take on two nailer lads to haul him through the locks now that Bill Perry was no longer capable and his vision so fogged that Janey and Annie were his eyes. Mind, it took two big lads to do the job Billy had done on his own. The boys dozed up the front, waiting till they came to the next locks.

The railway ran for the most part along the line of the canal northwest, sticking to the level ground and twisting round hills where it could. But the branch now being connected needed to ford a gorge just outside Nantwich to connect it to those running down from Liverpool and Manchester. The braces he was carrying were the length of three men and were to shore the sides of the stone columns constructed to carry the line over the chasm.

Where the canal rose and fell with locks or bored through hills with tunnels, the railway went straight over the top. Crushing everything underneath it, thought the Gaffer.

Still, the railway companies paid well and lines were being built everywhere. They called it the Rail Fever and fortunes were being made and lost in London speculating on the prices of the new rail companies. The Gaffer had read in newspapers that in this year alone 272 Acts of Parliament were passed to set up and commission new railway companies.

The change and growth and building around the basin where he kept his boats in Tipton made his head spin of late. Never a day went past when there was not men putting up scaffolding or pulling down the wooden hovels that teamed along the canalside. The peace that was once to be found out the back of the Champion on a summer evening was gone now. From his accustomed spot, sitting in the back of the barge looking west towards Bilston, he no longer saw any green at all. Most of the trees that once grew along the towpath had withered and died years before, their leaves stained black with smuts and iron dust. Further along, where there had once been a meadow, there were now heaps of black slag.

The town was changing too. A new rail station with classical columns holding its wide portico looked out onto the high street, where shops and emporiums seemed to open daily. The new co-operative store, a ladies' dress shop, a baker and ironmongery, even an ale shop. Where folk got the money to spend in them the Gaffer did not know, for in the crowded hovels and huts children still ran barefoot, hollow-eyed with hunger, and men and women still laboured twelve-hour days in the mines and nail shops. The pall of billowing black air still hung across Tipton most days.

But some had money. The fine people from up the hill who walked of a Sunday in the new Victoria Park with its recently erected statue of the Earl of Dudley, safe above the filth of the port whose view would soon be screened by the lime trees that had been planted in a uniform line along the southern railings. Few from the foundries where the railings were cast ever came of a Sunday to parade among the rose beds and bricked paths.

The Gaffer squinted ahead as he came out wide to line up to a bridge. He saw fewer and fewer barges on the canal these past days and seldom had to stop and wait for another craft to pass through. The drop in trade did have some advantages, he thought. As the bow went under the bridge, the Gaffer looked up and, pasted to the side of the bridge, was a poster: *Reward! The Scoundrel known as the Black Cloak . . .*

Now there was one who had money, thought the Gaffer.

Just the week before, two more foggers had been robbed on the Wolverhampton Road. They travelled in twos these days if they were carrying money. It was possible to take a train to Brum now, but the Gaffer suspected the foggers were saving a few pennies on their fare by walking, both clutching satchels for the nailmasters.

And they thought they'd be safe for the Black Cloak had not struck for some months, and both had carried charged pistols. They'd left the Champion at five o'clock, just as the light was fading, after an afternoon drinking together at a corner table there, for no others in the place would talk to them. The Gaffer, sat on his stool at the bar, had watched them go, one lighting a pole lamp as they set off up the long hill towards Wolverhampton.

There were scarcely any trees or hedges left along that road now, and the men travelling with money bags supposed that if the Black

Cloak were to commit a robbery he'd choose a route where there was more cover.

But they were wrong. The road skirted the church and the park, and as they came out into the open fields beyond the stacks of scaffold poles and piles of bricks that were stored at the edge of the new houses, they heard hooves coming from behind them in the dark.

A voice called, 'Turn, gentlemen!' The flash of a pistol and a boom.

The fogger with the lamp took a ball in the shoulder and spiralled away with the force of it, his lamp clattering to the ground and extinguishing as he called out, 'Murder!'

The other fumbled desperately in his coat to pull out his pistol. As he groped in the darkness screaming, 'Robbery! Murder!' he was run down by the rider's pony and trampled. His pistol discharged as he went down, a sudden flare that lit the scene a lurid orange for an instant, and the terrified fogger saw, frozen in the vivid glare of the powder blast, the rider dismounting and a gaping black cloak looming from the darkness.

The two robbed men fled back to the Champion where Annie tended their wounds. The robber's pistol ball had carved a smooth groove in the wounded man's right shoulder, but he was lucky: no arteries or bones were hit.

When the constable came and took statements from the men, he sighed and said, 'He'll be away beyond Brum by now. We'll patrol up there tomorrow. We'll tek lamps and see if he tries it again.'

The wounded fogger said, 'There's a twenty-pound reward for the man who teks him, sir.'

Constable Perkins shrugged and said, 'There's a lot of lonely little roads and lanes round here, son. Be a devil to trace him less you catch him at it.'

There was a growing sense of wonder amongst the assembled drinkers at the daring and skill of the robber. Jock Convey, a grizzled old Scotch miner, shook his head. 'He never kills – always a ball to the shoulder. He must be a braw shot with that iron of his.'

Susie Giout, perched on the knee of her big bearded husband Robin said, 'And in the dark too . . . in the dark he hits his man on the shoulder.'

'He'll be a soldier for sure when they catch him, man that can shoot like that,' said another miner, craning in to see the treatment of the wounded man.

Constable Perkins said, 'Well, he's got some nerve. I'll grant him that.'

Susie said, 'Long as he's tekin the nailmasters' money I'm not bothered whether they catch him or not.'

The uninjured fogger said, 'He's had your wages once, wench. It aint always landlord's money he's tekin. He's a big lad an all, knocked me flat with his pony.'

Annie pulled the constable a jug of ale and set to making up two beds in the back scullery for the foggers to stay over. She'd have a tanner off each of them for the beds and the tea and bread she'd give them in the morning.

Bill sat quiet in his chair by the fire that night, sipping his ale. He seemed lost in thought as the noise and the drama of the two robbed foggers played out around him.

The constable took his jug and sat down opposite him, and Bill said, 'Is that you, constable?'

The officer said, 'Aye, Bill, it's Jack Perkins.'

'If I could see better I'd find that robber for ya.'

'I know you would, Bill.'

'So what does you know of the lad?'

'Well,' said the constable, 'he's a big feller. Wears the black cloak.

The pony is a fast little grey. Speaks like he's from round here somewhere. And he knows how to shoot a pistol. And he knows how to get away and leave no trace of where he come from. Oh aye, and he wears a red ribbon on his left wrist. Lady Wilson-Mackenzie saw it.'

Bill sighed and leaned back, feeling the glow of the coals on his face. 'Honest, I wish the boy well, Jack, I do. You can't blame a man for robbing foggers the way they rob the rest of us.'

Constable Perkins drained his ale and said quietly to Bill, 'No, I suppose not. But we'll be out there now running about for him, especially once Sir Andrew hears there's been another blag so close to Ardleigh. He'll be sending notes to the Chief Constable in Brum, you watch.'

In a shelter made from branches and woven ferns in the most remote and wooded part of Tipton Heath that night the Black Cloak counted the money from the satchels by the light of his campfire. Six pound in coin in total. Not bad. But he needed more now that he was back in the district. There was money everywhere in these parts, he thought, as his pony stamped in the darkness.

18

The wench Paddy found to challenge us was called Molly Stych and she worked on the barges in Birmingham. The Gaffer knew her. When Paddy told me I felt all fluttery at the thought of a proper match with me the main draw, for everyone coming in the Champion started on about it.

Paddy wrote to Lord Ledbury, who would put up the purse of twenty guineas for Jem's fight and twenty for mine. There was no double purse: it was winner take the lot. There were bookies to come from all over to take the wagers and Paddy said his lordship was to place big wagers on me and Jem. Paddy had seen Ingleby Jackson fight and reckoned Jem would have no bother with him. Jackson called himself 'The Gent' and wore a proper collar and tie in the ring. Paddy said he was handy enough but he had no real power in him like Jem did and he was pushing thirty-five.

The Gaffer said, 'Oh, mighty Christ!' when we told him about Molly Stych coming in from Brum to fight me. He said, 'She's a great big bloody beast of a wench. You'd not have her for a wench but for the big bosom on her. Ugly? Our Billy's a Greek god compared to her. I've seen her pull a full coal barge on her own – she's stronger 'n a Shire. You've got your work set hard there, my girl. I mean it, Annie, she shall daunt you. I'd not back Billy to beat her. Think on it, Paddy – is it fair on the child?'

Bill said, 'Aye, but she aint trained, Gaffer. Our Annie's trained and honed. And she can read an all. I'll wager that Molly can't read a proper book nor say words from the Bible.'

He said it out to the room from his chair by the fire, smiling when he bragged about my reading. He was a queer one was Bill. He dint want me to fight nor to learn and now he was beaming about it. I went over and give him a kiss.

He said, 'I loves you, my Annie.'

I said, 'I loves you an all, my Bill.'

Paddy needed money for tipping the peelers to stop out of it when we had the bout. Fighting was illegal, and they were cracking down on it now. They broke up crowds at fairs if there was fisty and went after the bookmen too. The Chief Constable even said in the paper that 'pugilism is a threat to public order'. We got a paper once a week now and I read it to Bill while he sat by the fire. He liked it and it kept him quiet. Those days he was getting quieter and quieter as his sight went. Now and agin he stood roaring in the alehouse and made everyone salute the Queen, but he mostly sat quiet and sipped his ale, though he would still give it away if someone asked for a free ale, and it would still break his heart if he heard a sob story and he'd want to start doling out our money to any twister as caught him on with a tale. You had to watch him.

When I read him what the Chief Constable said about illegal fights he said, 'I'll bloody threat him! Never mind what the peelers say, I never fought a bout that wasn't broke up by the law at some point – they been doing it for years.'

Me and Janey kept it all ordered in the Champion. We slung fellers out if they give us trouble and we was a good team: I was all sweetness and soft words and Janey was a fury, slapping and kicking em. I used to say to a feller, 'You can get out with me telling you, or you can get out with her telling you.' And when they seen her looming up on em they mostly made a hasty exit. Slinging the wenches out was harder. Some as come in and got the worse wanted to try it with me and I flattened a few of them in the street outside under the painted sign that showed Bill in his prime.

I suppose it was all good training for Molly Stych, but I still did sessions with Janey out the back, and me and Jem sparred on a weekend when he rode over. I worked on moving my head, ducking out and turning. Jem worked on throwing while he was moving especially when he was moving backwards. It's hard to put power into a shot when you're moving away, and you have to get your feet right and push off the opposite foot you go back onto so you swivel and swing the shot in. It takes a bit of doing and you have to get the rhythm right and keep your eyes up and head down.

Me and Jem chipped in two pound each to give Paddy money for tipping the peelers. With the bills and suppliers paid coming up to Christmas, that was nearly the last of the money from the Hallow Heath Fair gone, and I needed the twenty guineas I could get for beating Molly Stych.

Jem needed his too. He was going to buy new horses for the summer fairs and he said he wanted to find a house for me and him when we was wed. I said we'd tell Bill after Boxing Day when we had the money and were all set. Jem said he would buy me a fine pony an all, and I dreamed of getting one but buying and keeping a good un was dear.

Miss Esther give me a look of pure horror when I told her I had sent the letter to the Bishop. For once she dint smile.

I was sat opposite her at the end of the school room. They had decorated a little pine tree with baubles and candles and Miss Judith was teaching the babbies a Christmas carol.

I was excited when I got there, bursting to tell her I had written the letter and sent it myself. But when I told her, her face dropped and she said, 'Oh, Annie.'

And I said, 'What have I done wrong, Miss?'

She said, 'Well, you really should have let us see what you had written.'

I said, 'Why? I dint tell no lies, Miss. And it was all spelled proper . . .'

'Yes, but . . . our relations with the Bishop are sensitive. He is a man with very fixed ideas about schooling for the poor. You have not done anything wrong, Annie, but it is essential for our father that we maintain a correct accord with the Bishop.' She pulled down the corners of her mouth and made a shrug.

Then I grew a little hot with her. 'And you think I must've said something to rattle his balls. Why? Because I'm a stupid gypo who lives in an alehouse?'

Miss Esther flushed bright red and gasped, 'Annie!'

I felt bad then. I felt like I'd fouled a lace bonnet. I said, 'Sorry, Miss, but I was proud of myself, writing it all correct and sending it. I paid for the stamp an all. I only done what you asked us and what you taught us.'

Miss Esther clasped my hands and said, 'Annie, I am sorry, I am sorry. I should have trusted you – I do trust you, Annie. And you are by no means stupid in any way. Please forgive me. I am sure your letter was simply splendid and the Bishop will be most impressed.'

Nobody ever asked me to forgive them before in my life, not even my mammy for selling us. I said, 'Well, I am sorry I said balls, Miss. We all speak rough where I live.'

Then she smiled. 'I know, Annie, but here we shall teach you to speak properly.'

I said, 'Will you teach me to curtsey, Miss? For I am to meet a lord just after Christmas.'

'And you feel you should curtsey to a lord?'

146

'It's decorum, aint it, Miss?'

Miss Esther looked down the school room. The babbies were singing 'O Come All Ye Faithful' and Miss Judith was pumping away on the harmonium. It dint sound so nice.

She turned back to me and said, 'Annie, we should show respect and deference to those who deserve and earn our respect. I do not believe we should simply defer and belittle ourselves to a person simply because of the station they have been allotted in life. A station allotted by man, not God. Simply because a man has inherited wealth and land and position it does not follow that he is worthy of unquestioning respect. In the eyes of God we are all equal and we are all worthy of equal respect.'

I thought, interesting. She sounds like a radical to me. I said, 'So you would not curtsey just cause he was a lord?'

'No. I believe I would shake hands. One must always be polite. Of course it would be dependent upon who the lord was and what he had done to deserve my deference. I fear I must defer to the Bishop because of the influence he has over my father. Who is he then, this lord? And how is it that you will met him?'

'Miss, he is not a man you would care to curtsey to. Nor do I believe I will now. I might not even shake his hand.'

'And how shall you meet him?'

So I told her. I told her about the match on Boxing Day and the purse and the wagering. I told her about Jem fighting and me fighting for the money to keep the Champion going and look after Bill.

When she heard of the purse she said, 'Twenty guineas! Good Lord!'

I said, 'I got to win though, Miss. The wench I'm fighting is worse than a gargoyle by the accounts I've heard.'

'And you are not scared, Annie?'

'No, Miss, I aint.' I was but I never told her I was.

She thought for a while and then said, 'I should like to come and see you fight.'

'I wouldn't, Miss. It is a powerful rough crowd, and there'll be a storm of trouble at the end of the fight – there always is.'

She thought some more and said, 'I do not approve of violence, Annie. But I must say I admire you. It is hard for a woman in this world. I do not believe I could make twenty guineas without marrying some dimwit approved of by my father.'

Miss Judith came over to us. The babbies were having their tea and bread sat on the long benches. The tea and bread was half the reason they all come.

Miss Esther looked up to her sister and said, 'Judith, Annie is to demonstrate her skills in the noble art of pugilism come Boxing Day.'

Miss Judith looked down at me and said, 'Oh . . . how alarming. I trust you will not be injured, Annie.'

I said, 'No, Miss. I know what I am doing.'

She dint look so sure but then she smiled and said, 'Abner said to Joab, *Now let the young men arise and hold a contest before us*. And Joab said, *Let them arise*. It is from the book of Samuel, Annie.'

Miss Esther laughed and said, 'Does it not talk of boxing as like one beating the air in Corinthians too, Judith?'

'I believe it does. You shall have to consult the Good Book, Annie, for there are some other verses about the sport. But, Annie, my concern is that you shall be arrested. I believe public fisticuffs, with men or women, is now illegal.'

'No, you're all right there, Miss,' I said. 'We've tipped all the peelers in Tipton so we shall have no bother with them.'

'And the purse is twenty guineas, Judith. Annie will be rich.'

Miss Judith said, 'Goodness. I trust we shall neglect to mention this to the Reverend, Esther?'

Miss Esther said, 'Of course we shall.'

Dint I think on that conversation as I walked back to the Champion. It was quiet the week before Christmas and snow started falling as I walked along Spon Lane. There were new terraces being built all along and off it that were to be rented by the works to the foundrymen. They were low mean little huts by the look of em. I dint want one of them when I wed Jem.

When I got back there was a to-do going on in the alehouse. Three constables were stood inside calling for a gang of fellas to go and search up to the heath with them.

The Black Cloak had struck again, they said. He had injured a constable who was patrolling on a horse up the lane and had come across him holding up three foggers returning to Bilston with rent money.

'Three this time,' said Constable Perkins. 'He's got three satchels. Our lad Clayton Samson saw the lights of the lamps and come across him with his irons out and the foggers all kneeling before him. He took a ball to the shoulder but he managed to gallop back down and raise the alarm. We need a crowd to come and search for him up the heath. It was not an hour ago and he will still be up there, so we can follow his tracks in the snow. I've sent a lad to Dudley to raise the dragoons at the barracks. We can flush him through that way.'

Bill was sat in his place by the fire and he called, 'Let the lad be, Jack! He's only took what was robbed in the first place!'

Constable Perkins said, 'He's shot a constable, Bill! He shall hang if we catch him.'

The door burst open, and there in a fine red coat and spurs stood Sir Andrew Wilson-Mackenzie, looking puffed and red-faced and holding his crop out before him. He boomed, 'I have just been informed, Constable Perkins . . . Come, come, we must hurry. You men there . . . there is a twenty-pound reward for the capture of this scoundrel. I have two of my grooms here, we have lamps and staves, and I have pistols too for you men. You shall not face this threat unarmed.'

When the miners in the Champion saw Sir Andrew, and heard his commands and entreaties to them they agreed to go. Some shuffled up like they dint really want to, but you could see they knew it would do them no harm to be part of the gang that took the Black Cloak.

Sir Andrew was in a fury shooing them outside and just fore he left he looked over at me behind the bar and said, 'Will you not join us, young woman? I am told you are fearless.'

I said, 'No, I won't, sir. I have an alehouse to run.'

Bill piped up from his chair, 'Good luck to you, sir. You shall catch the villain I am sure.'

They went off up towards the Heath Lane and the miners crowded onto Sir Andrew's cart. Sir Andrew was at the front on a fine black stallion, holding his crop aloft like a general leading into battle, and the constables followed on foot. The lamplight and the shouts faded off into the swirling snow.

I felt sorry for the bugger if they got him.

19

Janey and Annie saw Bill to his bed. He was, like most recent nights, drunk enough to need helped up the stairway to his chamber but not so drunk as to resist and call for them all to salute the picture of the Queen and sing 'God Save Her'. He was becoming more and more like a sick child, requiring dressing, undressing and washing. Janey took him into his room and Annie heard the great creak from outside the closed door as his massive frame settled onto the bed, and Janey saying, 'There now, Bill, let's get your britches.'

Annie locked the doors below and snuffed lamps and candles. She swept out the bar and set the ale jugs in a pail to soak overnight. She banked up the fire with coal for the night and made her way upstairs to her bedchamber.

In bed she read the Bible by candlelight. Outside, the wind was beginning to howl, and snow was drifting against her window. She wondered at the men up on the heath searching just two days before Christmas.

In the Book of Isaiah she read the verse, 'Give counsel; grant justice; make your shade like night at the height of noon; shelter the outcasts; do not reveal the fugitive; let the outcasts of Moab sojourn among you; be a shelter to them from the destroyer . . . ' before sleep overtook her.

She was awakened by a dull thud from downstairs. The candle had burned out and she lay with her eyes open, listening in the dark of the room. Then a crash and a rattle and chink as if the pail of jugs had been kicked over. The strongbox with the few shillings they had taken for ale that night was under the bar. It was locked, but those who knew the alehouse knew that was where Bill kept it. Annie was wide awake now and sitting up. She reached out and slowly pulled her door open. It was silence downstairs. Then she heard the slow creak of a leather boot . . .

Someone was creeping down the corridor towards the bar. She had no lucifer for her candle, nor lamp, but she rose silently from her bed and stood out on the landing, listening. Again the creak of the boot and a scrape as the bar door was pushed gently open. She'd no doubt now. They were being burglarised and the villain was after the strongbox. She moved slow and silent, gently placing her weight onto each foot as it met the step down. She wished she had a stave to clout the beggar. From the corridor she could see through into the bar. Silhouetted against the white glow of the snow outside the front window, she saw a figure. A tall man in a tricorn hat, the outline of his short black cloak was clear.

She caught her breath at the sight and stanced herself ready in case he rushed her.

His head turned slowly towards her and he said, 'Hello, Annie. Sorry about the pail.'

Though she could not see the face, she knew the voice. She said, 'Tommy.'

He removed the hat and stood with his arms open, and she ran into the room and hugged him. He smelled of cold mud and snow, and as he held her head into his breast he said, 'They're after me, Annie. I am the Black Cloak.'

With those words, he heaved off a heavy satchel to the stone floor.

Annie pulled away from him. She felt a sudden lurching anguish inside her chest and tears sprang to her eyes. She turned to fetch a candle, saying, 'I must see your face.'

'No . . . no lights,' he said. 'They harried me clean across the heath and I had to slap away me lovely mare and double back on em, but they'll get me trail soon enough unless the snow has covered me tracks. No lights. They might trace me back here and then we'll be in a hellish bind.'

Annie came close to him. She peered in the dim light from the windows, then put her hands up and touched his face. It was smooth, and his cold skin felt like a boy's. She held his cheeks.

'Oh, Tommy, what became of you? What became of Mammy? Here, sit.'

He moved in the gloom to the far side of the bar and sat on an oak bench. 'That satchel's full and it's yours, Annie – yours and Bill Perry's. Has he been a good father to ye?'

Annie said, 'I'll fetch you some ale. Are you hungry?'

'As my poor mare was when I had to set her off towards Bilston to lead them constables astray . . . I'm gagging, Annie.'

Annie went to the scullery and fumbled among the familiar shelves and pails, returning with a board of bread and cheese and a jug of ale.

She sat opposite him and he was but a dim blurred figure across the table. Before he began to eat he pulled two heavy pistols from his waist and set them with a clunk upon the table.

'I pray I have no more need of them tonight,' he said.

Annie whispered, 'There's a tale you need to tell us, Tommy . . .'

And in the darkness between gulps of ale and mouthfuls of bread Tommy told his tale. 'I know I have some road to close between us, my Annie. And I have come down a hard road since last I saw your face at the Hallow Heath. And our mammy is dead; she died near five years ago. And one by one the others too. Benny and Tass are as good as dead, and the little wenches.'

Annie sat for a moment in the silence, breathing in and out steadily. Then she said, 'What of the little babby?'

Tommy let out a long sigh. 'It was dead birthed, Annie. Not long after we left you. Mammy was half starved by then – you can't carry a babby starving.'

Tommy drained the last of his ale. Annie could hear the wind outside. She said, 'How did you not come and find me, Tommy? Come and visit even . . . ?'

'We bought a canvas-covered vardo and a pony after you went – with the guineas we got for ya, like Mammy said we would, and then we planned to go north and come up by Tipton and find a camp, and then come and find you. Mammy said we were to come and get ya and run for it. Go to Wales or down to round Bristol with ya. It was all she talked about, finding ya and springing ya. That was her plan, see . . .

'But then she got bad. She had a fever and she bucked about with pain. And we tried to see to her – the girls boiled up water and Benny took the pony and rode to Worcester to find a doctor. There weren't none of our people nowhere near us. We were in a wood north of Worcester. And then Mammy said, "This babby is coming," and we laid her flat on a blanket in the vardo and she told us to leave her. So we sat outside on the step listening to Mammy groaning and crying. I told the others all to say prayers for her and the new babby. And then we heard her cry out in a horrible voice, "This is a curse for selling my Annie!"

'We pulled back the drape and there she was, all twisted in pain and the new babby dead in her arms. It was a little girl, Annie . . .'

In the silence that settled on them Annie could see him convulse and stifle a sob. She said, 'It's all right, Tommy. This is a hard life full of pain for us to suffer. Least that babby's gone to Big Tom.'

Tommy said, 'That was the least of the pain to come, Annie, that was the least of it. Well, we buried the babby in the wood – me and Benny dug a grave with our hands for we had no shovels – and she was buried by a hawthorn so as the blossom would bloom over her in May. It was late for flowers but the little uns found yarrow and meadowsweet and Mammy laid them on the grave in a star of Solomon. She sat by it all night too, and there were shooting stars across the sky that night.

'And after that Mammy got sick and fevered again, and she was so queer with it she stopped in the vardo night and day. The little uns picked worts and leaves of all sorts to make her healing drinks, but they did no good. She just lay in the bunk there, staring at the canvas above her head and crying and cursing sometimes an all, and she said she was cursed for her sin.

'So now I was the guvnor and we stopped about there for two weeks. Me and Benny and Tass got some work harvesting for a week, and the little uns tended to Mammy. Then we moved on north, and the nights were drawing in and the days were getting colder and we had no winter camp and the shillings we had left from the fair money was getting less and less.

'Then we stopped about Kidderminster. I found us a meadow by the river. There was holly in the hedges and the water was clean and we tried to settle in there for the winter coming. We was all that stunned by the losing of you and then the babby, not one of us wanted to move and rove. All we wanted was our mammy back.

'But Mammy just lay in the vardo. She dint cook nor clean nor tell us what was what and what we had to do. Sometimes she cried and wailed, and sometimes she lay like the dead with her eyes open.

'And then one day when we was gathering wood we met an old man called Doctor Pettigrew. He was out walking and he got to talking to me. He said he was a doctor and I told him about our mammy and about losing the babby, and about Big Tom dying, and I even told him about you getting offered up.

'And I thought he was a good gorger. He was old but he was right kind and I liked it telling him all the woes we had seen. So he come to the vardo and saw Mammy and he saw the little uns all dirty and covered in mud.

'He tried to talk to Mammy, but she just lay there staring and not saying anything, and he said she was ill with a surfeit of grief. He had us say some prayers with us all stood outside the vardo with our heads bowed.

'Then he come back the next day and he had a basket with bread and cheese and apples for us. He said he wanted to talk to Mammy agin and he went in the vardo and I heard him talking quiet and slow to her and she dint say nothing.

'Well, then, he come the next day and said me and the babbies must all go and have a wash and bath at his house. He said he would save us from lice and diseases. It was getting cold then and we was having trouble by then an all. The pony had had near all the grazing in that meadow and the leaves were off the trees. So we left Mammy and we all trooped into the little town and we come to his house, and a fine big one it was too. They dint like the look of us in that town neither. The merchants wouldn't sell us fodder for the pony and they give us dirty looks in the baker's when we went for bread.

'But that Doctor Pettigrew, he dint mind us being Romi and neither did his housekeeper. She was a kindly woman who washed all the little uns by the fire in the scullery and then she give em bread and jam and tea. I washed an all, and she put a curtain round the copper bath for me as I was near a grown man.

'That doctor talked to me and said our mammy was suffering from a mania and she wanted treating by doctors to make her mind well. And he said if I wanted he would teach us to read. And I did want that.

'So we stopped there all over that winter. Doctor Pettigrew give us bread and cheese and sometimes a cake, and Benny and me and Tass snared rabbits and took partridge and pigeons with nets thereabouts, and we dint starve. We gathered the dried and dying grass from all over for the pony and she dint starve neither though no farmer nor dealer would give us hay. We bought oats in the town there for her an all, and she got through it, even with the cold.

'I thought Mammy would get better when the spring come and there were new flowers in the meadow, for all that winter long she sat in the vardo crying and sighing and tapping her forehead.

'And I went to that Doctor Pettigrew some days and he taught me reading. It dint take long till I could read the words from the Bible, Annie, and the doctor bought us penny papers so as I could read stories for the others. He give us a Bible an all, and he let me tek books from his library to read in the vardo. I read a treatise on veterinary medicine, Annie, so as I'd know about it for the pony. I had to keep walking back into the town there and going to his house and asking what a word meant or what the Latin was.

'Most I loved the stories in the penny papers. I read of Captain Jack Sheppard the notorious burglar and thief, and him robbing and escaping the peelers and rescuing his lady love Bess, and I read of Spring-heeled Jack who could leap a great wall to get away and got pots of gold from rich folk. I loved those lads, Annie. Me and Benny and Tass all vowed we should be highway robbers one day with fine horses and pistols . . .'

He picked up the pistol on the table and waggled it at Annie.

'What became of Mammy, Tommy?'

He shuddered and pulled his cloak round his shoulders for the fire had died to a dull glow and the fierce chill of the air outside had crept into the bar. 'She got no better come spring . . . truth be told she got worser . . .'

At that moment, they heard hooves and carriage wheels; the dancing light from lanterns bobbed at the window. The door was pounded and she could hear the voice of Sir Andrew calling, 'Open up! Open up, Perry! Ale for these gallant lads!'

Tommy froze and Annie rose, holding her hand out to him. 'Come, you must hide. Come up to my chamber and get in under the bed . . . Quiet now . . .'

They went quickly and quietly up the murky stairs as the pounding and shouting continued below. Tommy crawled under Annie's bed and she pushed his hat in after him, whispering, 'Stay there and make no sound.'

He said suddenly, 'Me irons, Annie! They're left on the table!'

Annie moved smartly back downstairs and snatched the two heavy pistols. She hid them under the bar with a cloth on top. Then she spotted the satchel lying in the centre of the floor. It jangled with coins as she hauled it back behind the bar. She pushed it down between two empty barrels, then she went to the door that was now vibrating with the blows being rained down on it.

The miners, four constables and Sir Andrew's two grooms all lurched in when she opened the door. Sir Andrew himself was last in, and as he entered he looked hard at her and said, 'The scoundrel came back this way, little Miss. Have you seen a fellow in a tricorn hereabouts?'

She said grumpily, 'I've been in my bed, sir, and Bill is still in his, so make less of a racket, all of you!'

Annie raked the fire and lit the lamps. The freezing men, shaking and stamping snow from their coats and boots, exhaled plumes of icy breath. Sir Andrew unbuttoned his heavy coat and said, 'Give these men ale and rum for the cold, and bring bread and cold meat if you have it—'

'I've no bread nor meat this time of the morning, sir. I can do you porridge. But this'll cost yer, mind,' she said, hauling a new barrel of ale up onto the bar.

Sir Andrew looked hard at her again; this time she could see his small blue eyes were set to flash in anger. He don't like being told by a wench, she thought. He breathed out hard and said, 'Very well. Hang the cost!'

The men settled with their ale, and Annie brought a bottle of rum through from the store and set it and nine glasses on the table. She put a pot of porridge on the stove in the scullery as Sir Andrew and the searchers settled in for a session. The rum bottle was quickly emptied and she fetched another and filled more ale jugs.

She prayed Bill would not wake and come down. This was what he liked, a big gang and drinking till the sun came up. She stood in the doorway of the bar to prevent anyone coming through to the back and past the foot of the stair. When a miner staggered towards her to go through she told him the privy was frozen and to go and piss in the canal.

Sir Andrew, warmed by the rum and ale, stood before the gathered group with his back to the fire and held up his glass. 'Here's to you, fine fellows. We nearly got him, I swear. And next time we shall.'

Constable Perkins said, 'It was a hard run, Sir Andrew, but his tracks come back this way. He is hereabouts, I know it.'

Another miner said, 'Aye, and no pony.'

Annie called across to them, 'Where did you find him then?'

Sir Andrew turned to her and walked across, sipping at his rum glass. 'He set his pony off towards Bilston to lay tracks, and we followed it, and shortly we came upon the lair he was using. It's a rough little hovel hidden away about the centre of the heath, and the pony led us to it. A fine little mare. Well looked after too.' His smile at Annie was thin-lipped and mean. 'And I will tell you now, Miss Perry, he is one of your people. Only a gypsy would bide in such a place. And he has the trickery and cunning of your tribe.'

Annie said, 'Well, he certainly tricked you, Sir Andrew. Perhaps he is gone towards Dudley, down the hills on the other side of the heath. There's many a quiet lane that way . . .'

'No, girl. He doubled back on us. We found a few of his footprints despite the snowfall. He came back this way – no doubt to seek help from his own kind. There were tracks not a quarter of a mile from here.'

'It would be a fool that helped him,' said Annie.

'It would indeed. The dragoons are still scouring back to Dudley. If he has gone that way they shall set hands on him before light. And we shall have him at the end of a rope before long.'

Annie had to stop herself looking up towards the bedchambers. The miners and the constables were now warmed with beer and rum, and she brought bowls of porridge through to them. One of Sir Andrew's grooms, a strapping lad of about seventeen, said to Annie as she set the bowls before the men, 'Are you fit for your match on Boxing Day, Miss Annie?'

She said, 'I'm fitter than you lot – can't catch a man in black in the snow!'

The miners and constables all laughed, and one called, 'I'll have a bob on you to win it, Annie!' and another shouted, 'I'll gie ye a bob for a kiss, Annie!'

They stayed until it got light, when Annie heard Janey and Bill stirring upstairs. She stood at the end of the table and told the party, 'That'll do you now, lads. We've to make ready for today and we've run out of rum. And you've woke up Bill an all, so I should scarper fore he comes down, for you know what he's like when he's missed a beano.'

They all cheered and rose to go, buttoning on their coats and cloaks and retrieving drying boots from the hearth. Sir Andrew was drunk enough to forget his previous hostility, and he warmly clapped Annie on the shoulder, pressing three pounds into her hand and saying, 'You are a fine young woman, Annie Perry – though gypsy you may be – and here is a reward for your hospitality.'

Annie felt like laughing as she took the money from him, what with Tommy hidden quiet up the stairs and the pistols under the bar. When everyone had left she ran up to her chamber. Her brother was fast asleep, crammed like a trunk under the bed. She brought the pistols up and hid them in her drawer under her petticoats and bloomers. They would be safe there for now.

When Bill got down and took his seat by the fire with his morning ale he said, 'You was raising a racket in the night, wench. Was that Jem over here? He'd better not be in yer bed . . .'

Annie said, 'No, Bill. It weren't Jem. But we do have a visitor.'

20

We kept Tommy in my chamber. Bill was cock-a-hoop at the game. Having the Black Cloak up the stair while Jack Perkins was supping his ale downstairs. I prayed Bill wouldn't let his mouth run off when he'd had a skinful of ale. But he was good as gold. Soon as the place was empty and we'd bolted the doors and pulled the drapes, he was all for getting Tommy downstairs and yarning fore the fire. On Christmas Eve he even closed early, shouting everyone out and stamping and bellowing till it was just him, me and Janey. As they all left, Jock Convey said to us, 'Is he sickening, Annie? I've never known him to close up early. Is he crook with something?'

I said, 'No, Jock, he's just getting old. He wants a quiet life.'

Once they'd all gone Bill clapped his hands and said, 'Let's get that Black Cloak down here and have some more tales!'

I used the money I took from Sir Andrew to get us a fine big goose for Christmas, and bought puddings and brandy too. Jem come over in the morning; he was dressed in a collar and a tie and his best coat, and I put on a bonnet and shawl, and we walked up to Saint Saviour's for the service looking like proper respectable folk. We never opened the Champion that Christmas and Janey had the goose and potatoes roasting while we was in the church.

We sat at the back. Jem was awkward and shifty. He dint know any of the carols and he wouldn't sing. He couldn't follow the service in the prayer book and he went all bashful with the number of ladies turning round to get a look at him. And he kept his cap on, and I had to pull it off his head for him.

After the service we all shook hands with the Reverend and his daughters as we left. I introduced Jem to Miss Esther and Miss Judith, and I could see the pair of them light up at the sight of him and his bonny blue eyes as they shook his hand. Miss Esther leaned in and said to me, 'He is a fine fellow, Annie.'

I smiled and said, 'He is an all, Miss.'

Miss Judith said to me, 'Annie, would you come to tea with us at the vicarage? We would be so pleased if you could. On the twenty-seventh? Come at two. Please say you will come . . .'

I must say I was flustered at the thought of it. Me at the vicarage.

Miss Esther said, 'Annie, Judith will introduce you to her young man. Won't you, Judith?'

'I am sure I do not know what you are talking about, dear sister,' said Miss Judith, flushing pink.

Miss Esther giggled and said, 'Please come, Annie.'

I said, 'I will, Miss, thank you very much.'

Then Miss Esther whispered to me, 'I will endeavour to come and see you tomorrow – I believe I shall never get another chance to see a female Hercules.' Her eyes sparkled as she said it and I could see she was all charged up about coming to the fight.

I said, 'Have a care, Miss. It is not really a place for a lady.' But her eyes widened, and she put her finger to her lips. 'Look, if you come I shall have Jem find you and watch out for you after his bout is done.'

She smiled even more and said quietly, 'I can think of no better reason to come than that, Annie.'

The Reverend was short with me when I come to shake his hand. He dint look like he was pleased one bit when he said, 'I am told we are to have your company for tea the day after tomorrow, Miss Perry. My daughters are keen that I see the butterfly they claim has blossomed from a grub.'

I dint know what to say to that, but I knew he was having a poke at me, so I said, 'I am most grateful, Reverend.'

As me and Jem walked down the long drive of the church a carriage stopped by us and Sir Andrew called out from the window.

'I have my money on you for tomorrow, Annie. Do not let me down, girl. And is this giant the Bilston Bruiser himself?'

Jem raised his cap and said, 'How do, guvnor.'

'You look worth a wager, my lad. Not too much ale today, Mr Mason, we need you sharp for the morrow.'

'I shall be sharp enough, guvnor – don't you fret.'

The grand-looking lady next to Sir Andrew in the carriage was shaking her head, but Sir Andrew laughed and called, 'Drive on,' and they rattled off up the drive.

Back at the alehouse, the goose was roasting and for once the place smelled lovely. Paddy Tacker had come too and he said he had Molly Stych and her two lady friends lodged at the Station Hotel ready for tomorrow.

We explained to Paddy about our Tommy and he said, 'I have no difficulty with the presence of this gentleman. It shall remain a sacred truth I will not divulge. I am honoured you have shown me such trust to enter me into your confidence.'

When Tommy came down we all cheered him and he sat down to a brandy bowl at the big table, which Janey had laid with white napkins, candles and holly. Bill sat at the head of the table and raised his glass to toast us all. He said, 'God bless me little family here at Christmas,' and made us all stand and toast the Queen, and then Janey brought in the goose she'd roasted with baked apples set round it.

That was the first time in my life I'd had a big feast for Christmas and it done my heart good to see Bill so happy and calling us his family. After the pudding we banked up the fire and all sat round and Bill asked for Tommy to tell us his tale of how he come to be the Black Cloak.

And Tommy started with what happened to Mammy. She got worse and worse and more and more madder through the winter and into the spring, and trouble started to come to the vardo there in the field by the river. First, Mammy started walking into the town and raving and shouting at respectable folk that she was the Devil and was being punished by God. Tommy begged the doctor to come and tend to her and sometimes he give her laudanum to calm her and help her sleep.

But some nights she would jump from the vardo and run off into the night naked. Benny and Tommy followed her with lamps, and some nights they found her and some nights they dint. One Sunday morning in March, she was found lying freezing atop a grave in the churchyard. The curate, thinking her dead, covered her with a shroud only for her to sit up and start raving and give him a turn an all.

Tommy was still taking his lessons from Doctor Pettigrew and earning pennies digging his vegetable garden and cutting wood for him. Tass and Benny started thieving hay from farmers' ricks about the area to feed the pony now that all the grass was gone in the field and none new to come till it got warm.

Charity and Mercy tended to Mammy and tried to stop her from running off when her queer mood was upon her. They struggled through that winter and early spring, and then fortune cursed them once more so as they fancied the Almighty had set his face agin them all and the Loveridges were of the cursed tribe of Cain.

In April, rains come hard and heavy for day upon day upon day. It was not like true and plentiful rain that comes in April to remake the land and bring forth the lovely green, it was a fearsome deluge visited upon the wicked in the time of Noah. The river flooded sudden overnight as they slept in the vardo and it was lifted and spun like a child's toy boat, and the pony washed away and drowned. Tommy had to swim and haul Mammy out of it as she cried of her damnation, and the little uns swam too in the swirl and churn of the boiling river.

The vardo was swept away and dashed against the stone of the bridge, and the water rose and rose, and all the few pots and pans and kettle and plate they had was swept away an all, and the breaking of dawn in the morning saw the six of them huddled in the rain on the bridge with the water just a foot below them. And dint Mammy take it all as a sure sign of their damnation for sin.

There was none from that town but the doctor who came to care for them, and he came and brought them to his house and housed them in his barn where they lit a great fire to dry them and their few clothes.

The doctor fed them then, and they stopped in his barn where it was dry. Tommy and Benny and Tass went back to the field by the river and tried to salvage the vardo, but the poor thing was just a mass of shattered wood and twisted iron axle. The canvas top was ripped clean off and the iron rims of the wheels bent and buckled and all by nothing but water sent from above.

And Tommy was the man of the family but he dint have no idea how he was to improve their woeful lot, for without the kind doctor they would have all starved. And Mammy never spoke for weeks and weeks, even when the sun came back and new grass and new pea-green leaves burst upon the May trees and oak thereabouts.

All the tales of burgling and robbing Tommy told Benny and Tass from the penny tales he read all the time and the books of adventure he borrowed off the doctor did no good for them at all. They got the notion to go out burgling and robbing. Benny wanted to bring Mammy some pretty silks and silver for he thought it would bring her out of her mania and make her smile. So they never told Tommy when they went sneaking out about the fine houses round the doctor and breaking in through casements and servants' doors.

One afternoon Tommy came back to the barn from his lesson with the doctor to find Mammy sat with silver lockets and pearl necklaces and silver spoons and a ladle, and silk and ribbon arrayed in her lap and the children all knelt before her.

He knew it was all burglarised and that it was a fearful sin that his brothers had done, but as Charity tied a pretty red ribbon into Mammy's hair she seemed to waken and see them all there before her, and she smiled gently at them and held up the pearls and stared at them. Tommy said it was the first smile he had seen her give since I got sold at Hallow Heath.

Benny and Tass told Tommy of a big house they had looked over the day before where there was silver plate and gold candlesticks and they would take a sack that very night and get them. Benny said they could sell them and get enough for a pony and a new cart. 'And we shall go to Tipton and get our Annie and then Mammy will be well,' Benny said.

And Tommy agreed for he had spoken at some length with the good doctor on the nature of right and wrong and sin and forgiveness. And the doctor had said that sometimes it was necessary to do a bad thing for a good reason. Sometimes, he said, a doctor must inflict grievous pain upon a body in order to make it heal. In fact, the doctor told him, the way the Lord had made this world meant that there could be no good without evil, there could be no gain without loss, and no healing without pain. And Tommy saw that him and the others had suffered for no fault and taken nothing but lost everything. He felt a powerful passion that he wanted to take something back, and even if it meant doing sins, them sins would give his mammy her smile and her Annie back, and that could not be wrong.

So Tommy asked the Lord's blessing on his brothers going out with a sack that night while he stayed with Mammy and the babbies. And while they waited, next to their little fire in the corner of the barn, he told Mammy that him and Benny and Tass would get money for a new pony and a new vardo and they would take them through the springtime lanes where there were bluebells and soon there would be May blossom and king cups by the river, and they would all go to Tipton and find little Annie. And while he spoke Mammy smiled and took the red ribbon from her hair and tied it about Tommy's wrist and kissed him.

But that weren't what happened. For there is no justice nor right in this life as well I know: the good are cursed and the wicked rewarded and only a fool or a lunatic believes that poor folk and wandering gypsies will get divine protection or even just a fair go.

The servants caught Benny and Tass as they clattered plate and candlestick into their sack in the drawing room of the house. A servant ran for the peelers, then they all came to the barn where it was well known the doctor let gypsies live.

They found the trinkets all spread in Mammy's lap and clapped the boys in iron cuffs while Charity and Mercy wailed and Mammy sat silent, shaking her head.

As the commotion in the barn unfolded Doctor Pettigrew came from the house. The gentleman whose house had been burgled came along with the peelers to see the den of thieves from which these ragged gypsies had sprung. He was a fat grain merchant who wore a woollen cap like a miner's and who berated Doctor Pettigrew saying, 'This is the consequence of your foolishness, giving succour to these vermin. Would they had drowned in the flood. You were better to let them starve. See how they repay your kindness by burgling your neighbours in the dead of night.'

Doctor Pettigrew stood in silence with his hand upon his head and regarded Tommy sadly as the peelers clapped him in cuffs. He said, 'Tommy . . . I thought better of you and your family. What am I to do now?'

Tommy said, 'It was all for good purpose, sir.'

They were taken first to the gaol and then to Worcester Assizes.

Before the magistrates the circumstances of the burglary were made known, and it was deemed that Tommy was not involved, for he had not been taken at the house nor seen to be in possession of the stolen items. He was ordered to the workhouse, having no other means of support, and Charity and Mercy were sent there too.

Worst of it all was that Doctor Pettigrew made a statement to the magistrates that Mammy was a lunatic and suffered from both mania and melancholia and was unable to care for her children and posed a danger to herself and others when her fits were upon her. She was committed to the asylum to be held indefinitely.

And Benny and Tass were sentenced to seven years' transportation, and before they could even say farewell to their mammy or their brother they were shut into a wagon to be taken to the hulks at Southampton to await their sorrowful voyage to Australia.

In just a few minutes the Loveridges were shaken, split and scattered like chaff in the wind.

Tommy and the little uns went to the new workhouse at Bilston where Charity and Mercy learned sewing and, for all they despised the place, they got fed and on Sundays they had Bible readings and a service. The girls was lucky to be lodged together in the women's house. But they both had broken hearts for losing their mammy and their brothers and me, and they was weak and sad for all the days they laboured there.

Tommy was sixteen then and got put with the able-bodied men where he worked. First he was out in the grounds digging foundations and drains for the new buildings, then he got apprenticed out to a tanner and spent his days in the stench of the tannery pits, slopping hides through vats of piss.

He wrote a letter to the superintendent of the asylum where Mammy was locked away asking for her and asking that he be remembered to her. The warden at the workhouse couldn't hardly believe he could write and read, and he was asked to do the readings on Sunday for the women's house, and there he saw his sisters sitting together in their grey bonnets on the long benches looking so sad and forlorn it broke his heart in two.

After a month he got a letter from the asylum that told him Mammy had gone over to her eternal rest, her death caused as 'a result of her own hand, the third of her attempts at self-slaughter following a deterioration in her mental state and severe aggravation of the mania with which she was afflicted'.

They said she was given a Christian burial in the grounds and the only goods to be forwarded to her next of kin was her stitched and ribboned shawl, which they gave to another woman in the asylum believing Keziah Loveridge to be without family.

When winter came so too did consumption to the women's house, and Charity and Mercy, both weakened with grief and sorrow, succumbed to it in less than four weeks, despite their confinement in the workhouse hospital away from the foul air of the main house.

Tommy heard from the warden that his little sisters were dead when he went to read Bible verses to the women on Sunday. He just nodded when he heard, but his chest burned with a fire that was shot with red and gold and lit his insides up. He vowed that there must be some reckoning with the world and them as owned and run it for the sorrow and grief that had come to him in his short life.

And reckoning there was.

He stole coins from the tannery cashbox and took a good heavy coat too and absconded on the Monday after he heard his sisters were dead. He had only a tanner's knife and a length of rope with him and he had only one idea and that was to find a horse and pistols and go to work like Captain Jack.

He ran into the woodlands that were left around the workhouse, where the trees were still to be cut for timber and props, and for some days there he camped and foraged for his food. Then under cover of a moonlit night he struck out on the road west towards open country, away from the forges and works where there were still woods and meadows.

To get his pony he used a Captain Jack trick. He strung the rope at head height between two trees at a bend on a road that ran along the edge of the woods, and sure enough after an hour a gentleman come galloping through. He caught the rope in his throat and was hauled off backwards while the pony galloped on. Tommy ran and caught her when she stopped to pull at the dry grass by the road-side, and she was a sweet little grey mare who came to him, and he friended her and made her his own. What became of the gentleman sprawled back on the road Tommy did not know. He mounted the mare and she picked through the woods and seemed happy not to be galloping with a great fat fellow atop of her. He went miles and miles into the woods and then stopped and made a shelter and a fire and burned all the papers he found in the saddlebag except one which was a five-pound note. Tommy never seen a bank note before and he said it was a good job he could read or else he'd a burned it.

They wandered then, him and the pony; sometimes they took country roads and lanes and sometimes they ranged through woods. He found the canal and they rode down the towpath. He burgled a farmhouse south of Worcester where there wasn't a body in on a winter afternoon, and inside he found two fine pistols and a horn of powder and caps and a bag of leaden balls. And hanging in a cupboard he found the old-fashioned tricorn, same as Captain Jack wore, and he took it and the heavy black cloak with a brass chain and lion's head boss at the collar.

He loved the pistols. They were very fine with inlaid barrels and carved stocks, and he spent days out in the woods practising with them. He tied his mare, first a long way off, then closer and closer in, as he shot balls at the trees, so as she'd not start at the boom of the pistol. But she stayed calm and just watched him filling and loading and priming the pair till he could shoot a sparrow off a tree limb at ten yards.

Some nights he treated himself to an inn where he could wash and have a hot supper, and his pony got fed and stable-bedded and brushed down by the ostler. He sometimes sat in the bar and drank ale and yarned about himself. He told that he was an army captain swindled out of his land by a villainous uncle while he was fighting for the Queen and now he was returned to claim his right. In another yarn he was the son of a nobleman who had left his family lands after the girl he loved drowned in the mill pond as she fled from the clutches of a wicked stepbrother intent upon ruining the girl. He said he now roamed the land searching for the villain to exact his revenge. Whatever tale he told it come from one of his penny papers and he was always the hero.

Whether those listening believed him or not he did not know, but he said they were mostly credulous country folk and some was even Welsh so he expected they did.

Soon his five pound was gone, he spent his last shillings on powder and caps and balls in a town in Mid Wales, and he knew he'd have to rob to get more.

His first was in Staffordshire and it dint go so well. Two big Irish lads he met in a tavern outside Stoke told him about a wages clerk for the potteries who carried a bag of coins and notes out to a clay quarry on the last Friday of the month; he was alone, they said, and he took a lonely road up over a wooded hill. Those lads were thinking of robbing him and they said it was easy money for the boy that carried the satchel was young and slow-witted. They had no pony to ride out to the spot, nor to get away when the job was done, so Tommy said he would do it and then meet the Irish boys later to square up for the tip.

So off he goes in the early morning and finds the spot, a curving lane along the side of a hill, and he waits in the trees for the rider. After an hour he hears the hooves of a pony and glimpses through the trees a fellow in a long coat and a satchel round his shoulders. Tommy puts on his tricorn, raises a kerchief over his face, and gallops out the wood and alongside him. He raises the pistol and says, 'Would you care to hand over that satchel, my good man?' Refined and polite like Captain Jack.

Well, that rider was neither young nor slow of wit; he was a great big grizzled bastard with no fear of a robber and he said, 'Out of my way, boy,' and whacked Tommy square in the side of his head with a riding crop. Tommy went down off his mare and the wind was knocked out of him, and the big fella turned and dismounted and walked round Tommy, giving him a good whipping there in the road. Were it not for that little grey mare Tommy would've been taken, for she reared up at the man's pony and it skitted and lurched off, and the big fella let go of the reins. Tommy jumped up on his mare and took off into the woods.

Mind, he got another leathering later from the Irish boys when he met them in the tavern and told them there was no tip nor coins coming to them.

After that he vowed he would always start by incapacitating the rider, and his shot was good enough to just wing a man and not kill him.

He tried that method near a tavern at Stafford and took a gentleman clear from his horse and snatched a purse of silver and got away.

He wandered more, and hid and camped in the woods, and slowly come nearer and nearer to Tipton Port as summer turned to autumn. He found the heath above the town, and a wild and lonely place it was, perfect for a camp and a hideout. He walked into Tipton wearing a cap like a miner and saw The Champion of England and watched for me; and it was then he saw I was now grown into a young woman who ruled the roost and flung out drunken nailers. His plan then was to get enough money from robbing to come to the Champion and buy me back off Bill: he wanted to offer ten guineas and then him and me would go to Liverpool and take a boat for America. He had read of America and he knew it was a place where a lad who wanted adventure and action would thrive, and he fancied I would marry a rich man and live comfortable and refined in a proper house with servants.

He said in America it dint matter if you was a gypsy or Irish or a Scotchman, or the poorest miner or nailer, you got a chance to better yourself, and in California there was gold in the hills for the taking.

He watched me and Jem fighting at the Tipton Fair in September and he was agog that I should have learned fisty and fine moves and tactics. He wanted to come to me then and tell of himself and Mammy and all the others but he vowed to wait and get the money to buy me from Bill. He dint know there was no chance of Bill letting me go anywhere, nor any chance of me marrying a rich American for by then I was betrothed to my Jem.

Tommy stayed out wild on the heath, and some nights he rode out and visited alehouses and taverns to find intelligence on the doings of men carrying money. In an alehouse in Bilston, a miner told him of the foggers twisting and robbing the nailers and carrying coins and notes to the nailmasters and ironmasters. He learned about the back lanes and roads away from the heath, and where there was likely quiet spots. He took close to five guineas from Sir Andrew and his shrieking wife, and he aimed never to kill a man, only knock him down so he was no trouble.

He was right proud when he saw the posters wanting him, but he dint like the name 'the Black Cloak'; he said he'd have sooner had 'Captain' before it. 'Captain Black Cloak,' he said, 'that's a true name for a heroic gentleman of the road like myself.'

Then he shot the peeler on the road near Tipton. 'That was a mighty misjudgement of mine,' he said, 'for they harried and chased me and I had no choice but to come here and reveal myself to Annie.'

We all listened to his tale sat there by the fire Christmas afternoon and Bill rose, felt for and clapped Tommy on his shoulder, and said, 'You are a fine lad, but my Annie aint for sale to no man. Still, you are a man of action and some wisdom . . . but this wench stays here wi' me.'

Paddy Tacker said, 'How much do you have in your saddlebags?'

Tommy said, 'There is close to twelve guineas in coin and notes in there, the fruits of all my labours these past years.'

Paddy said, 'Ye should wager it the morrow on your wee sister, you'd make a fortune.'

I said, 'He is not to come to the field tomorrow for someone would spot him and reckon him for the robber. He must stay here hidden in my chamber.'

Jem said, 'We can smuggle him onto a train for Liverpool, get him away for America. It is too hot in these parts for him.'

The Gaffer lit his pipe and leaned in and said, 'I know a captain at Liverpool who'd tek him, even smuggle him if we paid the right price.'

I dint know what to think then. If he stayed he'd rob and do villainy, sure as the oak beam he'd end up hanging from.

Tommy said, 'Let us all go! Let all of us go and make a new life in America.'

Bill scoffed. 'I'm staying here, boy, and I aint going nowhere that involves getting on one of them infernal trains. Annie, fetch me more ale.'

I got up to get Bill's pot filled and looked back across at Tommy there in the firelight. For all the world he looked like Big Tom, though he was still a boy with just a wispy beard growing upon his chin. I thought of my mammy and all the babbies dead or transported and I felt my heart would explode in my breast, and a reddening anger swelled up in me.

I had read Shakespeare with Miss Esther, a queer and bloody play called *Titus Andronicus* about a Roman whose daughter was raped and chopped up by the ancient Britons and he cooked a queen's sons in a pie and fed them to her. Miss Esther said it was a sinful play, but she read it with me anyway and thrilled at all the blood and raping in it. In one part Titus says, 'Extremity of grief would make men mad . . .'

That was me now, feeling there was just too much losing and dying to take it all in and my heart and my head would swell to burst before it was done.

I seen forward too, then: the fight with Molly Stych to come,

her a dragon breathing fire down on me and my hands melting
through the bindings and dripping like wax, then I seen train tracks
running away into the dark and Jem and me running along them
with a train behind us steaming and glowing red like a forge at
night, and Bill was blinded with his eyes bound like Samson,
swirling and punching out at demons swinging in at him from the
sky as he stood in a boat in a whirlpool sucking him down.

I heard him calling, 'Where's my ale, wench?' and I snapped
out of my seeing fit and brung it over to him and set it down on
the table by the fire. He held his arm out and cinched my waist
and said, 'I loves you, my Annie.'

And I popped him a play punch on his big twisted conk, smiled
at Jem and said, 'I loves you too, Bill, you drunken old bastard.'

We had early nights then and never opened up the Champion
Christmas night. Tommy slept in my chamber, and Paddy took a
bunk in the scullery; Bill and Janey went up to their room and the
Gaffer went out to his boat. Me and Jem made a bed on the floor
by the fire in the bar and we lay with arms about each other and
watched the coals dim.

21

There were iron braziers burning coal at each corner of the field behind the Champion on Boxing Day morning, and Paddy Tacker strung bunting along the rope fence that surrounded the field, a black slag-soiled square known locally as Tanner's Yard, one of the few plots not built on in the port. Paddy set a table and a chair at the entrance alongside the alehouse and took a halfpenny off each person who trooped through the gap in the rope to see the bouts. It was bright and cold, and the crowds gathered round the braziers. In one corner Bill and the Gaffer set a table with barrels on it, selling ale in stone pots to the throng, and in another Janey had a trestle table with a great steaming pot of faggots and peas and hunks of bread that she sold for a penny a time.

The crowd grew from nine o'clock. In the centre was the roped square where the bouts should take place, with steel stakes at each corner where the bookies hung the wagers they took. At half past nine a carriage pulled by a four with footman and postilion arrived, and from it came Lord Ledbury, two ladies in buttoned winter coats and his two pretty friends with their sticks and yapping spaniels. A few moments later Sir Andrew arrived on his horse with a tall, well-made servant lad behind on a pony. Sir Andrew wore a bright red jacket and fur gloves against the cold morning. He greeted his lordship with a bow and the two men stood talking next to a brazier.

Jeremiah and Josiah Batch came too in their black frock coats and wide-brimmed hats. They paid their halfpennies, made for the far corner of the field – Josiah with a Bible in his hand and Jeremiah with a wooden cross – and set to preaching to the crowd of the wickedness of the event they were to witness. The sin of wagering and not earning money from a fair day's work and the path to Hell was paved with the bones of Jezebels like the women who were to offend their maker by stripping for fisticuffs. The fair and gentle sex made by God to serve man, seduced into evildoing by the serpent in the garden, now to display herself in the unnatural pursuit of pugilism! Did it not say in Timothy 2:11 that a woman should learn in quietness and full submission . . . that she must not assume authority over a man? And was this monstrous spectacle of two women fighting not an abomination to the Lord and a usurpation of His authority?

Many foundrymen were astonished to see their employers addressing the crowd at such an event; most who passed by ignored or smirked at the Batches' preaching. A handful stood and listened solemnly to the brothers as they took it in turns to bellow their condemnation of the wickedness taking place about them and their breath rose in clouds into the frosty morning air.

Bookmen had now begun to congregate near the ring, each with a strong-looking lad at his side, and each holding a ledger where bets were recorded and winnings and losses reckoned. And already miners and nailers, stable lads and off-duty peelers were checking odds and wagering pennies and shillings on knockout, first blood, finishing round and number of knockdowns. Lord Ledbury laid a twenty-pound wager on Jem Mason, and a ten-pound wager on Annie to overcome Molly Stych.

Another carriage arrived and from it stepped a huge man, made taller by the top hat he wore. His whiskers were neatly curled over his top lip and his beard was trimmed tight to his chin below the shining bald head he exposed as he removed the topper to bow to

Paddy Tacker on the gate and announce, 'I am Ingleby Jackson, your honour, known as the Gent, and I have come as promised to take this prize.' Paddy shook his mighty right hand and ushered Jackson and his two cornermen through the crowd to one of the small tents behind the ring where the fighters were to change.

Then there came a commotion from the gate as Molly Stych announced her arrival at the field. She stood with hands planted on her substantial hips and bawled to the crowd, 'I am the famous Miss Stych from Brum and I've come to skin the gypo bitch. Put yer money on me, lads, and I'll not let you down.'

She was a broad woman of around forty years, her hair pulled back from her ruddy face in a bun, and her arms were thick and fleshy, ending in what seemed to some unnaturally large hands for a woman. She wore a billowing dress of green silk, with bunched sleeves and a floor-length skirt fringed with grimy white lace. Her wide flat face was coloured with rouge and thick powder, and her eyes and eyebrows lined heavily with black kohl. She looked more of a fit for the stage than the boxing ring.

Her movements were slow and heavy as she strode across the field followed by two other hefty ladies, both carrying carpet bags and parasols. Paddy crossed to meet her, and the fierce hug she gave him nearly choked the breath from the little Irishman. He ushered Molly and her companions to the ale table and supplied them all with pots and stood them by the brazier.

The referee and ringmaster, Mr Tyndale of Wolverhampton, arrived looking splendid in his Sunday-best black suit and top hat, and Paddy rushed along with him to meet and shake hands with Lord Ledbury and Sir Andrew before he went to the tents to meet the fighters for the first bout which was to begin on the dot of ten o'clock. Paddy checked his pocket watch and went quickly through to the tent where Jem and Annie waited. Jem was standing in his britches, a blanket around his shoulders, moving from foot to foot and gently shadow boxing with his bound fists. Annie sat reading on the low chair; she looked up as Paddy came flapping into the tent.

'We are all set now, all set and ready now. The referee's a good lad and I've tipped him in your favour, me babies. Now, Jem, that Jackson is a big fella, a big, big fella, and he's a hell of a reach on him. You got to stay back for the first few rounds, all right? You need to get him chasing you and tire him out. Just clip him and dodge till his arms start to go down – you got that?' Jem nodded and continued his slow deliberate warm-up. Paddy turned to Annie. 'Your Molly Stych is here an all – mercy, what a monster she is. She looks like a clown ready for the circus! She's a big tub of lard, Annie, you shall do her easy—'

Annie rose and said, 'I'm gonna get a look at her.'

Paddy said, 'She's at the ale table, you'll not miss her. Don't wear your ring gear out there, mind. Keep it for the show, all right?'

Annie said, 'It's there,' and nodded towards the corner of the tent where her ring gear hung on a wooden rail. A scarlet satin jerkin, sleeveless and set with white flashes at the side, and a pair of pure white britches with a scarlet belt and scarlet tags at the calf. Below them sat a pair of new white canvas pumps, with long scarlet laces.

The colour was as deep as blood and Paddy had declared the outfit 'the apparel of a slasher' when he showed it to her after he had fetched it from the tailor who made it up for him. He smiled. 'See them pumps? I had to send to Northampton to have them fashioned for you. You are going to give them a show that they'll talk of for years, Annie Perry.'

Annie pulled on her cloak, kissed Jem on the cheek, and left the tent.

Ingleby Jackson was ready for the ring and had walked across to the ale tent in his ring gear, a fine starched shirt with collar and white tie. The shirt was cuffed with gold studs and he wore a black cummerbund about his middle above the black britches and leather pumps. He still had on his top hat and he tipped it at the ladies as he crossed the field to the ale table. Upon observing Molly Stych he executed an elaborate bow, removing his hat and stretching his right arm out low before her. She and her companions giggled and Ingleby Jackson straightened, saying, 'Esteemed lady, I am Mr Ingleby Jackson, known as the Gent, and I am entirely at your service.'

Molly Stych laughed and bobbed in an awkward curtsey, saying, 'I am honoured, sir, and my, but you're a big bonny lad, aint ya?'

Jackson picked up an ale jug and downed it in one before saying, 'I am every inch of me a gentleman, dear lady, and I am bound to say that in all my peregrinations in the field of fisticuffs I have yet to see a fairer beauty than your good self . . .' He picked another pot from the table and downed it.

Molly and her ladies set to giggling again and called for more ale from Bill. He stood behind the table drawing jug after jug from the barrels and setting them atop the table. In the dim mist of his vision Jackson and the ladies appeared as no more than a shimmer, but he heard their talk and the chatter of the crowd around them about the forthcoming bout and he thought sadly, 'I am no name any more. I am no draw for a crowd. I am just the bloke who serves the ale.'

Annie watched Molly Stych from just behind the brazier, studying her wide painted face as it loomed through the coal smoke. She regarded Molly's body, and even wreathed in her dress she could see the woman was a lump. She even seemed to breathe heavily as she moved and shifted to fetch her ale from the table.

Annie wondered at the unfairness of this match, the peelers and the ref all tipped and his lordship set to take a pretty penny from the bookies to cover the purse money he had put up.

She watched Bill, stumbling and slopping the ale over the table, and, typical Bill, not taking a penny from those drinking. She walked back behind the table and put her arm around him, and he waved wildly to attract the Gaffer to fetch another barrel from the cellar. She slipped her arm around his thick waist, held him and said into his ear, 'You're not charging em, Bill. Tek tuppence a jug off em, or you'll have us in the workhouse.'

He grinned and said, 'I can't see the pennies even if they give em, Annie.'

She walked back towards the Champion and caught the Gaffer shouldering a barrel up from the cellar. She said, 'Go and help Bill. He's bloody giving away the ale again.'

The Gaffer said, 'Right you are, Annie. I'll sort the old bugger out.'

The bell from the ring sounded and the crowd surged over towards the ropes as Mr Tyndale, now in a striped waistcoat, announced the bout. Annie stood at the back and watched as Jem came out, stripped to his waist and skipping from foot to foot, looking to Annie like a fighting angel, his blond curls vibrant in the low winter sun and clouds of misty breath billowing from his nostrils.

Ingleby Jackson made a show of his entrance, bowing and doffing his top hat and drawing cheers and boos from the crowd as he capered about the ring before the referee. Finally he threw his hat to his corner, stanced himself side on and twiddled the ends of his moustache.

Mr Tyndale called the men to the centre and they shook. He held a handkerchief up over his head and let it drop to the black earth, and as it touched the bell rang and the fight had begun.

Paddy was right: Jackson had a good reach and he was fast for a big man, stepping into Jem straight away and catching him with two hard jabs to the head. Annie found it hard to watch as his big fists struck at Jem's perfect white cheeks, raising red weals. Jem was going back, moving his head and sidestepping as Jackson came onto him.

They circled each other for a few minutes, neither coming in and Jem watching the big man as he moved round him. Jackson began taunting him and calling Jem 'Charlie' for no good reason Annie could see. 'Come on now, Charlie . . . Come in for a look, Charlie . . . Come in for a peep at these . . .'

Whatever it meant, it seemed to rile Jem and he stepped forward off his right foot and threw a big swinging left. Jackson saw it and ducked away and came back up with two fast uppercuts that caught Jem under his chin. Jem stepped back and tried another left but he was stumbling from the two blows Jackson had dealt him and the left went wild again. Jackson got over him and jabbed down twice into the side of his face.

'He aint gonna be so pretty after this,' said a man standing next to Annie.

They called it a round and Jem went to his corner. Annie could see Paddy towelling him and yelling into his ear over the noise of the crowd.

The bell went and they were back out. Whatever Paddy yelled it seemed to do the trick and now Jem stayed back. He got a good skipping rhythm going, dancing in and out and letting Jackson follow him. The big man threw punches at him, but Jem sidled or stepped out of them, moving his head fast out the way and letting Jackson punch at the air. Annie knew what he was doing: there is only so long a fighter can throw at air fore his arms go, and for all his cool gentleman act Annie could see Jackson getting hot and angry. It don't pay to lose your temper in the ring, Annie knew that. When your passion takes you, you make mistakes and you stop watching and reading, and now Jem was reading him lovely, stepping just right to his moves and keeping a full guard up. Sometimes he dropped it to tempt Jackson in with a blow which he bobbed round or back from and Jackson flailed at the air.

Round two and three went on like that, Jem keeping back and letting the big fellow chase him. By the fourth Jackson had rolled up his sleeves, torn off his tie and opened his shirt collar. He was looking tired, his moves became more ponderous, and the cocky glint in his eye was gone. For most of round four he chased, sometimes stopping and calling to the crowd: 'Is Charlie a coward, ladies and gentlemen? He is certainly no gentleman for he fights like a frightened goose! Are you a goose, Charlie?'

Annie could see Jem was keeping calm, even when the crowd booed him at Jackson's taunts. Jackson then stood in the middle of the ring and held his hands out in a come-on-then gesture. Jem danced in towards him and the big man kept them down, then Jem did a fine trick Annie and Janey had taught him. He dropped his right shoulder and Jackson looked left expecting the big swinger, but Jem used the drop to come up with his right and snapped in under Jackson's chin. The man's belly came forward as his head went back and Jem gave him a stabbing one-two to the gut and the big man doubled. The bell went, and there was a roar from the crowd as Jackson hobbled bent to his corner.

In the fifth Jem continued his tactics, staying clear till Jackson threw, then hitting through the gaps he opened. He caught him five times with stinging jabs and another combination to the kidneys made Jackson bellow like a bull. Bar the two red cuts on his cheek from the first, Jem stayed unmarked, and as he turned at the edge of the rope away from a wild blow from Jackson he caught Annie's eye and grinned. She smiled back. But she was worried. She knew it was easy to get comfortable, think you were on top, and for all Jackson looked tired, he was still up on his feet proper and his hands were up.

Annie pushed through the crowd in the break between the fifth and sixth and she got to Jem's corner and just before he went back, she shouted into his ear, 'Don't get cocky, Jem. He aint done yet and he's still dangerous.'

Jem turned to smile at her and said, 'I love you, Annie Perry,' as the bell went. As if to confirm Annie's fear, he walked back into the ring and straight onto Jackson's right before his guard was fully up. The blow shook him, Annie could see, and he danced back, shaking his head. Blood started to pour from his nose and there were shouts of 'First blood, Jackson!' from the crowd. Some rushed to the bookies to collect and Jackson raised his clenched fist as if in victory. Annie had to fight the urge to look away as the blood flooded down Jem's front, spreading in tributaries across his belly. He grabbed the towel Paddy proffered from the corner and wiped away the blood as Jackson came back across onto him. He swerved his right again, twisting away from the ropes and backing with his guard up as Jackson came on again, throwing jabs at Jem's guard and pushing forward as Jem danced back into the ropes. He came in close and they grappled, each trying to punch at the other's sides. The crowd bayed and booed and the referee skipped around the clenched pair calling, 'Break apart! Break apart!' Jackson pushed out of the clinch and Jem ducked as he swung at him and hit him again in the gut. The crowd now roared as Jem nimbly stepped alongside the doubled man and hit down into his head.

The big farmer managed to straighten himself and throw quick jabs as he backed away from Jem. As he stumbled towards Annie's corner she could see he was breathing hard and there were cuts above both eyes. Paddy was calling, 'You've got him, Jem! Take your time . . . take your time . . .'

In Annie's bedchamber Tommy could hear the chatter and roar of the crowd and it grew too much for him to simply listen. He wanted to see his little sister doing as his father had done and he wanted to be there if she needed protection. He stole downstairs into the empty bar and from a hook behind the door took an old heavy coat of Bill's. It was soiled and scuffed enough to look like a miner's and, coupled with the cap he found next to it, he looked like any working man. He tied a muffler over his face and then returned to Annie's chamber where he took some shillings from the satchel stowed under Annie's bed. He pulled one of his pistols from the drawer. He quickly loaded power, wad and shot, and set a cap on the nipple, then tucked the gun into his belt.

As Tommy was preparing to slip into the field and watch the bouts, two others arrived at the scene: Miss Esther Warren in a long black cape and full bonnet and the stumbling, complaining Jessie whose hectoring high-pitched voice Tommy could hear as they walked quickly up the side of the Champion. 'Now I know your lark, Miss . . . I might've known it was a ploy asking to take a walk with me Boxing Day morning . . . I know your game, Miss Esther . . .'

Miss Esther stopped and turned to the older woman. 'Jessie, please! You may not approve but consider this an educational visit wherein we shall learn of the ways and entertainment of the working man—'

Jessie shook her head. 'I have no call to know the ways of anyone other than you, your sister and your dear father, and the poor man will be horrified if he learns you have come to this wicked spectacle not one day past Christmas . . . and you shall chill so in the cold.

Respectable ladies do not attend fisticuffs, child. Your father will be fair seething when he finds out you have been here—'

But Esther, ignoring the servant's entreaties, carried on determinedly towards the field where now a great clamour came from the crowd bunched around the ring, with men waving their hats and crowding around the bookies. In the ring Ingleby Jackson's two cornermen were carrying the huge form of their prize fighter away towards the tent and the referee was holding the bloodied fist of Jem Mason aloft.

22

It is the noise that hits you. It is a wall surrounding you and, in my fancy, I can almost see it – a sheer edifice bricked with cries and grunts and groans and throaty calls, limed with screeches, low callings and savage shouts, forever set to topple in on you and engulf you.

And there stood I in my get-up and the crowd yelling and trumpeting and screaming at me. *Whore! Filthy bitch! Jezebel!* Their twisted faces and gawping mouths melded into a flat shifting canvas of blurs and colours around me. And me in me scarlet satin and white britches like a circus clown. My hands were unbound, though Paddy fetched some red-and-white striped ticking he wanted them done with.

And before me stood Molly Stych. She had a fair clamour for her name when it was called and now she turned towards me, her great painted face above her laced corset and petticoat and her big hands bound in black ticking with the bony knuckles poking out. And she was smiling, a ghastly red smile showing me her few yellow teeth. In the smile I saw a face I knew for a second and it flashed in on me as she leaned and shouted into my ear, 'I know you, Annie Perry, and you know my poor brother Billy. Him you crowned and left half an idiot years back . . .' She stood back. 'The poor little lad come to me in Brum after you and that other whore had finished with him, half dead and half a madman . . . I am here to venge him and you'll not leave this ring till you're battered into his shoes, ya dirty gypo . . .'

Everything comes back to you in time, don't it just. And here was Billy Sticks' sister afore me. Stych, Sticks, now I knew where they twisted his name from. And what happened to him after we left him in that alley the night of the strike.

The crowd was wrapped round us facing each other when Mr Tyndale called the bout and the rules. Molly Stych was more of a devil when you seen her close up, bitter-looking and hard, with dragging grey skin showing from beneath the white powder. She was the height of me but double the width.

The cold sun was full up and the breath of the crowd formed swirling ghosts above us all; steam was rising off the ropes and the stakes, coal smoke drifting in.

Then a cold silence fell in my mind and the noise was blocked while I moved my eyes around the canvas, faces forming in the blur like leaves showing through melting ice. There was Lord Ledbury and his fancy lads, toasting me with claret glasses, and there was Sir Andrew blowing smoke like a dragon from his cigar, and there was Paddy clapping his hands and his face lit with the morning sun, and there behind him was Jem, solemn and livid-scarred across both cheeks from Ingleby Jackson's fists.

And here was yelling boys in caps and there nail wenches wrapped in scarves and miners holding jugs and clay pipes. One of Sir Andrew's servants was shovelling in faggots from a bowl.

And then there was our Tommy. He was stood looking sad and regretful in the throng, wisps of steam about his sharp brown eyes that peered over the muffler at us.

That shook us, but I was shook more when I saw that he was stood close by Sir Andrew, who was laughing and clapping Lord Ledbury on the shoulder. And more shook still as I slowly turned and saw not two yards from me Miss Esther's lovely face and bright eyes. She was beaming.

'Are you fit, Miss Annie? Are you fit to go now?' shouted the referee, and it broke through my reverie. The noise of the crowd roared back into my ears and Molly Stych was right in front of me, grinning with her big red mouth.

Mr Tyndale took our right hands and said, 'Shake for honour, ladies,' and we touched knuckles and Molly Stych spat full in my face. The crowd oohed and Mr Tyndale shouted, 'Now, ladies!' and held his hands up, but Molly was stepped back in stance, side on, her big white chin tucked in and her long fat arms stretched out at me. Fore Mr Tyndale could call a foul or ring the bell I planted one straight into her face and felt her nose go crunchy.

I said, 'If you want it like that, it'll be like that, wench.' And I skipped back, ragging the crowd with my arms up, and Paddy was shaking his head at me and calling, but I couldn't hear him amid the furore, and they were all shouting, 'Go on, Annie!'

There aint a prettier feeling in all this world than that, and fool as I was, I was lapping it up and took my eye off her. And dint she come back from behind and get me by the hair over backwards and give me her fat elbow in the mouth, and it thudded through me and I went down. She was on top of me then, her fat hands round my throat, screaming and spitting like a street cat, her nails digging trenches in my neck. I swung one round and got her face in the side, but the bitch was so heavy on us I couldn't move. There was bloody chaos then, Paddy and Jem and other men all piling into the ring, and Molly's lady friends swinging punches at everyone.

They got us both up, and Mr Tyndale cleared the ring and called for calm. I could see Sir Andrew and Lord Ledbury laughing and toasting the mayhem all around them. And our Tommy just stood silent next to them. I couldn't see Miss Esther as Mr Tyndale called fouls and voids and set us to start round one again. Molly had a nice snap in her nose and a white rag stuffed up under it to staunch it. I felt my teeth. They weren't wobbly so she never got us that hard.

We set to again, this time on the bell, and Molly was shuffling on her feet like she was trying to fight proper and no fouls. So now I settled to it and got ready to do the job the right way. I set to moving and bobbing and leading with my right and looking for gaps to jab through. Her guard was sloppy and she had no speed so I caught her three times with nice sharp little shots that made her face even uglier when she winced.

I sidestepped her and give her a hard left into the top of her right arm. I could see it hurt her and her right dropped and I banged a one-two into her that sent her staggering back. She bounced on the ropes and the hands of the crowd pushed her out again, and I got in a straight jab to her throat and she gagged and held her hands up like she was choking. I skipped about her while she heaved her breath back in and tried to turn and get her guard up, but I let her have a fast combination to the face and she doubled down and I crunched my left on the top of her skull, which was as thick and hard as I thought it would be. The bell went, and a great cheer went up for me as I skipped to my corner thinking this was too easy.

Paddy wiped me down and shouted at me, 'Not so fast now, Annie. Come on, give em a show. She's near a dead donkey after one more round, so kill her slow, Annie . . . Many of these folk have paid a penny to see this.'

Jem put his hand through the rope and squeezed my shoulder and said into my ear what I said to him, 'Don't get cocky, Annie. She aint done yet.'

In Molly's corner, they were giving her a good swig of brandy and one of her ladies was doing her powder over her flattened nose. She looked a lot better when she rose from her stool and held her arms up, and some of the crowd cheered her as she loped back into the centre.

Now here is where being young and pretty and clever like I was then is a curse. For I shoulda took the advice I give Jem and not let my head get so big and not be so worried on what Tommy was doing or what Miss Esther was seeing. For I liked the look of myself too much after that first round.

Back in there as the bell went, she come at me straight off, and she could put together a combination when she wanted to. She stood square on, and they come out of her fast and stinging hard. I dint expect it, I dint see it coming, and she hurt me.

And there shoulda bin a lesson, but where I shoulda steadied myself and got my rhythm back, I got a hot flash of temper and seen the red as she hit me, thinking, you're gonna bleed, ya bitch! And when you see the red, you don't think and you don't read.

Her blows had me going back and she came onto me. She was big and heavy as a charging bull when she got the upper hand, and I had to guard and take slapping one-twos to my fists and forearms and try to swing out the way, and she never let up neither as the crowd seemed to come on for her with each shot she got home. I couldn't break out to throw for she was raining on me fast and steady, my forearm clattered back into my nose, and she went for my belly, hitting hard and low, each blow making a smack-smack-smack in my ears.

I managed to turn and spin fore she had me on the ropes and I backed off quick to get some space from her, and I got side on and kept her back with a jab. There seemed as many shouting for her in the crowd as shouting for me, and I wanted to look and find Tommy but I daren't tek my eyes off her. She just planted herself like a big tree in the centre and held her hands down and swung up at me when I come near like she was in an alehouse brawl. A fella in the crowd was holding out a glass and shouting, 'Will ya tek a brandy, Molly?'

She called back at him, 'I'd rather have an ale, boy!' and there was laughter and hooting all around. I concentrated, got my movement nice and smooth, and I went round her jabbing. She turned slow to keep me in sight and see if I made a move, and we went on like that, in a dance. In the back of my head was a nagging that she had hurt me, and I hadn't never faced anyone that had really hurt me or put me down.

I caught her on the face and twice in the kidneys with jabs, but she dint seem bothered, and sometimes she was eyeing and grinning at the crowd or answering calls they made. If I got too close she swung, but she never got me, and I was wondering how long she'd take to get tired or punched out.

Well, the answer was a bloody long time, because we sparred and feinted at each other for the next three rounds, and with each round gone the crowd got uglier and more spiteful, especially to me. They thought she was a hero for staying round after round, and I was a loser for not putting her away with a slasher. *When are we gonna have a slasher, Annie? Give us a slasher!*

I got looks too, coming out from a duck when Molly swung at me. I saw Sir Andrew's red face all puffed and flushed with claret, shouting something I couldn't hear, and Lord Ledbury and his pretty boys stood clapping at me slow. Off to the side, Tommy was looking at them, a close steady stare.

I clipped Molly good in the fifth, and she stumbled back a bit, shifted her arms up for a guard, and I stepped in and got her in the gut. Truth was, I was getting tired and I wanted to finish her, but she was a bugger to knock over. A big wide thing like a beer barrel, when you hit her belly it was soft like a goose-feather pillow and it sucked your hand in.

When I got her stepping with the gut punch I come in close and smacked her under the chin with an uppercut and now she did move, but she swung and caught us again in the side of the head. It was a bloody hard clump, that, and I was ringing and spinning for a second, but she was still tumbling back out of it with her arms down and I got square and swung a big left into her face.

Her fat head went back and the crowd erupted. It was the shot they'd been waiting for, and there were cries of 'Annie . . . Annie . . . Annie . . .' I flipped back off her as she staggered away, then teetered and slowly toppled forward.

I turned to look at the crowd. They were throwing their hats up and Mr Tyndale was standing over Molly Stych and counting, 'Two . . . three . . . four . . .'

I turned my head to see Tommy. He was up on his tiptoes with his hands in the air like a preacher. And next to him Sir Andrew was not looking at me. He was looking up at Tommy's wrist, staring hard at the red ribbon Mammy tied on.

I dint have no chance to do anything, for Molly Stych had lumbered herself up on the count of seven, and dint look so much worse for the slasher she'd been served. She was shaking her head and saying, 'I'm fine, guvnor . . . dint feel a bloody thing . . .'

The crowd were roaring now – *Molly! Molly! Molly!* – and I looked across at Tommy again. Him and Sir Andrew were both staring at each other. Then Tommy suddenly broke and ducked back into the crowd as Sir Andrew held his hand up and shouted towards his lordship.

Molly Stych leaned over and tapped my shoulder and said, 'Are we on for this game then, gypo?' and Mr Tyndale shouted, 'No count . . . continue!'

I was too stunned by seeing Tommy racing off and Sir Andrew

shouting after him that I dint see when Molly slapped me hard across the face and shouted, 'Come on, ye bitch . . . I'm gonna finish ya!' The sting of the slap shook me to, and I let go with a combination at her face just as the bell clanged for the end of the round. Her mouth burst and blood shot out into my eyes, and I stormed on into her, feeling my fists drilling her fleshy cheeks and thudding and cutting on her skull.

There was a thunderous clamour now and it was all building and shattering around me, a great cacophony of screams and wails and then whistles.

Molly slumped, sitting, blood splashing out over the cold black earth, and then there were men all around me, whistles and peelers' uniforms and red-coated soldiers, bayonets flashing in the sun, faces of women screaming into mine and hands pulling at me, a low grunting report of a musket and more shrieking. I was being pulled back out the ring where the ropes were down and the stakes askew, and trampled into the earth as the crowd scattered.

Jem tugged at me and pushed me into the tent where Paddy was stuffing coins and notes into his carpet bag and shouting, 'They called the bloody yeomanry! The bloody army to stop a prize fight!'

I said, 'Our Tommy was there. Sir Andrew recognised him and he took off—'

Jem said, 'Jesus, they'll take him – there's soldiers and peelers everywhere.'

Paddy was kneeling on the bag to get it closed over the mountain of money inside. He said, 'So much for tipping the bloody peelers!'

Mr Tyndale pushed his head through the tent door. 'You owe me a fiver, Mr Tacker,' he said.

'And you shall have it, Mr Tyndale,' said Paddy, pulling notes from his pocket and holding them out to the referee.

Mr Tyndale said, 'I should clear out if I were you. They'll confiscate your takings if they get you.'

Paddy handed the carpet bag to Jem and said, 'Get this over to the Champion and hide it best you can.'

I said, 'What about Tommy?'

'They'll have him by now, Annie. Silly boy should've stayed hid.'

I was still covered in Molly Stych's blood. Outside we could hear the soldiers and peelers forcing people out of the field and down the road back into Tipton. I stepped out and looked at the ring, with the rope collapsed around it. There was a dark patch in the centre where Molly had bled but she was gone. The ale table was turned over and the faggot pot smashed; plates and ale pots were strewn about the field.

Up towards the heath I could hear the sound of horses.

23

Tommy lay still in the tree and listened. The light was going, and for more than half an hour he had not heard anything to indicate his pursuers were still below on the frozen heath. He had seen lamps in the distance and heard feet and hooves and the shouts of men.

After he saw the flash of recognition in Sir Andrew's eyes and fled from the field, he ran through a troop of yeomanry marching down towards the Champion. Headed by a captain on a bay mare, they ignored him as he ran at full tilt between their two ranks.

He ran up into the heath, cursing his lost grey mare and the satchel of money he had left at the alehouse, and thundered through the dead ferns and frozen bogs, circling to leave a wide confusing trail in the frosted grass and moss underfoot. He stayed well away from the previous camp he had made, and after running for nearly an hour he chose a sturdy oak to climb, shinning up into the topmost branches and using his belt to bind himself to a limb so he could lay flat along it. He was glad of the coat as he waited there, for it grew colder as the day wore on to evening and the setting sun. It took almost another hour before he heard the sounds of the men searching for him, the hooves and calls carrying easily in the still cold air. And, like Captain Jack, he lay and listened until the sounds passed away into the gathering dark.

The yeomanry and constables had been called by the Reverend Warren, who dispatched a frantic note to the magistrate in Bilston calling for the illegal boxing contest to be stopped. Minutes before writing it, he had stood astonished and appalled as one of his parishioners told him of his daughter's presence at the spectacle. The man, a God-fearing shop owner from the port, had been walking at Spon Lane and watched Miss Esther and the Reverend's housekeeper going into the field and paying pennies to the ruffian on the gate. The man ran up to the vicarage immediately to inform the clergyman. More than anything, he said, he was concerned for the young lady's safety in the baying throng that crowded the space behind the Champion.

Miss Judith affected to know nothing of the true purpose of her sister's morning ramble with the loquacious Jessie. She simply said, 'Oh dear, how troubling,' when her father told her of Esther's presence.

'Had you any idea that she was to attend this infernal gathering?' he asked.

'No, Father. Esther is quite her own woman and does not tell me of every fancy she takes.'

'And this fighting child, this Annie, is to come here tomorrow for tea? With Mr McLean?'

'As I understand it, she is,' said Judith.

When Esther returned to the vicarage in the early afternoon the Reverend made his disapproval of her action clear by staying in his room for the afternoon. Only at tea did he first berate Jessie for her complicity in the morning's events.

'Miss Esther lied to me too, Reverend, she's a wee besom. I knew nothing of her purpose till we were at the gate of the awful place. She was determined to watch the girl fight – and an ugly spectacle it was too,' said the housekeeper as she poured tea and set a plate of scones on the table.

The Reverend turned to Esther, saying, 'Well? How do you account for your mendacity and defiance?'

Esther said, 'It was an informative experience, Father. I watched Annie fight and I watched the way the poor are entertained. If I had told you I wanted to attend you would have forbidden it. And do not blame poor Jessie. She was an unwilling dupe, but I was glad of her presence when the yeomanry and constables attacked and dispersed the crowd. Father, women with children were beaten with musket butts before my eyes. The violence in the ring was nothing compared to the savagery of those trying to prevent it.'

The Reverend breathed out heavily. 'You could have been injured. You could have been arrested. And now the parishioners are aware that you were there. I don't doubt the news will reach the Bishop.'

'Father, you called the yeomanry, did you not? You sent a note to the magistrate. Did it not occur to you that there would be violence in the breaking up of the event and that I would be at the heart of it?' protested his daughter hotly.

'What was I to do, child, when one of my most devout parishioners made me aware of your presence? The whole thing was illegal! I understand that Mr Perry and his henchmen had even bribed some of the constables in Tipton to turn a blind eye . . .'

He placed both his hands flat on the table and looked heavenward. He said, almost to himself, 'This is what occurs when you begin to disrupt our Lord's natural order. Teaching that girl, reading Wordsworth with her? Yes, my dear, I know of your wide and uncircumscribed curriculum with the girl. She told the Bishop himself in her letter. I had a furious note from him this morning asking why we are using church funds to teach such wretches about the Empire and allow them to read periodicals? Informing them of things which can do them no good and create only want and discontent in them. And *poetry* – for a ragged godless gypsy! What possible use can Miss Annie Perry have for poetry? Robert Burns?

The man was a radical, a drunken adulterer, Esther. How is it appropriate to expose the child to such knowledge? The purpose of the school is to bring them to God through the Bible. They are learning to read so they can read the Scriptures. Anything else is close to sedition.'

Esther and Judith exchanged furtive glances. Judith said, 'I take it that your feelings mean we are to cancel Miss Perry's invitation to tea tomorrow?'

Esther said, 'No, Father, please . . .'

The Reverend thought for a moment and said, 'On the contrary. I believe I should like to talk with Miss Annie Perry. I should like to find out what it is about her that holds my daughters in such thrall that they disobey their father and put themselves at risk. That is, if the child has not been arrested and thrown into gaol along with her notorious father.'

Far over on the heath, Tommy unstrapped himself from the tree branch and nimbly dropped to the ground. He moved stealthily, crouching and listening in the moonlight as he made his way back towards The Champion of England.

24

We whispered and kept the candles low all night after Tommy came back, tapping at the back door and slipping in unseen despite the yeomanry about searching for him.

They had searched the alehouse in the afternoon after the contest was broken up and the ring and tents all dashed to the ground. Sir Andrew knew Tommy was something to do with me. He watched me hard when he arrived with the captain and two constables, and claimed to have seen the Black Cloak stood next to him bold as brass as I fought my bout with Molly Stych.

'I knew him by the ribbon and his gypsy look,' he declared as he stood in the bar. He caught my eye and held my gaze.

Bill started stropping off at him and the constables: 'You have no right to come in here and search! You have no right to treat us like we was criminals! I am a loyal subject of Her Majesty, and you and these villains have no cause nor evidence—'

'But you and your friends *are* criminals, Mr Perry,' said Sir Andrew, 'organising and running illegal boxing and abetting gambling. My friend, Mr Farmer the magistrate, is, as we speak, drawing up the documents to prosecute both you and your Irish friend—'

'Ha! You liked it well enough when you were watching and toasting with his lordship,' I said, crossing the room to settle Bill back in his chair by the fire.

'I liked it well, girl, and it is a shame you did not finish the big woman. Your fight was void and no bookman paid out, nor did you get your purse.'

'So you lost money, Sir Andrew?'

He shifted, a mite uncomfortable at the thought. 'I was moderately inconvenienced by your incompetence, Miss Perry.'

'Well, that shall be a comfort to us,' I said.

The yeomanry and constables found Paddy's carpet bag and confiscated it as illegal takings. It had everything we'd taken in it: the gate money, the payouts from Paddy's bets on Jem and Jem's twenty-guinea purse. Paddy sat in the bar and wept as the captain showed him the warrant giving him power of seizure.

After they'd gone I went up to check my chamber: Tommy's saddle bags and one of the pistols were still there, wrapped up in my petticoats.

We all sat round in silence. Janey brought in the last barrel of ale we had and tapped it. She drew Bill a jug and handed it to him.

He sat by the fire shaking his head. 'We are done for. We've a few shillings we took for ale and faggots, and then it's the workhouse. I shall go about all them I've subbed over the years – I must be owed a fortune in free ales.'

Paddy found an old bottle of port behind the bar and poured out glasses for us all. He sipped his with the look of a man who had wagered a penny and lost the world. We was all just silent then, thinking on what we'd lost and what we'd given. My face was red and purple around the eyes, there were little gashes on my brow, and my bottom lip was fat and livid. Jem, but for two small scars on his cheek, was as bonny as a new babby.

I lit candles and lamps when it got dark, then stood at the back of the Champion looking out across the field where we'd fought that morning. Two ragged miners were peering at the ground, looking for dropped pennies with a shutter lamp. I watched their light bobbing about over the black earth and I thought about our Tommy out on the heath. I had a knowing I'd see him again and I knew it would be in darkness but nowhere in my head could I see if he was safe from the soldiers and peelers tearing about on his trail. I said a little prayer then for God to keep him at liberty and for him to come back to us, and added 'in the name of Jesus', like the Reverend did at services.

And my prayer was answered later that night when I heard a tap-tap-tap at the window after Bill, Janey and Paddy had gone to bed. Jem and me were still sat up by the fire and I rushed to the back door to let him in. He was near frozen in Bill's old coat and cap.

He said, 'Sorry, Annie. I shoulda stayed put here but I had to see ya. You fight better than Big Tom ever did, wench – I was proud of ya.'

We got him in by the fire and gave him port and bread, and I said, 'Sir Andrew saw your ribbon, Tommy—'

He said, 'It's Mammy's ribbon and I'm not tekin it off for no man.'

We knew we had to get him away, get him to Liverpool and on a steamer for America. I went out and roused the Gaffer from his bunk in the barge and he come back through with us. He said, 'I can get him to Liverpool. And if he's got five pound we can get him aboard for Philadelphia. I knows a skipper who'll tek him.'

'He'll have to stay hidden in the bow all the way,' I said. 'They're looking for him all over.'

Jem said, 'We could get him on the train. The new one from Tipton goes to Manchester, and then he can tek another across.'

Gaffer shook his head. 'They'll be watching the trains and the coaches and roads. Nobody bothers about barges these days. I've near half a load of coal in there now; it won't look queer me shifting it tomorrow. Mind it'll tek us a near a week and I'll need this fella to come and do the locks and shovel coal.' He patted Jem on the shoulder.

Jem said, 'I'll go. I can look out for Tommy an all.'

Tommy took his satchel and counted the money he had from his robbing. He took ten pound of it for himself and his passage to America, gave two to the Gaffer and left me two in shillings and coppers.

The Gaffer took the notes Tommy gave him and looked at them. 'If the world was right this'd all go back to the nailers it was twisted out of,' he said.

Tommy said, 'Aye, but the world's not right, and no amount of giving back'll make it right.'

We stopped awake by the fire then, and when it got light the Gaffer started the steam engine and stretched the canvas right across the load. He piled bales and sacks on top of the coal to make it look like it was full under the cover and made Tommy a berth in the centre with hay bales. I gave em bread and tea and cheese from the scullery and Tommy kept Bill's old coat. He took one of the pistols from his saddlebag and handed me the other, saying, 'You never know when you might need an iron like this, Annie, especially in your game.'

He was right an all, so I stashed it away in my bloomers drawer.

When the light came up and the barge was full on steam we went down to the canalside. In the light Tommy saw my blacked eye, bent nose and the little cuts on my forehead from Molly Stych's bony knuckles. He held my face and said, 'Give it over now, Annie. I don't want you getting hurt no more. I will write to you from America and you and Jem can come – even old Bill could come.'

I laughed and hugged him hard.

Jem come and took me in his arms and kissed me and said, 'I will be back in just past the week, Annie. And I love you more than a sane man should love.'

I held his sweet face and said him some Burns, which is the best for parting from your love: *And I will luve thee still, my dear, Till a' the seas gang dry. Till a' the seas gang dry, my dear, And the rocks melt wi' the sun; I will luve thee still, my dear, While the sands o' life shall run. And fare thee weel, my only luve! And fare thee weel a while! And I will come again, my luve, Tho' it were ten thousand mile!*

I thought Jem would cry at those lovely words, for Mr Burns' songs could make a stone statue cry, and I did see tears spring into his eyes, but he simply turned and got onto the barge.

Tommy waved and went below into the hull, the Gaffer let the throttle go, and the barge chugged out into the cracking ice of the canal.

Then I went back inside and set a copper pot to boil so I could take a bath in front of the fire before Bill and Janey and Paddy awoke. For that morning I had an invitation to the vicarage for tea.

25

The drawing-room windows looked out onto the red-brick walled garden. On that cold December morning, the newly planted trees were bare, the rhododendrons and azaleas shone with frost, and the lawn was trodden to frozen mud by the feet of the workmen who had so recently completed work on the building. Even at noon the candles on the drawing-room table were lit, for the low cold sun did not strike the rear of the house in winter. The room was silent as Jessie set the tea things on the table: a brightly coloured Welsh Gaudy set, the cheerful primary colours and swirling flowers of which so delighted the late Mrs Warren. It was the treasured best china of the working man, she'd told her husband, and good and fitting for the modest needs of a vicarage. There was another fine porcelain set kept in the sideboard cupboard, but Jessie had decided that today's guest did not warrant it, nor the unwrapping and dusting.

Miss Esther entered first. Annie followed in her Sunday-best white dress and plain black pinafore, grey leather boots and her long black hair in a neat chignon – pinned by Janey that morning as Bill and Paddy cursed the summonses they had been delivered. The fierce bruises that had bloomed on Annie's face the afternoon after the fight with Molly Stych had begun to go down, but around her eyes there was still a purple tinge, and over her brow a small cotton dressing across the worst of the cuts.

Esther touched Annie's shoulder and said, 'Sit here, dear Annie, next to me. I am so glad you came. Oh, your poor face . . . but it is still lovely. Was it very painful for you?'

'Aye, Miss, she could throw a proper one, that wench.'

'Yes, she could, couldn't she? Annie, I confess it was the most thrilling thing I have ever seen, but my father is furious over the whole thing. Please forgive him if he is a little curt with you.'

Annie looked down and said, 'Pretty china, Miss.'

Esther picked up a teacup and said, 'It was my mother's favourite. She said it was the pattern that miners had in their dressers.'

'I aint never seen a miner with pretty china such as this, Miss – nor a dresser.'

'My sister and my father will be here shortly. My sister's young man Mr McLean is coming. I am sure you will find him handsome, Annie. He is an engineer at the works and can be rather dull if he is allowed to talk about steel production.'

Annie smiled and said, 'Do you have a young man, Miss?'

'I do not, Annie. Nor do I care to have one. I believe I shall not marry, for it binds a woman so and I have plans for my life. And I certainly would not care to be fawned over by someone as tedious as Mr McLean, handsome or not.'

The two women smiled at each other.

Esther said, 'And what of your young man?'

'My Jem is away to Liverpool on a coal barge. We are betrothed though. He is an angel, Miss Esther. Just this morning I told him some words by Mr Burns fore he left and it brung him near tears . . .'

'Oh, how romantic! Imagine, a man who is moved by poetry!'

'He is the one true blessing in my life, Miss.'

'And he is a fine-looking fellow, Annie. I saw him at the field yesterday.' Miss Esther flushed slightly and added, 'A fine-looking fellow.'

'He's a beauty, aint he, Miss? He's a fine stallion!' said Annie, and the two women laughed as Esther took Annie's hand and squeezed it.

'Oh, Annie, how I shall miss our talks.'

'We shall have many more, Miss Esther. I have not yet finished the whole Bible.'

Esther looked at her. 'My father feels you are now too old to come to the school. He says there are younger pupils who need my attention. I am so sorry . . .'

'Nor does he think well of me. Or my place of residence.'

Esther lowered her voice. 'My father is a traditionalist, Annie. He is hidebound by his background and his station. When my mother was alive she was able to soften his more conservative views and attitudes. And I am sorry for you and your people that he called the yeomanry.'

'The Reverend called em out, Miss?'

'Yes. I'm afraid he did, Annie. He was furious that I was there and he sent a note to the magistrate. I fear he means to continue trying to curtail any repeat of the event at the Champion. He is not well disposed to your father.'

'Then, begging your pardon, Miss Esther, but I must curse him for my enemy. I am Romi, Miss. We don't forget and we don't forgive,' said Annie, looking down.

'Oh, Annie, do not say that! You must forgive or you cannot enter the Kingdom of Heaven, and it is heathen and wicked to curse anyone. You must live by Christian principles, Annie.'

Annie raised her head and stared at the young woman sitting next to her. She seemed about to say something when the door opened and Judith entered, followed by Mr McLean.

The Scotsman wore a formal tie and short buttoned jacket and bowed to Annie and Esther.

Judith said, 'Father will be here shortly. Annie, this is Mr James

McLean. Mr McLean, Miss Annie Perry. Our star pupil at the parish poor school.'

Not knowing that she should stand and shake hands with Mr McLean, Annie nodded and said, 'How do, sir,' and the young man dropped his outstretched hand and said, 'Very pleased to meet you, Miss Perry.'

Judith said, 'I shall go and tell Jessie to bring the tea,' and left the room.

Esther said, 'Annie is a great admirer of your national poet, Mr McLean. She is able to recite Mr Burns' fine lines from memory.'

The young man shifted in his seat. 'Ah, very good, Miss Esther. I am not really an admirer of poetry if I am to be truthful.'

Annie and Esther exchanged brief amused glances and Esther went on playfully: 'Well, I hope you will be very truthful, Mr McLean. I expect there is scant need for poetry in your foundry.'

'Just so, Miss,' he said.

'What is even more remarkable about this young person is that this time last year she was utterly illiterate, unable even to write her own name. Is that not so, Annie?'

'It is so, Miss,' said Annie.

'Her progress in education has been astonishing. She can now read and quote the Bible, she knows the kings and queens of Britain, even the prices of coal and iron in the stock markets of London.'

'That is admirable indeed, Miss,' said Mr McLean.

'Perhaps you might make your employers aware of her great achievements? They have, after all, provided some of the funds for our little school.'

'I shall indeed, Miss. May I ask if she has been instructed in mathematics?'

'We have covered some rudimentary arithmetic, have we not, Annie?'

Annie looked puzzled.

Esther spoke in a Black Country accent and said, 'Reckoning.'

Annie nodded. 'Aye, Miss.'

Judith returned and sat next to Mr McLean, saying, 'The tea will be here in a moment. Oh, where is Father?'

Mr McLean said, 'A sound knowledge of mathematics would be most beneficial to the boys coming through your school, Miss Esther. We have new processes coming into the works that will need men who can subtract and multiply numbers quickly.'

Esther said, 'Just the boys, Mr McLean? Do poor girls have no need to know their numbers?'

Mr McLean smiled and said, 'Well, perhaps to count their children . . .'

Annie leaned towards the Scotsman and said, 'And maybe to reckon them when they die, sir. There's a lot of babies die from the smog from your foundry down the port.'

Judith gasped. 'Annie!'

But her sister smiled and said, 'Well said, Miss Perry. Perhaps Mr McLean is unaware of the effect on infants of the gases and the steam belched out by his works.'

'I am very well aware of it, Miss Esther, but fail to see why it should be a concern of yours here on the hill,' said Mr McLean, peeved at the turn the conversation had taken.

'My daughter's views have taken a radical turn this last year, Mr McLean. Forgive her hectoring – she has been allowed too much freedom in her reading,' came the Reverend Elijah Warren's voice from the doorway. He crossed to the head of the table, saying as he sat, 'I fear it is my failing as her father.'

There was a brief awkward silence before the Reverend nodded to Annie and said, 'Aha, the protégé we have heard so much of. How do you do, Miss Perry?'

Annie said, 'I do well, sir. How do you do?'

The Reverend smiled and said, 'I too do well. I trust my disruption of your entertainment yesterday did not cause you too much inconvenience.'

'No, sir, but my father is to be summonsed to the court.'

'Then he shall perhaps think twice before he inflicts such barbarity on the parish again,' said the Reverend.

Jessie came in with the trolley and set a teapot, teacups and saucers, scones, cakes and a plate of tiny white sandwiches on the table. The gathered group said nothing as she fussed over where to place each item, and Annie, catching the older woman's eye, received a look that said she did not belong here and was not welcome. Jessie muttered to herself as she circled the table until finally the Reverend said, 'Thank you, Jessie. That is perfect.'

Miss Judith poured the tea and Esther lifted a plate of finely sliced cake to Annie, saying, 'Here, Annie. This is Jessie's famous sponge.'

'And how is your diligent study of the Scriptures continuing, Miss Perry?' enquired the Reverend. There was an edge to his voice and a disdain for the girl that he found hard to hide. Annie could hear it, and in her mind already had him cursed. She waged a brief mental fight with the voices in her mind suggesting she just clock him one and walk out of the drawing room back to the Champion, where if folks didn't like you they told you straight with no fancy words and airs.

She said, 'My study of the Scriptures has opened my mind and my heart to the love of our Lord Jesus, Reverend, and has taught me that all men should be treated fair and equal, for we are all equal in the eyes of God and the poor are the most blessed.'

Miss Esther looked for a moment as if she would burst with pride at Annie's speech.

The Reverend said, 'It is to be admired that you know the beatitudes, child. You will also know that our Lord said it is your duty to turn the other cheek. A difficult thing, I expect, for a pugilist.'

'It is not difficult for me to provide for my father, sir, and that is why I fight. I honour my father as commanded.'

'I fear my daughter's radical ideas may have infected you in the school room, Miss Perry. And I say that there shall be an end to that come the new term.'

'I aint no radical, sir. I am a loyal subject of Her Majesty, and your daughters have given me the greatest gift in teaching me to read the Word of God. I trust you will agree with that, sir.'

Mr McLean said, 'We had previously been discussing the merits of teaching girls at all, Reverend. I am sure you will also agree that it can lead to the creation of problems in a community.'

Miss Esther looked hard at her father and said, 'Your answer to that remark will warrant very careful contemplation, Reverend.'

The Reverend smiled and said, 'When my daughter very much disapproves of me she refers to me as Reverend.'

Judith put down her teacup and said, 'Come, we are in danger of boring Mr McLean with this talk. Let us discuss more gentle and less personal matters.'

The Reverend took a sandwich and said, 'I agree, Judith. Let us hear no more of the events of yesterday nor the role of education for young ladies. Mr McLean, what think you of these new buildings here on the hill? As an engineer, what is your view of their construction?'

'They are most well made, sir. The church is a fine example of modern building techniques. I noticed on Sunday that heating pipes have been installed, which I fear would not have been so in the period of church building it is imitating.'

213

'There is a coal boiler in the basement, Mr McLean. The days of freezing pews are past. Gentleman may even remove their coats before the service.'

'Is it a steam or hot-water system, Reverend?'

'I fear I do not know. The verger, Mr Plant, attends to such things. There is a vast copper water tank down there, that I do know. I am told it cost a good deal.'

Esther looked at Annie and raised her eyebrows, and Annie wanted to giggle. Judith too was amused by the banality of the exchange between the two men, and she glanced across at Annie and her sister and smiled.

Esther said, 'Father, we shall take Annie for a turn around the garden while you and Mr McLean discuss pipes and valves and suchlike.'

The Reverend and Mr McLean rose as Judith, Annie and Esther left the table. The women went to the hall where Annie put on her long cloak and the sisters buttoned up thick winter coats.

Esther said, 'Do not allow Jessie to believe that you will be at all cold, for the thought of a chill sends the poor woman into ecstasies of concern.'

'I doubt she'd be much bothered if I got a chill, Miss Esther.'

'Oh, I am sure she would, Annie. Chills are her greatest fear.'

Jessie said, 'You will know, little Miss Perry, that chills will kill a bairn, coming from where you abide. I expect you've seen it.'

Annie said, 'Aye, you are right there. It's the poor ones who stay cold while they heat the churches for fine folk.'

In the garden they walked along the bricked paths past the leafless trees and drooping shrubs. Judith said, 'Will your father suffer greatly from the summons?'

Annie said, 'Well, they took all the money we made from the fights and they'll fine him, but we've nothing to pay a fine with. I expect we'll manage. It won't be the first time we've been penniless, Miss Judith.'

Esther said, 'But your young man is working? He's on a coal boat to Liverpool.'

Judith said, 'My father means you no harm, Annie. He finds it hard to adjust to the way the world is changing about him. He is still greatly affected by the loss of our mother. I hope you will forgive him and learn to look on him kindly.'

Annie said, 'I know what it is to lose a mother, Miss Judith, and I feel for the man if his heart is broken.'

'Then you will not put a gypsy curse on him, Annie?' said Esther, laughing.

'Esther, what a thing to say!' said Judith.

Annie laughed too and said, 'No, Miss, I shall not put a curse on him.' Then her expression hardened. 'Though I could if I had a mind . . .'

Judith looked appalled. 'Annie, we do not speak of such things here.'

Annie smiled and walked on, away from the two young women.

26

I hadn't never bin served and waited on. I hadn't never bin called Miss Annie so much neither. And I liked it well there, with the pretty china and the sweet sponge cake. But I knew I dint belong there, nor would I ever go back there. Nor would they ever want us again, lest it was to skivvy for them.

Fact was: I dint really belong nowhere. I felt no catch and hold to the alehouse. I loved Bill and I felt warm and kind to Janey for what she taught us and how she looked out for me. But the reading and knowing had made me see over it all, all the dirt and the struggle, the clacking of nails and the thunder from the foundry. Anywhere I once belonged was gone now.

And I weren't going to curse the Reverend. Though my mammy taught me curses you could put on a body or lame a horse with. Or make milk go sour or mould come on wheat. They were just like prayers you said in church, little rhymes and skipping words, and sometimes you drew a double star on a rag and wrapped a lock of a woman's hair or a bit of a man's beard in it, and then bound it with monkshood stems.

But I dint hold with that now, though I liked the way a gorger quaked if you muttered at him. I used to do it on Bill all the time.

But whoever was turning the wheel of fortune over us at the Champion had a good hard grip on the handle. Bill got fined thirty pound and Paddy the same at the court, and they kept the takings and purse money. Paddy scarpered off back to Brum and we dint hear nothing from him till spring.

Me and Janey tried to keep the alehouse going, for Bill was smitten with melancholy after that fine and he sat all day long not speaking and just sipping at his ale. He stopped shouting at everyone and he stopped demanding we all sing 'God Save the Queen'.

Then Janey went back to nailing to earn pennies and I began to take in washing from those about us. I used the big copper pot to boil it all up and I had strings of washing drying out the back in all the smutty air. There weren't nothing ever got returned white no matter how much caustic I used. I got sick scrubbing washing in the filthy black air and started coughing up black specks when it was damp.

Jem was back over at the farm, and it looked like me and him would never be wed. He'd come out on a Sunday and bring a few pennies I used to pay off bits of Bill's fines, and we would walk up the heath and have a grapple in the bushes.

But we slid into debt over that spring. Soon we owed the brewery, the baker, the butcher and the grocer, and I was forever robbing one to pay the other. For a while I got barrels and barley, and me and Jem mashed and brewed our own ale in the backyard. It weren't so bad – we sold it for tuppence a jug. The nailers went out on strike again in April and there were more radicals and Chartermen speaking in town and outside the mine gates. There was less and less call for the nails in those days. They said they could be got cheaper and better from elsewhere and the foggers were always screwing down the money they paid out. And they were still starving in the lanes where the nailers had their forges.

I never saw Miss Esther or her sister after I stopped going to the school and I ran out of books to read and had no money to buy any.

Jem borrowed books off Mrs Fryer at his livery; she had a soft spot for him and she liked to read novels and stories and sent to

Birmingham for them. He started bringing me one a week when he come over on Sunday and I read everything. I was done with the Bible by then. I read a book called *Two Years Before the Mast*, in which a gentleman recounted his life in the Navy with all the lashings and rum you could want. I thought it a fearful hard life on a ship, and I thought about Benny and Tass transported to Australia.

I read Mr Edgar Allan Poe's story 'The Tell-Tale Heart', and I shuddered in my bed in the candlelight at the horror of that story, told by a madman who is driven madder by the sound of the beating heart of the man he killed and hid under his floorboards. Mr Poe had a terrible imagination that he could think of all that fear and horror and write it down as if it were true, to bring terror into the heart of them reading it.

In those months, as we got more and more bogged in a mire of liability and arrears, the only time Bill was happy was when I read to him as he sat before the fire. And I liked it too an all.

He wasn't one for stories or adventures: he liked history best, especially *Lives of the Queens of England* by Mrs Agnes Strickland. I had to read it him twice. He clapped his hands with joy when I told him of how Queen Elizabeth by her resolve and faith defeated the Spanish Armada in the year 1588.

I liked Mr Dickens' books for he knew and wrote well of the poor and them as are victims of the cruelties of fate for no wrong done by them. I loved the sorrowful tale of the orphan Oliver Twist and the hardship of the workhouse he endured. It broke my heart thinking on Mammy and the babbies in such a place. It likened to my own family tale, as our Tommy turned to crime like Oliver when he escaped the misery of that temple of despair. I knew my story would not end like Oliver's, mind, for Loveridges have no rich relations to seek them out and make all well.

Bill liked the American poem I read him called 'The Wreck of the Hesperus'. It was about a proud sea captain who kills his own daughter by tying her to the mast in a storm. The poem come in one of the periodicals Mrs Fryer sent over for me to read and I thought it gloomy and tragic and with no beautiful wording like the English poems by Mr Wordsworth, Mr Keats and Mr Burns I had read with Miss Esther. I wondered if perhaps Americans do not speak so beautifully as the English do.

In April, the magistrates removed Bill's licence to sell ale and demanded he pay his fine for organising illegal fighting and abetting illegal gambling at a regular rate of five shillings a month or he would be called for a bankrupt and go to prison. We couldn't find five shillings a month and not starve.

Then one day a fine-dressed gentleman came in the Champion and said he was a lawyer. His name was Mr Matthew Goodwin and he stood over Bill as he sat before the fire and showed him a long letter which he said was a purchase agreement for the alehouse and the field at the back. I read it for him and it said a client would pay thirty pound for the property.

Bill sat listening and nodding as Mr Goodwin explained: 'It is well known, Mr Perry, that you are in some difficulty, and my client is willing to pay you a very good price for this property and the small piece of land at the back. Since you are now forbidden to run the property as a licensed house it would seem sensible to accept a sum with which you could discharge your current responsibilities and avoid the debtors' prison.'

I said, 'Who is the client who wants our property?'

Mr Goodwin said, 'He is a business gentleman and he wishes to build a new factory and houses on this site. It is an excellent location for such a venture, being so close to the canal and the railway.'

I watched Bill, and his misty eyes flashed for a minute, then he stood slowly and dint he then swing his big left hand up and catch Mr Goodwin square in the jaw, sending him sprawling across the floor. The gentleman did not see that this might be Bill's reaction to his proposal, but I could've told him, and perhaps I should've done.

A day later, a magistrate arrived with a constable and served another summons on Bill for the bodily assault of Mr Goodwin. He stood well back as he handed it to Bill lest he was served the same as the lawyer. The constable said, 'Them fists of yours will see you in the gaol, Billy. That there was Sir Andrew's lawyer.'

Bill held his fists up and said, 'These are all that give me the power to stop them as have from tekin from them as have not, and I shall not desist in letting them talk on my behalf, constable. The fellow insulted me and wanted to tek my alehouse, and he nor no other shall do that – sir or lord or gentleman though he may be.'

So now we had another fine of five pound, and this was to be paid immediate, and no time or credit on it. I felt we was about to sink and Bill go to the gaol and me to the workhouse like my Tommy had.

And that night, as we sat before the fire fretting on how we were to pay all the debts we had accrued, we heard a carriage arrive outside and there was a smart rap at the door, and there stood Paddy Tacker.

He had Jem with him and the show wagon all repainted and two good horses. And he said, 'I have a solution to all your ills and wants, Bill. Shut up the alehouse, lock the doors, and hang those who hound you for money. We are to go on the road.'

27

For Annie, it was like the time before Big Tom died, when she and her family ranged and wandered through lanes and country roads in a painted vardo pulled by Cobble the pony. Bill's melancholic mood lifted as the five of them travelled from fair to fair. Paddy drove the wagon, and beside him sat Jem and Annie. In the back rode Janey and Bill, Janey stitching Annie's show gear and Bill enjoying the warm May sun on his battered old face and breathing clean country air.

There were May fairs and summer fairs far and wide, and Paddy had a list of those they could show at, moving first west into mid Wales, then down through Monmouthshire and Gloucestershire towards Bristol and then into Somerset before they turned and followed the River Severn back towards Worcestershire. Each day's travelling was slow and calm and each night they camped and cooked round a fire like true gypsies.

Paddy had worked for months carrying bets for Birmingham bookies and fencing bits of gear lifted from the silver quarter in the city to raise the few pounds he needed to buy two good ponies and repaint the wagon with the legends they used at the fairs for the boxing booth. Then he sent word to Jem, and finally came out to Tipton. He had not envisaged taking Bill and Janey on the trip, but the magistrates and debtors were after the old fighter (as they were after Paddy too), and he convinced Bill to join them on the road and to leave his debtors to whistle for a month or two.

Paddy knew there was money to be made from the show they

had. There was no other woman in a boxing booth in England, and it seemed that their fame and the marvel of their show spread as they travelled.

Janey coached the two fighters of an evening, and at the fairs Bill was a good man for dealing with challengers who wanted their shilling back. Few pressed their claim when they were told they'd have to get their money off Bill, who sat at a table at the side of the booth and was in charge of the takings. A look from Bill could still make ladies scream and strong men quake. He still needed his ale, but they took close to three pound at each fair and nobody begrudged the old man a jug or two. He'd brought his picture of the Queen with him and proudly displayed it at the booth, sometimes demanding that stray passers-by salute it and sing 'God Save Her'.

Annie and Jem fought a play bout against each other at the start of the show: Annie kitted out in her Slasher's Daughter garb of scarlet and Jem stripped to his britches, drawing admiring looks from every dairy maid and fine lady who clapped eyes on him. The spectacle drew in the crowds, and soon Paddy was calling for a-tanner-a-time challengers and they came, both men and women. Neither Annie nor Jem had much bother. Paddy never paid the prize that whole summer. In Kidderminster, a mighty farm lad stayed up with Jem to the last second of the five minutes, and Paddy made that stretch with his hand poised over the bell amid the bellowing of the lad's gang of friends. Just at the moment when Paddy felt he could no longer hold off ringing, Jem swung a great clattering right into the boy's head and knocked him cold. There was a brief altercation with the gang until Bill stood up and bellowed blindly at them to move on, which they duly did, carrying the prostrate giant between them.

After that fair they stopped outside the asylum where Annie's mother had died. Annie knelt and said a prayer for her mother's soul, still in her show gear, and Bill, always prone to tears, knelt and wept alongside her, and prayed piously for the dead woman whose daughter he had bought.

At Tintern Abbey they stopped and spent a day walking and exploring the cliffs and quiet valley where the ancient monument lay. Annie and Jem led Bill up to the high rocky outcrop where Wordsworth had contemplated over fifty years before. Annie recited some lines from the poem for Bill: *These beauteous forms, through a long absence, have not been to me as is a landscape to a blind man's eye: but oft, in lonely rooms, and 'mid the din of towns and cities, I have owed to them, in hours of weariness, sensations sweet, felt in the blood, and felt along the heart.*

Bill listened and then said, 'Aint I but a soul in wonder at you, my Annie, and at all them lovely things that reside there in your head.'

Further down the valley, Annie and Jem left the camp to swim naked in the quiet river as the evening sun set and clouds of mayflies tumbled above them. They lay in each other's arms on the long grass as the dusk light turned the bankside oak leaves amber and gold, and Jem looked down at their two entwined shining bodies and said, 'These beauteous forms,' and Annie laughed and kissed him.

Paddy kept them away from towns where there were mines and works and kept to country places where the air was fresh. The sun shone warm and full for the whole of May and early June as they moved about the fairs. Sometimes they met other show people on the road and travelled side by side with troupes of Italian tumblers or Romi fortune-teller wagons.

In the second week of June they made their way back towards Wolverhampton. Their money bags were full enough but could have been fuller. There was still not enough to pay all the debts and fines that Paddy and Bill had hanging over them, but there was enough for barrels of ale and a party at the Champion to celebrate the betrothal of Jem and Annie. The young lovers had told Bill of their intention to marry as they came back towards Tipton and he had given his blessing, though not without an impassioned plea to not break his heart by leaving him. Annie said they would always stay close to him and Jem promised to look after her and always be true.

Warrants and summonses were plastered over the door when they opened up the Champion. Bill had been called to a debtors' prison in Birmingham. And two more letters awaited them inside. The first was an offer and contract from Lord Ledbury for a boxing show to be performed at his Midsummer Night's Dream fair in the grounds of Ledbury Court, to be held over three days from the twentieth to the twenty-second of June. The contract promised the astonishing sum of fifty pounds for Annie and Jem to attend and had provision for Paddy to act as referee and timekeeper.

Paddy said, 'The man has more money than he knows what to do with. It is a most auspicious event, mind. There's gentry from all over and all the society folks from London to come. We'll take enough to keep Bill out of prison, I wager.'

Paddy sent a note to his lordship confirming that they would all be at his grand fair, and they prepared to leave the Champion once again.

The other letter had come from America for Annie. It was stamped with marks of Pennsylvania State and the American postal service, and had come across the sea to Liverpool by steamer.

28

This was Tommy's letter:

My dearest sister,
I have been two months in America at this date and the winter
snows are still upon the ground all around the State of
Pennsylvania where I have settled for the last months since my
arrival. It is said here that Spring will come soon with a great
melt and rushing of the rivers. The rivers in America are wide
and mighty and flow back into the interior for thousands of
miles. The Delaware River is like the sea at Philadelphia and I
took a barge from there up into the state, and come here to
Lakawanna Valley where I have work in a foundry and bide in
a rude shack with others who labour here. We make steel with
hot blast from the coal which is all around and iron ore mines
everywhere. It is like Tipton and Bilston, only here it is wild
and rugged country with high cliffs and endless forests and
Winter is colder with great falls of snow.
*   The pay is good but the conditions of our life are harsh here,*
with so many crowded into the shacks along the valley side, and
more arriving each day.
*   There is a saloon, as they call an alehouse in America, and*
there you shall hear the tongues of a thousand countries spoke.
Most are Dutch, German and Irish, but there are Scotch,
Italians, Spaniards, Frenchmen, Jews from Poland and Russia,
Moslems from Turkey and Egypt and Greeks. There are Romi

too. Most come tinkering and selling to the foundrymen but I have seen none we knew from our days on the road with Big Tom and Mammy.

I was blessed to meet up with two fine Staffordshire lads on the great steamer that brought me here. They are good fellows and we joined up together to seek work and a place to stay. It is fine for me to hear the voice of home in their speech and the three of us rattle in Black Country in the saloon so even the other English boys think we are foreigners speaking in a strange tongue!

I wager you will be pleased to know that I have not yet resumed my previous occupation in America, for though travellers carrying sacks of dollars and gold are common, here they move in a fortified coach with steel doors and lockboxes, and armed guards ride atop as they carry money to and from the banks in Philadelphia.

It would be a fool who tried to rob one of these. It would take an army. My old iron is stored safe away in my pack and shall not see use I hope. I pray you have kept the other I give you, for you may need it in your life of fisticuffs.

My plan is to work here for this year and save my dollars. Then me and my Staffordshire lads shall buy horses and go West. We have heard much talk of California which is a Promised Land where gold is to be found lying in the fields. The journey there will take a full year and we shall have to learn of the trail from men who have done it, and these men can be found in the State of Missouri, where a great river takes you to the South of this land where men possess African slaves and live in palaces.

My work is hard. I shovel coal all day long and unload coal wagons. There is a railroad being built here at this time, and if a fellow likes not his work in the foundry, he can walk to the railroad and get as many days' work as he pleases. So the guvnors hike up the wages to keep the lads at the foundry, for our iron and steel is much needed for the railroads which they say will one day run all across America.

I shall have a day's holiday for Easter in a week and me and the Staffordshire lads (their names are William Stack and George Sandman) will take a coach and a steamer to Philadelphia where I will mail this letter to you to be carried on the steamer to Liverpool.

I mean no dishonour to Big Tom but I have used Bill's name as my name here and I am known as Tommy Perry, for to call myself by my birth name might bring misfortune upon me from them arriving here from our country who know of the adventures of the Black Cloak, who must keep the truth of his daring doings a secret. I discovered both William and George had heard of the Black Cloak when we talked of home and they resolved to keep my secret.

I can buy and read the stories of adventure I like so well here, and there are fine tales of frontiersmen and Indian fighters in periodicals. There is a church in our valley and a store where we can buy tobacco and our bread.

I teach William and George to read of a night in our shack and we stay away from the saloon until Friday. I like to go there for I have gone soft on the saloon keeper's daughter. She is a very pretty German girl called Stella Beck and me and the boys talk to her and make her laugh and, truth be told, we all three are in love with her.

My Annie, you would be set well if you came here for ladies have fisticuffs bouts all over. They tell me there are boxing matches at all the summer fairs here and the champion of the

227

*ladies in the State of Pennsylvania is a Dutch wench named
Bertha Bakker who lives in our valley and works in the mines
at Slocum Hollow. The saloon boys say she is a mighty strong
wench and she fights men and has knocked out everyone she has
taken on in a challenge fight. What would she make of our
Annie, I wonder? The men here fight often. There is a square
at the back of the saloon where they stage bouts and money is
wagered almost every Saturday night. I do not wager for my
money is being saved for my adventure to the West.*

*I must fight in my thoughts my terrible sadness over
Mammy and the others. I wonder and dream of the fate of
Benny and Tass, and I still say prayers every night for the souls
of Mammy and the babbies we lost so tragic.*

*I pray for you too, my Annie, for we are the only Loveridges
left. I pray you will marry your Jem, who is the finest fellow
and who I would be proud to call my brother, and if you have
a boy first born you must name him Thomas for our dear
father.*

*Though we are all ripped and cast to the winds, still I have
my memories of our little tribe and I hold you close in my heart.*

From your most loving Brother,

Tommy

*You can send correspondence to me here. It will take a time
and cost some shillings but you can send to Tommy Perry,
Scranton Furnace and Steel Works, Lakawanna Valley,
Pennsylvania, United States of America, and I shall get your
letter. And I will send word when we go out West.*

Holding Tommy's letter in my hand, I stood before The Champion
of England. They were building all around, more rows of mean

little houses, and fellows were cobbling in the street and the back lanes. The alehouse wanted painting; it was filthy brown. Nobody had washed the windows in months and the image of Bill on the sign was scarcely visible beneath the grime. Paddy, Bill, Janey and Jem were all in the wagon and the horses were stamping to move off.

There was a sudden rush into me of a knowing that this would be my last time in these parts. Bill had made me write out his will the night before as the party was going full tilt. All the regular twisters and free ale merchants had crowded in to wish me and Jem well and celebrate that the alehouse was open. We had no licence, so Bill was justified in giving away all the ale on this occasion. A fiddler and concertina player come, and there was singing and dancing till it got light.

In the middle of it, while Jem was sweeping and swirling every wide-eyed nail wench around the floor, Bill made me sit with him on the bench out front beneath the lamps and he told me his wishes.

'I have nothing, Annie – only this that you see. When I go you shall have it, but I want to provide for Janey an all. Though we are not wed she has been a true wife to me.

'So I wants to say, in this will, that you and Janey shall jointly own The Champion of England alehouse and the land out the back an all. The two of youse shall have all the fittings and the tables and chairs, the goods in the scullery and the ale store, the barn, and all the plate and china and glass.

'Forgive me that I can leave you no money nor other property, but I have been a profligate soul all me life.'

I kissed him and said it dint matter nothing and that he was to live and fetch me trouble for a good while yet to come. We paid Jock Convey two shillings to lodge the will with a young solicitor, Mr Garrow, who had just opened his offices in the port. Old Jock swore he would execute his task and Bill said you can always trust a Scotchman when it come to monetary and legal affairs.

So as I stood on that June morning, with a thick head from no sleep and too much ale, I had it known deep in me that this was the last I should see of The Champion of England and these streets. I dint know what was to happen nor where I was to go after we fought at Lord Ledbury's. I knew that things were shifting in me and shifting about me, the port and the hill up from it all quivering with navvies and wagons and cranes, red brick upon red brick covering everything over, and still the forges and foundry bellowing steam and smoke above us.

29

For Bill it was the end. Having to leave the alehouse again and go out on the road, all the long road to near Worcester which he knew from years past and years when he pulled barges and slapped lads down if they were in the way. Years with the Gaffer hauling coal and timber and charcoal and ore. The Gaffer said the lord they were going to perform for was a bad un. He said all in the region knew it: that he was a libidinous and salted lad, possessed of the morals of a barge rat. His lordship had put up the guineas he had used to buy the alehouse all them years past on the day he bought Annie and lost to the Irishman, but let him try it, thought Bill, with my Annie or with her Jem or with any of us. Let him try it! He would make sure Paddy got the money and they'd settle all the bills and the fines and it would be back to the old days of The Champion of England, when Annie mopped his brow and he sold ale to all the lads who came in.

And here we was now, rattling along in the wagon, Janey with her head lolled onto his shoulder, feeling every damned creak and bump and the steady pull of the ponies. That is where he was now: unable to sit comfy and every bone in his body aching and complaining as the wagon jumped and rolled over the road. There would be none who would ever know the swirls and swimming in his head, how each day was a fog and a brew of mist before his eyes, which once had seen and reckoned everything around him.

He thought then of his whole life. Of his days as a strong young buck who bargemen paid to clobber fellows out of the way at the locks, and then as a fighter in his britches, his belly scrolled and hard as he bobbed and swung with the odd gait that puzzled his rivals.

He remembered his lovely dark-eyed beauty of a mother, who held him and whispered tales in Romi to him, and his father, a great cursing monster with a mass of swishing blond hair and hands the colour and feel of iron. He remembered the long walks to Mass after his mother passed, his father striding ahead in the lanes where he felt hemmed and trapped by the height and majesty of the hedgerows either side of him. His father said they were to hear truth as he clipped and slapped him into the church where they bobbed and crossed before entering the pews, and the Father talked in lovely words of the beauties of Heaven and they chanted 'Our Father' and 'Hail Mary'.

To Bill all women were blessed; he grew to feel a crushing desire to protect and honour them, and never mind the dirty words the barge lads used, never mind the great wrong of their position in the world. He knew and felt in his soul that a man who could not love and respect and protect a woman was no kind of man at all. He loved the way Jem Mason hovered over Annie, his eyes alert and wide for any threat to her, the big gentle hand over her shoulder. That was a real man, Bill thought; never mind the fighting and laying out lads, a real man loved and looked after his woman. He had tried to do that all his great bumping ale-swilling life. So much was a blank to him.

All the ale over the years – the great rushing pleasure as it cascaded down his throat, swishing and cleaning his inside, and the sharp clench of hops as it hit you and everything became possible. He was born with a powerful thirst that it seemed no amount of ale could quench.

As the wagon rumbled down Spon Lane and he sensed the Champion getting smaller, he felt that something was ending, something was shifting about in his misted vision. Then he felt Janey's hand on his face and he smiled as she pushed a flagon of ale into his hand.

30

Anthony William Percival Grainger-Hyde was known to his friends as 'Percy', to the workers on his vast Worcestershire estate as 'your lordship', and to the wags and gossips of London society as 'Sporting Percy' – reference to both his love of pugilism and the energetic bouts of physical exercise he was said to indulge in with both ladies and gentlemen at the lavish parties he held at Ledbury Court, the substantial Palladian mansion which had been the seat of his family since the early seventeenth century.

Mr Theodore Hook in the *Sunday Bull* had taken to writing scurrilous accounts of the bacchanalia alleged to have taken place at Ledbury Court, which carefully avoided libel by use of such euphemistic phrases as: 'We believe his lordship was most exercised by his sporting indulgences with various enthusiastic young persons.' A series of paintings he commissioned of naked Greek boxers that hung in the central hall of the house were referred to by the newspaper as 'painting most indecent and mollified'.

Semi-clothed Greco-Roman figures stood in the niches and exedra of the hall, and a handsome marble reproduction of the *Boxer of the Quirinal* sat as the centrepiece of the covered-bridge folly which crossed the serpentine lake at the front of the house.

His lordship relished his scandalous reputation and was amused when the periodicals made reference to his eccentric behaviour – such as allowing imported Arctic wolves to roam the woodlands of the estate and slaughter the sheep which grazed in the rolling fields, or indulging the troop of Macaque monkeys that colonised the stable block and terrorised the kitchen staff.

His lordship's love of dangerous and challenging sports included staging and riding in his own steeplechase around the estate each year, taking wrestling lessons from a huge mute Turk whom he housed in a distant corner of the estate, archery where the targets were frequently various pieces of fruit balanced on the heads of tremulous estate workers, and the art of pugilism. He had been instructed by Tom Sayers himself, who stayed as a guest at the house for an entire summer while he coached his lordship. He retained a full-time fencing master at the estate and a man who was employed to walk over his naked body in heavy boots so that he could practise the Indian breath- and pain-control techniques he had read of in lurid accounts of the subcontinent.

In London he was known for his propensity to challenge other young men in combat – his most recent attempt to engage a cavalry officer in a duel with swords was breathlessly reported in the columns of the *Sunday Bull* – and he would seek to insult potential adversaries in the many private clubs he frequented. Most society men knew of his penchant for thrills and did not take him up on his challenge.

Anthony Grainger-Hyde had no parents to answer to, his mother having died when he was eleven years old and his father and older brother shortly thereafter in a shipwreck as they returned from the family plantation in Barbados. Upon their demise, the young boy inherited the title and the entire estate. The Grainger-Hydes were, like many slave-owning families, the recipients of lavish sums of compensation when slavery was abolished in the British West Indies in 1833, and this money, added to the income from the estate and the family's investments in iron and steel, made him one of the richest and most eligible young men in England.

His circle of friends were as all rich and, largely, idle as he, and they cultivated a foppish effeminacy of dress and manners, which they took delight in subverting by their quickness to combat and fisticuffs. His lordship had been barred from numerous taverns and gentlemen's clubs as a result of his proclivity for brawling.

Two elderly aunts arranged a procession of eligible young ladies to meet him, consort with him at parties, and even to visit him at Ledbury Court, but their attempts to secure a wife were in vain. He much preferred the company of other young men and would often behave in a deliberately insulting way with these potential brides. His only regular female companion was a Mrs Jenny Fraser, a Scotch actress some fifteen years his senior he'd met at a London theatre and whose presence at Ledbury Court outraged both his aunts and his servants.

And today Mrs Fraser was at his side as he welcomed each carriage that pulled up in front of the house.

Of all the parties he threw, the most celebrated and gossiped about was the Midsummer Night's Dream fair he staged every year. The *Sunday Bull* reported that the whole of London society had decamped en masse to Worcestershire for the three-day extravaganza, which featured a steeplechase, canoe races on the lake, a re-enactment of the Battle of Austerlitz, archery, wrestling, pony jumping, the hurling of hay bales on a pitch fork, and, this year, in a specially built boxing ring, the chance to see and challenge the famed Bilston Bruiser and the Slasher's Daughter.

Mrs Fraser looked out across the expansive lawn from the raised terrace where she and his lordship had just had lunch. Black-coated manservants scurried about the terrace clearing the plates and glasses. She stood and breathed in the vastness of the place as he came to her side and touched her elbow. His lordship held out a small glass of bitter laudanum, which she took and sipped, with a smile.

He said, 'You will be most pleased by the spectacle, Jenny, and by the young fellow from Bilston who is to perform tomorrow. He is the sort you favour.'

She watched the men erecting tents and painted poles on the lawns and said, 'And you too favour him?'

Lord Ledbury said, 'I shall challenge him when he fights. I shall savour the smell of his skin close up. You should challenge the girl, Annie Perry – she is a rare beauty, one to be enjoyed.'

Mrs Fraser smiled again.

31

We set our camp in the woodlands. Me and Paddy walked up through the trees and great sweep of grassland to the house. The fine ladies and gentlemen were already gathering on the lawns, taking wine and watching jugglers in the June sunshine. There was a ring set with wooden poles and sagging tape. We wandered through the crowd. Some of em bowed as they seen us and one young buck even spread himself before us and said, 'We are honoured by your presence, Madam.'

Paddy found his lordship and talked money, and I looked out upon the scene from the terrace. I never knew there were so many rich folk in this world. There were scores of em, all sauntering about the place in their finery, and the ladies all demure with their ringlets and ribboned bonnets and voluminous skirts.

Paddy come over to me with his lordship, who looked quite the lad in his silver and pearl waistcoat and a coat the colour of blue sky. No hat, so his long blond hair swung and swept about his shoulders. I couldn't deny he was a looker and I am shamed to say I felt a twinge of yearning as he strode towards me.

There was a most pretty lady with him in a green silk dress. She was a fine beauty, with the look of a child about her, yet her eyes were rimmed with kohl, her face powdered white and her hair tucked into a jaunty sailor hat. Everything about her was what I wanted for me – the look of her and the proud way she walked. I felt a right lump in my old pinny as she came towards me, smiling.

His lordship bowed to me an all. He said, 'We are honoured to have you here, Miss Perry. May I introduce Mrs Fraser, the most celebrated London actress.'

The lady stepped in to me and caught me about the waist, and in full view of those about, she kissed me hard on the mouth, slipping her tongue in. What did I feel then? I dint push her away, I will say that. I could smell the powder on her cheek and feel the warm June sun on my back. Her mouth tasted fruity of wine and her lips were hot and soft upon mine.

His lordship applauded, stepping back from us, and Paddy said, 'Well now . . .'

The lady smiled at me and said, 'You taste exquisite, Miss Perry. I hope we shall meet again in the ring.'

I said, 'You shall not take such liberties with me in there, Miss.'

She and his lordship laughed and clasped each other, and his lordship said, 'You may leave your prudishness behind here, Miss Perry. This is midsummer, and while you and your parties are here, I trust you will take part in our pleasures. There will be some surprising sights and events to divert you during your visit.'

Paddy come and stood by me and took my arm. 'Well now, your lordship, Miss Perry is charmed to be here but she must go and prepare for her performance. Might I just mention to you the matter of the fee we've agreed for this entertainment . . .'

A crowd of young dandies and ladies now stood about us. The gentlemen all wore bright embroidered waistcoats and shaped jackets in silk and velvet, and the ladies wore gowns that showed their shoulders and were cut low to their bosom. Most of the gentlemen were beardless and wore their hair long like his lordship. They all seemed to regard me as if I were a new foal in a stable – with a mix of endearment and disgust at the slick from the mare's womb that clung.

Lord Ledbury clapped Paddy on the shoulder and said, 'You shall get your fee, Tacker, but first we must see the entertainment.'

A lady from the crowd stepped forward to me and held out her hand and said, 'May I observe?' She lifted my hands to examine them, and others began to crowd around to look, and there were cries of 'Such a size!' and 'How rough they are!'

One young lady said to the man next to her, 'I imagine these feel a little rough upon a person,' to which her companion said, 'I should like to know the feel of them on *my* person. Perhaps they are gentle and caressing when not delivering jabs and crosses.'

The crowd laughed and I whipped my hands away, for I knew they were mocking me and I dint like the look of them gentleman and the way they regarded me. Some of the ladies too looked hungrily at us, and, although smiling, I could feel they wanted to take liberties as Mrs Fraser had.

Lord Ledbury clapped his hands and called, 'Ladies and gentlemen! Let us go to the far terrace for wine and tinctures, and then the entertainment shall begin . . .'

He turned to Paddy and pulled a bundle of notes from a silver purse he kept about his neck. He counted out five of them and handed them to Paddy. 'Here, Tacker . . . half your fee to ensure you all behave agreeably while you are here. The rest shall come when you and your fighters have drawn a little blood.'

Paddy hurried me away back towards our vardo in the woods. He said, 'They are a rum lot, Annie – you shall have to watch yourself amongst them. For money is no bar to these fellows and they believe they can buy anything. Did you see how much his lordship carried in that purse of his? The bundle there was surely two or three hundred. A man who can sport himself about like that carrying so much coin may not be a man you can entirely trust.'

I said, 'How much did he give you?'

Paddy never liked talking about how much he'd been paid, but he stopped and said, 'Well, it was twenty-five pound. We shall have the rest after the show. I know how you and Bill need this purse, Annie, and we shall get it.'

32

At Ardleigh Chief Constable Southwick stood before Sir Andrew's desk in the study that overlooked the lawns; in the distance, the familiar pall of steam and smoke hovered over Tipton Port.

Sir Andrew entered, crossed to the desk and held out his hand to invite the constable to sit. 'Chief Constable, you have news for me?'

'Well, sir, I must first apologise for the time it has taken for us to glean this information, but we have undertaken certain enquiries and I am now satisfied that the Black Cloak who robbed you and shot our constable is indeed the brother of Miss Annie Perry. His name is Thomas Loveridge and he is a gypsy like Miss Perry. The workhouse at Bilston confirmed that the lad, who would be about twenty now, absconded from there two years ago when he was employed by the tanneries. We questioned the officers at the workhouse and he did indeed wear a red ribbon upon his left wrist; in fact he favoured the left hand in all things, and our lad swears he fired with his left. Now, his sisters died in the workhouse and the mother committed suicide in the Worcester asylum, and it was shortly after these events that he ran off.'

Sir Andrew said, 'He held the pistol in his left hand when he took from us, and the ribbon was the same sorry-looking scrap I saw at the prize fight on Boxing Day.'

The policeman continued: 'The workhouse had another letter from Miss Perry herself, who was enquiring after her family, and that said they were all Loveridges. I have it here . . .'

He handed Sir Andrew the letter.

'Well, the Reverend Warren could certainly be a little more circumspect about the backgrounds of those his daughters choose to champion at their school. And the boy Thomas was indeed at the workhouse, so I conclude that they must have been hiding him in the alehouse those months he was robbing. Or, at least, giving the villain succour and shelter.'

Chief Constable Southwick said, 'We believe Bill Perry bought the girl from a fair in about '38 – it is not at all uncommon amongst the Romi to sell their offspring. If we can prove Thomas Loveridge is still about them, hiding as a servant or a hanger-on, then we shall have all of them in a noose. I have no doubt the boy still wears the ribbon; it was tied onto his wrist by his poor lunatic mother according to the workhouse officers. He was by all accounts a clever lad: he could read and often gave the lessons at Sunday services.'

Sir Andrew looked once again at Annie's letter and shook his head. 'It makes one wonder at the Church, does it not? This is all rather fine, Chief Constable, but where is the boy?'

'Well, it seems that after getting into substantial debt from fines and unpaid bills, the whole party of them, including young Jem Mason from Bilston, went off and about to the fairs with their boxing booth. They returned for two nights just a day ago and then they were off again. The alehouse is shut up once more. It seems nobody is within, but with a warrant I could force entry and search for Thomas Loveridge. I have sent to the magistrate. William Perry is called to debtors' prison so we may assist those he has wronged if we can find him too.'

Sir Andrew said, 'Call on the magistrate and get the warrant. But if they are not there, where might they be?'

'Our constables have been told by the locals craving for their ale that they were called to the annual midsummer fair at Ledbury Court. It seems his lordship is fond of their boxing show.'

'How very convenient! I am to go to the fair myself tomorrow. Allow me to lead a party of constables down to Ledbury and we shall have them!'

'Well, sir, should we perhaps secure the alehouse first?'

'Very well. Do it this afternoon. Once secured, the place will be seized for sale to cover Perry's debts. And then find me a good party of fellows with strong horses to ride there. And make sure they have pistols and are able to use them.'

'I wonder if his lordship cares to have his party disrupted so? Perhaps we should wait until his guests are gone and intercept them on their return?' suggested Chief Constable Southwick.

'Oh no! Percy will think the whole affair an absolute hoot! Armed constables and fleeing desperados at his party? He will be thrilled by it.'

33

The weather turned thick and warm in the afternoon as Jem and me prepared for our bouts. Paddy had the ring set up as he wanted, with a bell and his pocket watch upon a table. He was set to ask the challengers to pay, notwithstanding the fee we were getting off his lordship. Paddy always had his eyes open to the opportunity of relieving people of their money. He hummed and hawed, and amended the price on his board with chalk. 'I'm thinking, with the kinds we have here, that five shillings a bout shall not be unreasonable and beyond their means.'

Bill took up his seat by the ring. He saw nothing now save shifting shapes about him. A footman from the house fetched him two big flagons of ale and he looked happy enough in the warm afternoon, tipping his cap to ladies and gentlemen as they passed by, saying, 'Ow do, squire?'

There was a lavish luncheon on the terrace with row upon row of ladies and gentlemen seated at tables and servants clad in togas serving wine from Grecian pots. After the meal Lord Ledbury announced the first sporting entertainment of the afternoon: a group of gymnasts would tumble and roll on the lawn, forming pyramids and doing flips and dives.

Me, Jem, Janey and Paddy walked over to the rope to watch from below.

His lordship announced to his guests: 'This troupe shall perform in the ancient classical Greek style, ladies and gentleman. Behold the gymnasium and I trust you shall appreciate their beauty.'

Then six big lads, entirely naked but for a red kerchief each wore about his neck, come running out of their tent. Seeing them run and tumble onto the lawn, the crowd above gasped; there were shrieks and cries, with gentlemen holding up their glasses to toast the scene.

Even Janey shrieked and clapped her hands and called, 'Ooh, what a fine spectacle!'

Paddy flushed and said, 'By God, he must've paid them a fortune to perform like that! It is indecent . . . I wonder how much they got—'

Jem said, 'Forget it, Paddy – I aint going nuddy for no amount!'

I watched, and I had to laugh when I saw a feller's feller swinging about, but Jem covered my eyes and went, 'No, Annie, you are not to see this.'

I said, 'Bugger off.'

Janey shouted, 'Blond one is a big fella, aint he!'

'For God's sake, nobody tell Bill,' said Paddy. 'He'll try and run in there and stop it. It is a blessing he is blind!'

I turned away from Jem and looked back across the field. Bill was sat happily by the fluttering bunting of the ring in his chair, sipping his ale and smiling into the warm afternoon.

On the terrace, it seemed the gentlemen and ladies were most inflamed by the spectacle; they all stood up toasting and shouting as the six lads went about their show, rolling and somersaulting and climbing upon one another, flipping backwards and forwards.

A young fellow from the terrace leapt down onto the lawn shouting, 'I am enlivened!' and stripped off his coat, waistcoat, shirt and britches, and ran into the middle of the gymnasts. His eyes were swirling with wine as he chased the fellows about. The crowd roared and applauded him as Lord Ledbury stood on the stone wall of the terrace, arms outstretched and calling across the lawn.

Jem said, 'This is getting out of hand here, Annie. What on earth shall they expect of us?'

I said, 'It will be all right, don't you worry. We shall do our show, get the money and leave.'

The naked guest had now pulled over the biggest lad of the troupe, and the two of them were wrestling upon the ground as the other gymnasts tried to prise them apart.

Paddy shook his head. 'Well, they tell me this is how the Greeks did it – the dirty bastards!'

The mood of wantonness and leaving the Devil his due proceeded into the afternoon. Me and Jem did our sparring show and the crowd gathered about us. Many of the gentlemen had stripped to their britches, and the ladies too had cast off their bonnets, shawls and coats, loosened their stays and collars, and were lolling about on the gentlemen or in the embrace of other ladies. Servants with trays circulated the whole time with champagne and tinctures in small silver cups, which the guests took and sipped. Paddy said it was laudanum – a potion which could relieve the most terrible pain but was wont to enslave a body to its effects.

The first challenger Jem got was a big foolish-looking stable lad who his lordship put up and paid the tariff for. Jem looked right sorry as he knocked the boy about the ring, whispering to him, 'Just go down and stay down.' The idiot boy got the message eventually, though his face was cut bad.

The gentlemen booed and ragged the poor fellow as he left the ring, and next up was another servant, a tall footman urged and pressed up by the cheering gentlemen and ladies. He made a better go of it: he even got a shot to Jem's belly, but Jem just skipped about him, almost shadow-boxing him, and every now and again he'd look over at me and shrug, as if to say, 'What are we doing here?'

After the footman was downed – and sensible enough to stay there – a great boo from the crowd welcomed a scrawny lad in a workshirt and britches pushed through the ropes. He was no more than twelve, and when Jem saw him he seemed to lose his head a bit. He ran around the ring shouting at them, 'What about you, gentlemen? How about some of you fine gentlemen gie it a try? I'm not knockin down no workin man nor babby neither . . .'

He bundled the lad from the ring and Paddy came shouting over to him, 'No, Jem, come on! You must take on all challengers – take on all!'

Of course Paddy dint mind who Jem hit as long as he got his five bob.

Then came a great roar from the crowd as a shirtless man with long auburn hair climbed in. He was one of the gentlefolk's own, and they began shouting, 'Come now, George! Come now and show this peasant how to do it!'

A little fat man, near naked but for his undergarments and top hat, and soused to past Monday with the wine, yelled, 'He is an ignorant turnip top, George! Show the bricky lad how his betters will keep his kind underfoot!'

Amid the shouting and cackling and laughter, the fellow strode about the ring like he was born in it, holding his hands up and striking poses for their applause. He wore a gold sash about his waist and he wasn't a bad-looking specimen for a toff. He liked well the look of himself, mind, and at first tried to provoke Jem by blowing little kisses to him with elaborate hand gestures and little winks and smiles.

The crowd whooped and cheered, and I could see all Jem wanted was to knock his head loose. The man could move a bit, and he set to dancing about trying to get a spot where he could come in.

He made a few moves forward, but Jem had him seen and he got two sharp jabs and a nasty cross to his head for his pains.

When the blood came the young buck roared and wiped his mouth and smeared it across his body. Why he did that I do not know for it seemed a powerful loopy thing to do in the middle of a fight, but the action sent the crowd wild with appreciation. They were calling, 'A savage! A savage!' and 'First blood!' and 'You are a noble savage, sir!'

Jem let the fellow caper some more before his friends and then flattened him: right under the chin, head back, lights out.

There was booing and jeering, and more of Lord Ledbury's young friends stepped up to challenge, each more mincing and womanly in their movements than the last. When he had clouted three more down Jem come over to me and said, 'I could knock these rich bleeders out all day, Annie.'

Then there was a trumpet call and the crowd parted to reveal Lord Ledbury looking like a Roman emperor in a purple pleated cloak and gold laurel wreath. He held up his hands and called, 'Ecco inimicus vulgo!' as he paraded towards the ring, and the call was taken up by the crowd who clapped along with it.

Once in the ring, his lordship shed the cloak to reveal himself naked but for a tiny leather cloth across his privates and leather bindings about his hands, forearms and legs. The crowd hurrahed more and called, 'Inimicus vulgo,' and I wished I'd done Latin with the Miss Warrens.

He began the bout by going straight in for a clinch when the bell went. He was near a head shorter than Jem and they grappled back and forth. I could see Jem dint know what to do with him as he clung about his middle; he tried to get him in the kidneys with a few shots and then simply lifted him, feet off the ground, and spun him round and let him go flying into the ropes. There was a mighty bellow from the crowd and cries of 'Foul!', and Paddy stepped in and gave Jem a warning like he would in a real fight.

Jem nodded, and then his lordship nipped in round the back of Paddy and clouted Jem hard on the jaw before dancing away, waving his arms to the crowd. I could see that one stung Jem but he kept control of himself and backed away, getting his feet proper and crouching right. He let his lordship come onto him. They moved around together eye to eye and the crowd began to hush more, waiting for a move from one of them. Then his lordship let out a great cry and came in wide open, throwing his right hand. Jem could've decked him then easy − I would've − but he kept calm and sidestepped away and cracked him with a few little jabs. Then he slowly came round him, just stepping right to jab him and you could hear the little smack-smack sounds over the crowd.

A few started up the 'Inimicus vulgo' chant again and 'Come along, Percy!'

From where I was it was clear what the problem was: his lordship was half cut, his eyes wouldn't focus and he was staggering after only a few little clips. Jem could see it too and he called to Paddy, 'If I lay him out, will we get paid proper?'

His lordship heard that and laughed uproariously. 'I shall lavish money on you, my beautiful brute,' he said.

'What's his game, Paddy?' Jem said, and he stepped in and jabbed him again, a nice clean snap that opened up his cheek.

'Again, again, Adonis − it is exquisite!' his lordship called to him, and he dropped his arms and went front on.

'Put your hands up there, boyo! I aint hitting a man with no guard!' Jem shouted to him.

I was thinking, just clock him, Jem, get the bleeding job done. The crowd started getting mouthy again then; some were shouting at Jem to finish him and some were calling to his lordship to go in hard.

Paddy stopped and whispered something in Jem's ear as Lord Ledbury turned to the crowd and bowed, holding up his hands to show the blood that was now streaming from his cut.

Like the gent before him, he wiped his hands across his face and chest, bloodying himself, and then spat blood on the grass and called, 'I submit to the giant! I offer myself to him. I will be his Patroclus.'

There were hoots and cheers from the gathered gentry. A man handed his lordship a bottle of champagne and he swigged it greedily. Then he called, 'A wreath for the hero!' They handed in the gold wreath and his lordship tumbled over to where Jem stood with Paddy. He pulled Jem into the centre of the ring, placed the wreath on his head and held his hand aloft, shouting, 'Vulgo grand-inem!' and the cry went up.

Jem looked at his lordship and said, 'What does that mean then, squire?'

'I am hailing you, Jem Mason. You are my Hercules, my Achilles.' And with those words he clasped Jem's head and kissed him hard on the mouth.

Jem pushed him away and swung his left, but his lordship had his wits about him when he wanted to, for he ducked and jumped away, and the crowd went even more wild and raucous. Lord Ledbury stepped back through the ropes into a sea of cheering faces and clapping hands as Paddy held Jem back from going after him and starting a riot.

'I aint doing this no more, Paddy. That's it,' he said. He was in a strop about the kiss and no error, and I went to him and said, 'They have some queer ways these folk, Jem. Don't let it rattle ya. It was only a kiss.'

Janey was laughing about it an all, shouting, 'I'd have kissed him for ya, Jem!'

Even Paddy started laughing. Then he said, 'Come on, Annie. It's your show now . . .'

He called to the crowd and led me into the centre of the ring, shouting, 'Ladies, gentlemen, discerning sports lovers all – I now call on all challengers from the ladies here present! I give you Britain's foremost and greatest woman pugilist . . . I give you . . . Annie Perry, the Slasher's Daughter!'

34

Lord Ledbury had paid a succession of dairy girls, maidservants and stable lasses five shillings each to challenge Annie for the entertainment of his guests. And as each climbed into the ring to try her mettle against the Slasher's Daughter, the assembled throng of increasingly dissolute revellers cheered themselves into ecstasies of excitement.

Annie showed none of Jem's compunctions about who she would or would not hit and duly flattened each woman in turn until seven bruised and battered opponents had left the ring to the jeering of the crowd.

Only one lady of a higher class came forward to challenge Annie: Mrs Jenny Fraser.

She appeared through the crowd after the seventh challenger had limped, bleeding, from the ring, and like his lordship she made an entrance with a trumpet blast. She was a fearsome sight and accustomed to commanding an audience.

She was wreathed in a scarlet cloak and gold headdress, and clad in a white toga cinched at the waist with a thin gold belt. Her hands and feet were bound with gold thongs, and she carried the goatskin shield, bearing the face of the Gorgon and fringed with the heads of snakes, of the goddess Athena. Her face was whitened with heavy powder, her cheekbones highlighted with spots of rouge, and her eyes lined with sooty black.

She strode into the ring, discarded her cloak and shield, and paraded before the baying crowd, arms aloft. Finally she turned to face Annie.

The two women's eyes met, and a sudden thrill seemed to go through the audience. They hushed as they stepped forward to shake hands.

Mrs Fraser gently pulled Annie in to her and whispered, 'It is a show, my dear. It is an illusion. Let us not hurt one another. Let us try to thrill them. I shall go down whenever you command me to.' And she smiled in a wicked way that made Annie smile too.

Annie said, 'Very well, but mind me jab. I should hate to scar your pretty face.'

As a performance it was one of Mrs Fraser's best. She had learned the stance and fluid movements of the best fighters, and in her years on the stage had perfected the art of watching, reading and reacting to the person playing opposite her.

The two circled and shadowed each other in what became a kind of dance, each mirroring the other's motions and gestures. As Annie jabbed, Mrs Fraser moved back, so the blow was often the lightest and most gentle touch. When Mrs Fraser swung at Annie's head, the younger woman pivoted and the blow, though appearing to connect, swished past her face. The bewitching fluid ballet they staged ranged between moments of a fragile delicacy and brief hectic flurries. They floated and darted like two mating butterflies chasing one another through a summer garden.

In one clinch Mrs Fraser whispered breathily into Annie's ear, 'Do you see how they are enchanted, Annie? Do you see how our beauty enthrals them?'

Annie said, 'I do, but mind you shall have to drop in a bit, and I might have to make it a true one.'

As they parted Mrs Fraser said, 'I shall savour your touch.'

The felling blow when it came was preceded by a knowing nod from Annie as she fixed Mrs Fraser in the eye and then suddenly quickened her left so she caught the older woman with a crossing uppercut on the tip of her chin. Though she tried to pull the punch, it connected and Mrs Fraser gave a sharp 'Aah!' as it spun her to the ground.

She lay smiling up at Annie as Paddy counted to ten. The crowd of onlookers, who had watched the encounter in awe, burst into applause and cheers.

Looking on as Mrs Fraser rubbed her bruised chin, Annie said, 'That is payment for the kiss you stole, Mrs Fraser.'

Still smiling, Mrs Fraser was raised from the ground by Paddy and stood before Annie. She said, 'All is illusion, Miss Perry. Do not ever forget that.' And she leaned forward and kissed her again.

The delighted shouts of the crowd enveloped the two as they embraced, and Mrs Fraser turned and held her hands aloft.

After the boxing show had finished the crowd moved to the lake where there was a chaotic series of canoe races. Revellers fell and dived into the water, and the lawns and house echoed with their delighted screams. A soaked and semi-clad procession was then led by Lord Ledbury to the house, wherein a munificent banqueting table was set for the evening's festivities.

Annie and her party returned to their wagon in the woodland beyond the lake. Jem made a fire and they boiled water in a kettle to wash. Jem took the two horses out to a patch of grass to graze and hobbled them.

Bill Perry was helped to his place by the fire, and he sat with Janey and Annie as the skies above them grew darker. Thunder clouds were approaching and a warm breeze was rustling the leaves of the spreading oak they camped beneath.

Paddy returned, carrying flagons of ale, a bottle of champagne and two fine glasses. He set them on a box before the fire and said, 'Well now, I shall get no sense from anyone up there till tomorrow, and maybe not even then. His lordship is indisposed.'

Annie opened a flagon and handed it to Bill. She said, 'Have we got our full amount?'

Paddy said, 'No, my girl, we have not. The gentlemen and ladies are carousing in the main hall. I think we shall have to wait till I can catch his lordship and persuade him to open his silver purse once again.'

Bill said, 'It was a fine show, you children. A fine one. I could hear a bit.'

Jem settled on the grass next to Annie as Paddy lifted the bottle of champagne and said, 'Here . . . for you two performers. I swiped it from a table on the terrace.'

Jem, unsure how to open the bottle, handed it to Annie. She twisted the cork, and they all gave a small cheer as it popped. Annie poured the champagne into the glasses and handed one to Jem. The glasses were of a clear and ringing crystal with grapes and vines engraved on the bowls, delicate stems and gold rims. Annie held hers up and looked at the straw-coloured champagne. She said, 'These are probably worth the twenty-five quid he owes us, Paddy.'

Paddy said, 'No, girl. We shall wait. His lordship is an honest man for paying and the two of you put on a fine show for his guests.'

Jem said, 'Aye, and the bugger kissed me. Kissed me!'

Paddy said, 'Rich folk are queer in these things, Jem. They do not have the morals of others. But they do have the money.'

Bill held out his hand and said, 'Annie, tek me hand.' The girl did, and he held her bruised knuckles to his face. 'What is to become of old Bill, I wonder? We cannot go back to the Champion for I shall be took for prison. Are we to wander like your people? I think it might be time for you to leave old Bill, my love. You and Jem could go and wed and find a life together somewhere. You could go to your Tommy in America.'

Annie said, 'I aint leaving you, Bill, you old bastard. What would become of you? You can't fight no longer and every bailiff and magistrate in Staffordshire is after you.'

Janey said, 'With Ledbury's money we can clear off the debts, Billy. We can go back and run the alehouse.'

The gathering wind was breaking the dark clouds above the park; huge boiling grey cumuli drifted like galleons across the evening sky. The lowering sun slanted through the gaps and shone amber on the tree trunks and waving grass, and a bright full moon seemed to be gliding gracefully in the opposite direction to the shifting clouds.

Bill asked Annie if she had brought Tommy's pistol with them. She said she had. He said, 'Fetch it for us, will you?'

'What use have you for a pistol, Bill?' said Paddy. 'You have no call for a pistol.'

'You couldn't see what you was shooting at, Billy,' Janey said and laughed.

The old fighter grew angry. He slapped his knees and shouted, 'Just bring it to us! I have a fancy to protect us all this night. It is midsummer's night and a full moon and I feel trouble blowing in at us. I cannot use me fists no more, but I can sit here with the iron and scare any queer folk or witches what come in on us . . . Fetch it! Fetch it to me now!'

Annie shook her head and went to the wagon where she pulled Tommy's pistol from her bundle. She came back to Bill and handed the weapon to him.

He looked up and said, 'Is it charged?'

Annie said, 'Aye, it is. Not much use not charged, is it?'

'Now fetch me my picture of Her Majesty and set it in front of me, facing out from us . . . No fairy nor beast shall assault us if Her Majesty presents her lovely face to them.'

Shaking their heads, but accustomed to Bill's queer fancies and demands, they arranged him as he asked, facing out towards the woods and the house beyond with the pistol in his lap, a flagon of ale in his hand and Queen Victoria at his feet.

They sat watching the scudding clouds above glimpses of the brightening moon. Then a sound of running feet came to them from the direction of the house. Bill raised the pistol and called, 'Who is there? Who troubles us?'

A voice came from beyond the nearest trees. 'I bring a most important message for Miss Annie. It is from his lordship. He charges me to give it only to her.'

It was the young stable lad who Jem had refused to fight. He walked gingerly up to the group holding a folded and sealed note in his hand. When he saw Jem sitting before the fire he nodded to him, and Jem smiled and nodded back.

Annie stood and said, 'Give us it here then.'

35

Bill was right. There was something coming on us.

A full moon on midsummer night meant something, but I didn't really know what.

The note said:

Miss Perry,
My thanks and felicitations to you.

Your performance was splendid as was that of young Mr Mason who shall remain in my heart as a worthy contestant comparable to the heroes of Antiquity.

It would be most advantageous to you in financial terms if you would indulge a fancy of mine and come to the Greek Temple at midnight tonight where I plan to stage an entertainment which very much requires your presence and participation. Nothing shall be required of you that may offend or endanger you.

If you come to the Temple just before 12, beyond the lake and along the marble walkway in a small grotto amongst the woods, I shall pay you both your outstanding fee and a further consideration for your much appreciated presence.

Mrs. Fraser would be most amused and pleasured to re-acquaint herself with you.

There is but one proviso to your receipt of the money I promise you – you must come alone and leave those of your party at your quaint camp. If this proviso is not fulfilled it may not be possible to furnish you with the outstanding fees.

*Please do not disappoint me and grant my trifling request.
You need not bring your fisticuffs outfit as apparel will be
provided.*

I reiterate – please come alone.

Please pass on my regards to your eminent father,
LEDBURY

When I read them all the note, Jem went, 'You aint going, Annie.
Hang em and their entertainment. You aint going.'

Paddy said, 'Well now, he is a man of his word, Annie. If he
says he will pay, he will pay, and a further consideration an all. It
would not do to offend the gentleman.'

Bill said, 'They mean you no good, Annie. You must stay here
with old Bill and we shall watch the midnight moon.'

Janey said, 'I should go, but tek the pistol in case they try any
funny business with ya.'

Jem said, 'I am your betrothed, wench, and you shall not go!
Never mind the money – you're bound to obey me.'

Paddy said, 'Well now, let's not be so hasty, Jem.'

'Paddy, you were the one who said we couldn't trust him, and
now it's all right to send her off alone to him?'

Bill come in with, 'There is more to life than money, Paddy, and
I want my little daughter kept safe.'

Then the three of em started at it, shouting and calling each
other out. I looked at Janey and she shrugged. I stood and listened
to their hollering at each other and then I bawled, 'Right! Shut it,
all of you!'

They all stopped and looked at me.

'This concerns *me*, and *I* shall decide how it will go,' I said. 'We
need all the money we can lay our hands on, so I am going to go.

I can defend meself if need be. I don't need no pistol. Janey and Bill, you taught us how to fight – well, now you've got to let me go and do it if I need to. Jem, I love you but you aint going to tell me what to do, and I aint going to obey no man for no good reason, and if you want to wed us you have to warrant that fore you do . . . Paddy, what's the time?'

He looked at his pocket watch. 'It is a quarter before midnight.'

I said, 'If I am not back here by half past one then you can come and look for us, but not till then, got it?'

I turned and walked away, and I dint look back at em.

It was quieter now; the breeze had dropped and the clouds had stopped racing and the moon was bright and full. You dint need no lamp. Across the lake I could see the lights in the big house and upon the terrace.

Near the bridge I found the marble walkway. It ran, curving and snaking, across the open pasture with statues of gods and goddesses along it on raised plinths. There were arbours every so often of white steel bedecked with tumbling roses. Everything looked bright silver in the moonlight, like there were no colours in the world, but I got the pleasing scent of the roses as I passed under them.

I wasn't scared nor worried. If you can fight you don't get scared and if you can read what's what in a fix you feel full of vim about it. Truth told, I was excited. I liked that they just wanted me, just little Annie Loveridge, the gypo whose mammy sold her and who'd skivvied, and I liked the knowing that I should gain an all. For I had lost a fair load or two over the years and now I wanted to get something back. I resolved to ask his lordship for two hundred from his silver purse before I would agree to any part in his entertainment. Two hundred would service all the debts and buy me and Jem a cottage with a stable for ponies and a cottage for Bill near, where he could sup his ale and we could keep him out of trouble. I could even send some to America for my Tommy to take his trip west.

The shining path went down a hill where the sparse trees came closer and closer together until it disappeared into a dip, and there I could see a glow of orange light among the trees.

The wind picked up again, driving the clouds across the moon, so sometimes it went almost black, and then the moon appeared like a night-time dawn and lit everything silver.

As I got closer and I entered the wood, my bare feet still on the cool marble of the path, from beyond I heard voices and strange singing and chanting and shadows flickering in the trees.

I came to a clearing, and there at the centre was the round temple with great scrolled columns holding its domed roof. All about there were torches burning and figures in togas flitting and skipping and dancing, and on the curved stone benches sat more figures, drinking from goblets and singing. One played a curved harp, and the notes tinkled lightly across to me.

All was shot with a weird shifting orange and silver light. When the moon went the firelight painted the temple and the figures around it in red and black, and then when the moon came back the scene was washed with silver and grey. The wind was stronger and the trees were rushing with it. I heard a clap of thunder some way off and the crowd about the temple oohed and aahed.

His lordship rose from his bench and came to me. He was in a toga that barely covered his privates, and a twisted headdress of green leaves and berries. He held out his hands and said, 'Ah! Our Diana has arrived. You shall have some quarry tonight, my goddess.' He knelt before me with his arms spread wide. Some of the others did the same, calling, 'Our goddess . . . hail Diana!'

Mrs Fraser, still wearing her Athena costume, came to me and kissed me. Other gentlemen and ladies, all in Greek and Roman garb, greeted me; some of the ladies had their breasts uncovered like statues and some of the men wore nothing at all bar headdresses of twigs and leaves.

His lordship said, 'We have an opponent for you, Miss Perry – a most worthy and terrible creature. We wish to see the clash of the gods to celebrate midsummer. Would you oblige me by donning this for the bout?'

He handed me a short dress made from calfskin and a twisted-twig headdress with bird bones and feathers and tiny arrow heads in it.

Mrs Fraser handed me a goblet of wine and smiled. 'Be sure he pays you well for your skills, Annie,' she whispered.

So I said, 'I want two hundred pound for this, your lordship, in cash, up front. You owe us the other half from today an all. I will fight whoever you want and I will dress as queer as you please for it, but I want pound notes in me hand fore I do.'

The others whooped and cheered at my speech, and his lordship, whose eyes were swirling and darting about as he spoke, cried, 'You are a formidable negotiator, Miss Perry! Very well, you shall have it!'

He signalled to another toga-clad gentleman, who handed him the silver purse. He dug about in it and then counted the notes into my hand as if he was dealing cards. Twenty-two ten-pound notes and a five-pound note. I aint never seen so much money in my life.

I was near giddy with it, and I slipped off my pinny and chemise and petticoat and put on the tiny dress of skins. It only just come over my privates, so I rolled up the legs of my bloomers, tied the waist good and tight, and stuffed the notes down inside them. I dint bind my breasts nor nothing. Under that little skin dress I was as near naked as a newborn. I thought, well, he's paid for it, might as well give him a show.

The thunder cracked again, and a flash of lightning lit up the sky over west of us. The crowd thrilled to it with shouts and screams, and Lord Ledbury grabbed my hand and led me into the centre of the temple. All around me the audience frolicked and disported themselves across the stone benches, some languishing on one another and all drinking wine from silver goblets.

The wind was whipping in now, and the thunder rumbled in the distance as his lordship held my hand and paraded me in front of the guests around the circular floor. He called, 'My friends, how fitting for tonight here in this forest that we are to see a contest never before written of . . . a contest of Roman and Greek, of goddess and monster . . . for here, behold the goddess Diana, of the hunt, the moon, the woods and the wild! And behold her opponent . . .'

From the back of the seats came two men with a figure beneath a blanket. They pushed it up into the temple and Lord Ledbury pulled back the blanket. 'Behold the Gorgon!'

It was Molly Stych.

She was dressed in a flowing ragged gown of black and red, with her hair plaited into lots of little tails, at the end of which were silver snakes' heads that swirled and clacked about her face when she shook her head. She was made up in a most fearsome way with huge gold and red triangles about her eyes and black lips. She would've scared Bill Perry.

There was a burst of applause and the thunder rumbled and his lordship pulled the two of us together.

'I promised Molly a chance of revenge for Boxing Day,' he said. 'I shall referee this contest, and I don't enforce Jack Broughton, so do as you will, ladies. The more blood, the better. I will ensure things are fair and run as they were in the days of the Romans.' He gave me a nasty grin and clapped his hands in delight.

Molly looked at me and said, 'He promised us an extra tenner if you bleed first. These'll help. They're sharpened lovely.' She swung her head again and the silver spikes on her plaits flashed past my eyes.

I stepped back and stanced, watching her hard, for I knew she was tricky and strong. She kept her hands down and we circled, her shaking her locks at me as the audience hushed and tensed. Out the corner of my eye I could see Mrs Fraser; she was kissing a thin girl in a flimsy toga, pressed against one of the columns. I looked for half a second too long and Molly was on me. A fast jab into my brow and two hard crosses threw me. I felt the second snap a crack in my cheek, and fore I could get away and get my guard back she swung her head and the silver snakes clattered into my face. I felt a thousand stings ripping across my eyes. I was gasping for air and blinded with the blood so I clinched her into me and we went over, rolling and clasping. She got on top and had me flat with her hands holding me down. She shook her head again and the snakes' heads rattled down and slashed my forehead. She had her full weight on me, but I bucked under her and she wobbled. Her hand loosed on my left hand and I swung it up into her face. There was a mighty crack from that and she screamed. I rolled and jumped up and give her two more while she was down, both shuddering head shots that made her silver snakes jangle. She went over onto all fours, shaking her head and spitting blood out onto the white marble.

A normal referee would've stopped it then, but I looked up at his lordship and he was just stood looking at me with his thumb turned down and a soppy expression on his face. The audiences were baying now. 'Finish her, finish her!' I dint know what to do.

If I hit her hard into the back of her head when she was down I would kill her.

I backed off and stanced, shaking the blood and sweat out of my eyes. Molly was still on all fours, screaming and shouting she was gonna kill us. Mrs Fraser leaned in from her column and held out a goblet to me. Molly was beaten enough for me to be cocky, so I took it, held it up like a lady and then drained it. It was warm and sweet, and it shot through me, and I felt like the Queen of England.

But for a big bride Molly could be quick once she was up, and the next second she was before me, flailing her fists. I crouched, got my guard up, weathered her few blows, and then snapped jabs at her to keep her bloody head well back. I was liking it, stepping about her now. She had a gaping cut over her eye and the blood was pouring down her face. She only had one eye that could see, so I got on that side of her as she came on swinging again. I went for the cut eye and it splatted when I got it with a jab. She hollered and staggered, and I give a fast one-two-three; the third went into her gut and she stumbled back into the crowd who were now up and filling the spaces between the columns. They took her weight and pushed her back into me as I came at her. I jabbed her again, and she had her arms down and was stumbling like a drunkard.

Then his lordship sprang into the ring and got between us. He held up his hand and called, 'Stop . . . stop . . . The Gorgon is almost beaten . . . Praise to our Diana . . . But we must make this fair, must we not?' A cheer from the crowd. 'We must assist the monster against one so young and lithe as our goddess of the wild. She is a wild animal . . . must we not assist the Gorgon?'

The crowd roared yes, and his lordship pulled a short sword from his belt and held it out to Molly by the blade.

I said, 'No chance, squire . . . I aint—' And next thing I knew

Molly swung it at me. I tried jumping back, but the tip ripped across my belly, slicing the thin dress, and I felt the burn of the blade slit my skin. His lordship skipped away from us, clapping his hands, as gleeful as a babby on Christmas morn.

Blood was seeping out my belly, and I was backing and backing now, away from Molly. She was still staggering but now onto me, and she was swinging that blade through the air and it was flashing white in the moonlight.

I thought, this is gonna get nasty in a minute, and I looked for a way out, but the crowd was packed into the space around me. They were like savages now, some streaked with the blood that had sprayed about, calling, 'Occidit ei, occidit ei!'

I dint know Latin but I knew what that meant.

Molly was muttering and yammering and shouting she was going to do me, and I was backing. But when she swung, she left herself open, and she was tired and groggy and I could see her swings were not that fast, so when I skipped away from one I came back into her face before she could swing the next. It was a nice straight left and her nose collapsed under it, blood spraying back and up, leaving great black streaks of it on the marble columns.

Lord Ledbury was stood with his arm about a young naked man shouting, 'Bravo, Diana!'

Molly stayed up and raised the sword to swing down on me, and I went to push off my left foot to swing a left at her, and I felt it slip from under us on the bloodied marble floor.

I went crashing forward between her legs as she swung down, but toppled with the force of the miss, she fell flat on her face. Then the two of us skidded and grabbed at each other in the slick of blood. I was thinking, if I get that bloody sword off her I am gonna stick it up her arse.

We fumbled about, unable to stand for the slime, and she

launched herself onto me, her great bulk flattening me down. She managed to straddle me, and I felt for her hand that held the sword, but my grip slid from it. She shuffled and pinned me, with her knees on both my arms. She was sat above us now and she lifted the sword with both hands, pointing it down at my face. The crowd were chanting, their calls and screams and hoots battling with the boom of the thunder.

And I saw the sparkling silver tip of the sword there above my throat and I knew I was going to die.

For a second it all froze. The sounds and the smells went, and I could not feel her knees crushing down on my arms. Molly's twisted face was still before my eyes . . . And I had a sharp and sudden knowing it was my end, and all my fighting and loving and losing had come to this. And I felt no panic on the knowing. I felt only sad. In that moment before I died I felt a mute sadness well up in me. Sad I would never touch Jem's firm arms and soft lips again. Sad I would not see our Tommy cross America and find gold. Sad I should not be able to bring Bill his ale and call him an old bastard. Nor ever read a book or walk in a summer sunset on the heath.

Then came a boom and a flash, and the din of the crowd and the thunder flooded back in, and it raged.

Molly face jerked away from me and the sword clattered, and there was Jem's lovely face above me, his hand reaching down. He pulled me up and shouted, 'What the fuck is going on?' and dragged me out of the temple. Two of the guests tried to bar him from between the columns but he flattened them both with one punch.

As he pulled me out I looked back, and there was Molly Stych sprawled on her face on the blood-soaked marble.

Jem said, 'Good job I dint do as I was told, innit? She was going to kill you!'

Lightning was flashing close in now, and Lord Ledbury came round the temple with a crowd of his people, all bloodied and dishevelled in their togas.

He called, 'Fine show, Miss Perry! Mr Mason, I believe you may have killed Mrs Stych. That was quite a blow.'

Jem said, 'You stay away from me, or you'll get the same.'

I felt down in my bloomers and then said to Jem, 'It's all right, Jem. I got the money.'

Lord Ledbury called something to me, but it got lost in a mighty thunderclap above our heads. We turned to walk away, but he shouted again: 'I say, Miss Perry! You may wish to know you shall have another visitor this evening. Sir Andrew and a party of constables are to arrive to arrest you and Mr Perry. He was kind enough to inform me with a note this afternoon. I asked him to delay until we had finished our entertainment. I shall inform them of Mrs Stych's demise and perhaps they can arrest Mr Mason at the same time. Aha! Here they are!'

We looked up the path and saw a group of horsemen trotting towards us. There were six of them, with Sir Andrew in his red coat at their head. The constables all carried pistols and lanterns. For a second they were framed in the blinding glare of a lightning flash, and then great fat drops of rain began to smack onto the ground around us.

I grabbed Jem's hand, shouted, 'Run!' and we took off into the woods as the rain pelted down and the drops danced off the white marble path.

36

Sheltering in the temple, Sir Andrew listened to Lord Ledbury's explanation of how he and his guests had been out in the woodlands enjoying a Grecian-themed picnic when they chanced upon Annie Perry and Jem Mason, covered with blood and standing over the dead body of the woman who lay with a broken neck on the temple floor.

'Some strange gypsy rite for the midsummer, I expect,' said his lordship. He then provided Sir Andrew and his men with directions to the Perrys' camp.

Annie and Jem were running wildly through the pitch-black woods when a lightning flash illuminated the wagon and tethered horses amidst the driving rain. They ran for it.

Bill had remained in his chair as the rain battered down on him, happily singing and mumbling to himself as Paddy and Janey sheltered inside. Beside him a storm lantern glowed in the murk.

As Annie and Jem ran into the camp Bill called, 'Who goes there?'

Annie shouted, 'It's me, Bill! Sir Andrew and his constables have come and mean to arrest us! They are over by the temple now.'

Paddy rushed from the tent and shouted to Annie, 'Did you get the money?'

'I got the money, Paddy, but it's all gone wrong here. We need to shift out now!'

Jem hurried to the horses, unhobbled them and led them by their halters back to the wagon.

Bill was raving. 'No man shall take me! No man shall take Bill Perry! I aint going to a prison!'

Annie said, 'There's no time, Bill. I have all the money we need in me bloomers. We must fly now, or they shall get us!'

But Bill refused to move, constables or not, he said. He was happy where he was in the rain with his pistol and his ale. 'You go, my Annie. You and Jem tek them ponies and run for it. Leave me here and I shall delay these constables.'

Paddy shouted, 'We need to go now, Bill!'

Bill said, 'I aint shifting.'

Janey came to him and said, 'I'll stay with him. You three get gone and we'll keep em back for a bit. You can send for us when you're safe.'

Jem had the ponies bridled as the rain began to ease and the thunder rumbled further off. He said, 'Come on, Annie. They shall hang me for that wench I clouted.'

Annie kissed Bill, and the old fighter smiled, rain glistening on his face. She said, 'I have the money to buy you from a debtors' prison. We shall come for you and all will be well, Bill.'

'I love you, my little one,' said Bill.

Beyond the trees, the constables and Sir Andrew had broken into a gallop as they followed the marble walkway towards the lake.

Paddy shouted, 'I'll come two up with you, Annie.'

Annie mounted the pony and Paddy jumped up behind her. Jem turned his mount and called, 'Come on!' Annie looked back for a second through the driving rain at Bill sitting in the dim light of the storm lantern. He was holding the pistol out before him, pointing it towards the trees, and at his feet was the soaking portrait of the Queen.

The three of them thundered away into the night.

Bill could hear the hooves of the constables' horses nearing the campsite. He shouted, 'Janey, get in that tent and hide!'

Janey shouted back, 'Do not shoot nobody, Bill! The powder'll be wet.'

Bill sat smiling as he sensed the direction of the approaching horsemen. He called to them, 'Come on and try it! I am the Champion of England and let no man gainsay me! You will be in a mighty bind if you pass this way, gentlemen.'

The riders broke through the trees.

The powder was not wet. By some miracle it had stayed dry through the downpour, tucked in Bill's jerkin, and now he raised the pistol to fire blindly at the men. There was a flash and a crack as the red-hot ball left the barrel and a plume of smoke rose above Bill's head.

It would later be called blind man's luck, for the ball flew through the sodden air and struck Sir Andrew Wilson-Mackenzie square in the chest, knocking him from his horse and sending him thumping to the ground, stone dead.

The constables dismounted and took position in the trees, squinting into the rain at the faint light from Bill's storm lantern.

Bill heard the whump as Sir Andrew's body hit the ground and he turned and called to Janey in the tent, 'I think I got one! You don't get past Bill Perry!'

He started to sing 'God Save the Queen', and at that moment a constable took aim and fired. Bill Perry slumped forward with a pistol ball in his head.

37

Thank God Jem could ride like he could, for we just followed him as he thundered up the hill away from Ledbury Court, Paddy clinging onto my waist and calling over the swish and thunder of the galloping pony, 'Sure you got the money? Sure now?'

The track was soft and clagging, and mud splattered up at us, and the high grass and cow parsley whipped our faces as we hammered up there, but they were strong little cobs, those two, and we kept up a good pace. The rain kept lashing in my eyes, and the rump of Jem's pony blurred and melted before me. When the lightning flashed I could see the track before us, leading into a thick copse. It lit up silver like a road into Hell and the storm screamed like the demons welcoming us.

I could hear Paddy muttering behind me, and I caught a snippet of words between the thunderclaps and there he was praying! Mumbling prayers for our salvation!

As we reached the hilltop the rain cleared and the fierce wind dropped and a huge flat strawberry moon shone down on us, with little wisps of cloud whipping past it. We pulled up and looked down at Ledbury Court in the moonlight. At the bottom of the track there were four riders coming up after us. We could see their lanterns bobbing as they cantered up the track.

Bill dint hold em off for long, I thought, and I had a sudden sick fret for him and Janey.

Jem kicked his pony into the copse, and we snaked through the trees on a badger path, our little ponies surefooted and true as you like. There is nothing as certain in this life as a surefooted pony. You can trust em with your life.

The path led down through the woods to a meadow and a river. There was an old stone bridge and on the other side a village. We could see a church spire glistening with rain in the moonlight as mist began to form and drift above the river.

I knew we needed to wrong-foot our pursuers – not do what they expected. Just like in a bout when the other thinks he's read you and makes the move you expect him to.

There was a stone wall running along the riverbank and Jem's pony jumped it. I followed and yelled, 'Hold tight!' to Paddy, who screamed, 'Holy Mother of God!' as we sailed over. On the other side, a path ran one way to the bridge and the other way into a thick hedgerow. Jem turned his pony to head for the bridge, but I shouted and pointed, 'No! Not that way! Here . . .'

I jumped off and helped Paddy down as Jem shouted, 'What you doing?'

I said, 'Gallop up that way and put some tracks up to the bridge then come back here.'

'Is this a gypsy trick, Annie ?' He laughed.

'Aye! Just you do it!'

He tore off on his pony up to the bridge and beat the grass and mud down, then returned the same way in his own tracks. He dismounted, and we all crept into the hedge. I could hear the riders coming from the copse above us. They were calling to each other, and I heard the rattle of lanterns on poles, though the moon was now bright as day. They were slow getting to the wall and then only one could jump it; he was on a big hunter and called to the others, 'Go round and find a gate through!'

We could hear them muttering and cursing at their horses for shying at the wall. Paddy held the ponies steady, and me and Jem peeked out the hawthorn to see the rider looking down at Jem's tracks. 'This way . . . they've gone over the bridge!' He thundered off towards the village.

We followed the path along the hedgerow, leading the ponies to make lighter tracks. It was silent under that moon, just the drips from the hedges and the gentle murmur of the river that shone a sliver of pink in the weird light of the strawberry moon.

For a mile or more we moved quiet as we could till Jem said, 'They'll suss we sent em wrong soon, Annie, and they'll be back down this way.'

Up ahead, the hedgerow stopped, and behind a gate a meadow ran down to the river. On the far side there were two vardos and ponies tied. There were withy batches stacked all about and baskets of every kind strapped in bundles to the roof. The fire was smoking in the damp, and an old woman, wrapped in a white shawl, sat fast asleep on the vardo steps. Even from over our side I could see her big gaping gob.

Jem said, 'Romis, Annie. They might help us out.'

I was still half naked in the calfskin dress his lordship put me in, so I took Paddy's jacket for decency and walked across the meadow to them. The horses skitted at me coming there through the moonlit misty field, and the old woman sat up awake and made the bad luck go-away sign and shouted, 'Manny!'

A tall dark fellow came out of the big vardo in his britches and a jerkin, and he looked across at me. I don't know what he thought he was seeing, me mud-spattered and smeared with dried blood, dressed in skins and barefoot under Paddy's red jacket.

He stood with his hands on his hips and laughed and said, 'Never! It's never Annie Loveridge.'

I hadn't seen Manny Lee since Big Tom was alive. I remembered him teasing us though when he was pals with our Tommy, and we met at the fairs and chased through the stubble and played on the hayricks. His people were Lees and they were all over, though many had gone to America, my mammy told me, years ago. And they all knew Big Tom.

We brought Jem and Paddy and the ponies over, and he got the kettle on, and his wife Lidja came out with their new babby, the most beautiful little black-haired thing I ever seen. She was called Lavinia.

There was a long telling of my life and troubles, and all the Lees knew I'd been offered and Mammy had died in the asylum. They knew the boys had gone too but I never told them of Tommy in America. We said he had gone off into Wales with a band he met with and they were in the north there, trading horses.

Paddy was shifty about his satchel of money and kept it clamped to him. But I knew they'd look after us and do us no wrong. Paddy made a little fire of his own away from the vardos and sat drying off the notes and counting the coin till the sun come up.

Manny said, 'We'll not see you wronged no more, Annie Loveridge.'

They got a stew on, and I was ravening with hunger, and we all wolfed down the turnips and rabbit and black bread. Manny and Lidja and the old woman were on their way to Gloucester to sell baskets at fairs. The old woman would only speak Romi and she had her eye on Jem and kept rubbing his hair and saying, 'Shukar . . . shukar . . . Me gamau dut.'

Jem said, 'What's she on about, Annie?'

I said, 'I think she's saying you're beautiful . . . and she loves you.'

It was strange hearing it spoke; it was like birdsong heard from a long way off. She dressed and treated my cuts with grasses and plants they took from the roadside and the woods, just like Mammy did, and they found me a skirt and chemise and shawl. Manny gave us his big vardo, and Jem and me slept in the back bed and Paddy made a bed on the floor, and the three of us went out like lights.

I woke to a banging on the side of the vardo and Manny calling, 'Keep it quiet in there. There's riders coming.'

We listened to them trot up and a man say, 'We're hunting three runaways wanted for murder. Who have you seen come this way?'

Manny said, 'Only us, squire. We're just packing, ready to move. Nobody come down here.'

I heard the man drop from his horse and say quietly, 'Just as well, gypo. We don't want you lot round here. The one we seek is the fighting wench, Annie Perry. She's one of you lot, aint she?'

Manny said, 'Never heard of her, squire. We come down from Chester only yesterday.'

The man said nothing. He walked away from the vardo. One of the other men said, 'Give us a pail of water for the horses, boy. We bin trotting all night.'

Manny said, 'Right you are, guvnor.' And I heard him fetching a pail from the rain barrel at the back of our vardo. The old woman started muttering Romi curses on them and the man said, 'Shut her jabberin.'

The first man came back saying, 'Two of them ponies been ridden hard recently, eh, boy?'

I held my breath and Jem pulled me in closer to him. Manny said, 'I took both for a blast along the river first thing. They been pulling for days and getting creaky. I gotta sell them. Bet they could outrun your old nags there, if you want em. Good price and I'll throw in a basket or two. I'll clean em up if you want em.'

One of the constables laughed. 'You don't miss a trick, do ya?'

The first man said, 'We don't want your ponies, gypo, and we don't want you in this parish. You get yourselves gone before midday or we'll do you for vagrancy.'

I listened as their hooves pounded away and the old woman shouted foul curses after them. Paddy slept through the whole thing, his arm curled tightly round the money satchel.

We travelled with the Lees for two days. They crissed and crossed the country until we come into Birmingham and the railway where the engines heaved and clanked and billowed out steam.

They left us by the canal, and Paddy said we could scoot up into a district he knew well. I offered Manny money for taking us but they said no, so we gave em our two good ponies and he was well pleased. They embraced us. The old woman gave Jem's crotch a squeeze when she kissed him bye-bye. Manny said he would never let on he helped us, and I believed him, and I felt good that we were helped by one of my own.

There were posters all over for us. And the papers reported that Bill was killed by an armed constable after he had shot and murdered Sir Andrew. Jem and me were wanted for the killing of Molly Stych and the aiding and abetting of the highway robber Thomas Loveridge, known as the Black Cloak. We were also wanted for the theft of two hundred and twenty-five pound in banknotes from Lord Ledbury.

I read the reports to Paddy and Jem by the candle in the tiny windowless room above the canal in Birmingham where we stopped for two weeks while Paddy and the Gaffer arranged to get us to Liverpool and passage to America.

Under the title 'Outrages at Ledbury Court', it said I was a woman prize fighter of renown and Jem, known also as the Bilston Bruiser, was my betrothed. It said we had killed Molly Stych in revenge for her defeating me at an earlier bout. It did not say what she was doing at Ledbury Court nor why she was dressed as a

Gorgon. It stated we had been illegally camping on the land belonging to Lord Ledbury, the famous sportsman and society host.

The reports said we were thought to be in the company of a Mister Patrick Tacker, an Irishman and a dealer in stolen goods. Paddy cut his hair and shaved off his beard, and he was free to come and go and fetch us food and drink. We had to piss into a bucket, and Paddy had to go down and empty it into the canal for us.

Paddy paid acquaintances of his to take notes to Tipton, and we learned that Janey had run and hid after Bill was shot. She'd got herself back to the port and was living in a nail shop. I had to argue with Paddy over how much we sent her. In the end we sent forty pound, enough for her to get a house to live in with some left over. The Champion of England had been seized by Bill's debtors and the land sold to Sir Andrew's mining company to build a new coking works.

And old Bill was gone and I dint know what I felt. I wept over it for a time. But I also knew it was right and how it happened was the way it was meant to go and the way it was going from the day he stood before me as I was held up by Tommy at the Hallow Heath. And I did bring him happiness in his life: he had more joy and laughs with me and Janey and Jem than he would've had he stopped on his own. He had a life and then it was over and those as remember him remember him and those as don't don't.

I knew these things, but in that tiny room with Jem those weeks we hid in Birmingham I fell into the deepest and most abiding melancholy. Never before, not even after I heard of the fate of Mammy and my brothers and sister, had I felt such a dead leaden press come upon me. Mr Keats said it came 'sudden from Heaven like a weeping cloud, that fosters the droop-headed flowers all, and hides the green hill in an April shroud', and all of a sudden any green hill in me was wrapped and smothered.

I lay on the straw mattress in the hot rank air of that room and did not, could not, move. It was not that I felt sadness nor anguish nor the tearing pain of loss. The worst of it was that I did not feel anything. For days I thought I was dead; only the stench of the air and the clatter from the streets outside reminded me my senses still worked and I was indeed alive. It seemed a most herculean effort even to speak when Jem came to me with tea or bread or candles. He chattered away to me and he held my hand and wiped my brow. My state drove him to tears and he begged me, 'What can I do, Annie? I will do anything to get you back chipper.'

Not even the tears on his lovely face moved me out of my stupor, and the truth was there was nothing he could do. When Paddy came in to see me he said, 'The poor lassie is swamped, Jem. It's an overload of everything she has endured these past months. Tommy, her mammy, the boys, the wee sisters, fearing the work-house and the fights, nearly dying in there with Molly Stych, the running and ducking and hiding, and then Billy gone and us on the run. It's done her. One blow too many has knocked her out.'

I heard his words like they were spoken quiet down a long alleyway and I saw the things he spoke of play inside my mind like the characters in a fair show moving silent on a dim stage.

Jem said, 'Don't say that, Paddy. Get a doctor for her. Fetch a doctor.'

38

In Liverpool, the Gaffer found the mate of a steamship who said he would see Jem and Annie onto the ship next time it docked to load for Philadelphia. The man took ten guineas on top of the usual fare and provided the Gaffer with tickets and papers for travel. He reserved a cabin in the name of Mr and Mrs Williams of Birmingham. The docks were plastered with posters offering a reward for the apprehension of the pair, and the Gaffer found he simply had to trust the man. He was a good Staffordshire lad who had started on the barges with him donkey's years back, and sometimes, he thought, you just have to trust a fellow.

In Worcester, the county coroner recorded a verdict of unlawful killing by one William Perry on Sir Andrew Wilson-Mackenzie and a verdict of lawful killing by Constable Steers on William Perry, the celebrated pugilist. The death of Molly Stych by a forceful blow to the head was recorded as an unlawful killing by Annie Perry (also known as Annie Loveridge) and Jem Mason.

Evidence was heard from Constable Steers, Sergeant Evans, Constable Greenley and Constable Macklin. Lord Ledbury was not called but was reprimanded and fined five guineas for staging an illegal boxing bout. Sergeant Evans told the court how he and the other constables chased the fugitives into woodland during a heavy storm but lost the trail.

A magistrate sitting with the coroner ordered warrants for the arrest of Annie Perry, Jem Mason and Patrick Tacker and instructed that posters be distributed and hung across Worcestershire,

Warwickshire and Staffordshire. A reward of twenty guineas would be offered for information leading to the arrest of any one of the three.

In Tipton, nailers, miners and foundrymen held an impromptu street party in the lane outside the abandoned alehouse on the brilliant summer day Bill Perry was buried in the newly opened Tipton Parish Cemetery. Barrels of ale were tapped and fiddles and squeezeboxes played while the former clientele of The Champion of England thronged the roadway. A dancing floor of planks and hay bales was constructed, and chief amongst the revelling mourners was Janey Mee, who had arranged the funeral and led the raucous chants of 'Bill Perry, Bill Perry – you made us all merry!' The faded sign was lowered and set on a trestle, wreathed with lilies and dark red roses, and Bill's portrait of the Queen and his favourite jug were placed before it.

There were chants and songs celebrating the death of Sir Andrew Wilson-Mackenzie and a local balladeer performed a new song called 'The Fearsome Slasher Bill' to a cheering crowd. Janey challenged any man there to go a round with her in memory of Bill. Only old Jock Convey took her up, and the pair staged a farcical mock boxing match before the delighted revellers, which ended with Jock feigning a knockout, dumped down on his bony old arse. Chartists from Birmingham came and addressed the crowd, hailing Bill Perry a hero who fought for the rights of the common man against those of power and privilege.

The dancing, chanting, drinking and fighting went on until constables came to break it up, but, plied with ale, they stayed to see it through till dawn.

At St Michael's on the Hill, Sir Andrew's interment in a white marble tomb was attended by Lady Wilson-Mackenzie, Josiah and Jeremiah Batch and Mr Pottage from the parish council. It was conducted by the Reverend Elijah Warren. Within an hour of the funeral, the wind changed and smuts from the port began to fleck the new marble with dirty big brown spots.

39

The doctor gave me laudanum, and I dreamt Jem and me flew in a golden vardo across the sea and soared above America where the mountains and forests went on for ever and rivers of liquid gold snaked across the land. Then we settled in a fine white house made from marble that looked out across a vast lake where swans swam and eagles soared. Bill was there in a robe like Moses, holding a golden jug. Big Tom and Mammy, Tommy, Tass, Benny, Mercy and Charity all floated like angels above us as we stood on a sweeping green lawn holding hands as an amber sun set before us.

Then I was tiny, and I climbed up a towering teasel, swimming across the water pots it carried in its leaf stems and pulling myself up the spines to the waving head where I fed the seeds to linnets who fanned me dry with their wings.

Jem said I slept for two days. He kept checking I was breathing. And when I woke I could feel the blackness had lifted from me. As sudden as it come it seemed to melt, and I could move again. I even smiled when I saw Jem's face. He said, 'I been praying for ya.'

And I said, 'Well, them prayers are answered.'

He said, 'Wherever you been, don't go there again, my Annie, for I shall not survive it.'

The Gaffer sent word. He would meet us in Liverpool and get us onto the steamer for Philadelphia and he give us a date.

Now we knew it was time to shift again for that room would kill us if the hangman dint. Paddy had been taking the notes and changing and spending them about the city. He said it was called washing the cash so as nobody could trace it to us. After we sent money to Janey and Paddy was through with his washing we had a hundred and sixty-two pounds left.

I knew we had to present ourselves different before we left the room. So Paddy went into Birmingham and bought a fine suit of clothes for Jem, with a shaped checked jacket, a stiff-collared shirt and tie, a high-buttoned waistcoat and a good short top hat. He bought fine brown boots and a leather case. Jem looked a right toff in his get-up, and Paddy took him out to a barber's shop and he had his beard and whiskers shaved and his hair clipped short. He found him a pair of clear spectacles to wear and a nice ebony cane topped with a silver finial, and when he was done up he looked like a professor from the university. In his waistcoat pocket he carried a gold watch, made by Sanders of Birmingham.

Paddy was always dapper, and he had a good eye for a fashionable gentleman's look.

Then Jem and Paddy went to a dress shop, Paddy making out he was the servant and Jem the gentleman searching for a respectable outfit for his sister. They bought me a long dark-blue bell-shaped silk dress and a large-collared cape, stockings and chemise, and a lovely bonnet that tied under in grey silk. They bought a little purse on a chain and a crucifix for round my neck. I washed best I could in the filthy water Paddy carted in, and then dressed in my finery. Then Jem gave me a gold wedding ring to wear. Any fine lady who was wed would wear one, he said.

For my small case they bought a ladies' set with silver hairbrush, mirror, comb and button hook. The shoes I got were high soft buttoned boots that felt like wearing velvet on your feet. Paddy said the boots alone cost ten pound.

We divvied up the rest of the money. Paddy got fifty pound and said it was a fine score for him, and he would go to London and set himself up in business and find a decent fighter to manage. He said he would send to us in America news of how he fared. He hugged Jem and said he was the finest lad in all the world. He turned to me and said, 'Annie Perry, you are the most gracious lady I have ever met in all my old life. I salute you and your courage and fortitude. And this boy here is to be envied that he shall have the honour to be your husband. I have no regrets for our adventures and nor should you. We shall part devoted friends.'

Both me and Jem started weeping then. Jem couldn't talk at all for it, and I had to dab my eyes with my new linen hankie.

We stood on New Street outside the grand canopy of Birmingham Station and Paddy turned to walk from us, saying, 'And you young people will without a doubt hear from Mr Patrick Tacker again.' He bowed and was gone into the busy crowds around us.

For a few minutes we strolled together, holding our cases and feeling like proper gentlefolk. Nobody paid us much mind, but a little beggar girl ran up alongside me and said, 'A penny for me mother, pretty lady.' I gave her five bob.

On the corner was a book emporium, and I took Jem in there and sat him on a chair while I perused all the volumes. I whispered, 'Don't open your mouth, or they'll know you're a rough bugger from Bilston.'

He smiled and said, 'They'll know you too for a Romi sharper. You can't get Tipton out of your mouth, wench.'

But I could. I fashioned my speech on the sounds Mrs Fraser used, her lovely silken words said with breath in them, and shortened my *oi*s to *eye*s when the gentleman of the store come over and said, 'Is madam searching for a particular volume?'

I said, 'I seek stories of adventure, sir. And poetry. I should like Mr Wordsworth's *Lyrical Ballads* for one. And a volume by Mr Burns.'

The gentleman said, 'Aha, madam has romantic taste.'

I said, 'I do, sir. I long for a more beautiful world.'

He said, 'I am sure I agree with you, madam; it is the desire of all of us who love the written word. Allow me to find you the volumes!'

I winked down at Jem, who grinned at me and shook his head. It was true what Mrs Fraser had said: all was illusion.

I looked at Jem's watch, for he could not tell the time, and it was half an hour until the train went for Liverpool. We paid for the parcel of books and strolled back towards the station, and as we rounded the corner of Regent Place, there upon the steps of the Unitarian Church was a group of ladies holding banners and flags and chanting, 'Votes for all! Votes for all!' Before them was a large poster reading:

THE BIRMINGHAM FREEDOM AND REFORM LEAGUE

A Campaign for Freedom to vote for ALL PEOPLE of this Kingdom, no matter their Station, Sex or Income.

Women and the Poor must have their Say.

Join us in our Campaign for Freedom and Justice for all Subjects of Her Majesty.

Sign this Petition for Parliament to be presented in the New Session.

CALL FOR A NEW REFORM BILL

FREE THE WORKING MAN AND WOMAN

And there at the front, in a wide straw hat, holding a board and pen out to passers-by was Miss Esther Warren. She looked as lovely as when I last saw her gaping at me on the path of the vicarage. Her eyes were full of sparkle as she called out to the people crossing the square.

Jem and I stood before her, and she looked up, saying, 'Madam, would you care to support us?' Then she clocked me and almost shrieked, 'Annie!' Panic flared in her eyes.

'Oh, we must talk, Annie . . . but not here.' She turned to her ladies and handed one the petition board, saying, 'I have encountered a very dear friend. I must go and speak with her for a moment.'

We went into a narrow close off the square, and there she took my hands and smiled. 'Oh, Annie, how do you do? They are all a-bluster in Tipton for you and Jem. They say you murdered and robbed.'

'We did neither,' I said. 'But they may say what they will. My father is shot and killed, and we are bound for America. I trust you will not betray us, Miss Esther.'

'Never,' she said. 'I do not believe a word written in newspapers, Annie. Though I fear my father does. The Reverend and I are estranged. In part, I confess, over you. I have taken rooms here with my friend Miss Gulliver. My sister is to marry Mr McLean in September.'

She made a face and I laughed.

'Tell me you are well and thriving, Annie. I have missed you so. You look so splendid, and Mr Mason too.' She glanced at the ring on my finger. 'Are you wed?'

'No, not yet, Miss, but we must keep up appearances for our voyage.'

'You must always keep up appearances, Annie,' she said, laughing. 'I feared you were hurt or killed. We were questioned by constables over your brother. The Reverend was livid. Was he really the Black Cloak?'

'Oh, I have no idea. Peelers have a lot of funny notions,' I said. 'I aint seen our Tommy since I was nine, Miss.'

She said, 'Please, call me Esther, Annie, for we have much in common now. My father has cut me off without a penny and my rooms are tiny and I work in a laundry in Snow Hill.'

'And you are a proper radical now.'

'I am a reformer, Annie. I fight to free the working man and woman. We have formed a union of washerwomen!'

'Do you need money? For we have plenty.'

She laughed and said, 'No, no, no, Annie. Your money was won fair and square by your own labours and you must use it for a new life.'

She glanced at Jem and blushed. 'Mr Mason, you are most handsome in your suit . . . You will both thrive in America. It is a republic; there is no king or queen.'

I smiled at her and said, 'Esther, I will be forever grateful to you and your sister for teaching me to read.'

'And I learned a great deal from you too, Annie,' she said.

We stood for a moment and looked at each other, and then we embraced warmly.

We said goodbye, then me and Jem walked across the square to the station to take the train to Liverpool.

40

The SS *Pennsylvania* juddered and lurched like some great iron beast. The creaking masts and the snapping flutter of the flags and bunting along the rails filled the air as we slid from Liverpool Docks. Then the rumble of the engine swelled and the steam whistle hooted, and I felt the shift of the thing beneath me, grinding iron through the water, heaving itself west.

And us with it. Mr and Mrs Williams of Birmingham.

Liverpool was lit up gold in the sharp morning sun: the spire of the big church gleamed and factory stacks and sail masts and mizzens spiked the air; the jutting arms of steam cranes slashed across the skyline; and we looked back and England ebbed away from us.

We had tickets for the second deck where a body could take tea and dine in a narrow galley. Our cabin was tiny, with two unsteady little bunks and barely enough room to turn.

From our deck we could see down to steerage where crowds of poor wretches sat and loafed about under oilskins to shelter them from the rain and spray. The men were muffled against the wind and the women wrapped in shawls, some cradling suckling infants. They were mostly Irish and had the hollow haunted look of those who had starved, but there was no unseemly clamour when the crew brought trays of bread and cups of clean water, only a quiet shuffling into line. They looked that beaten I wondered how they would fare when they got to America. I knew most would end labouring in mines and foundries till they dropped down dead.

That seemed to be the fate of so many – but I knew it would not be mine nor Jem's.

After my melancholy fit had left me I had the eyes of a man who'd woken up at his own funeral. Things were new and shocking to me. From the moment Jem clouted Molly Stych off me, the world had become too bright and scary. Up till then I don't think nothing had really frightened me. Now, part of me was scared all the time.

I kept our money tied tight in a cloth bag about my waist for it seemed to me that that was what it was all about. Money. There was no other force that drove us. Or drove me all those days.

Despite what Miss Esther said about the love of God, everything that happened to me and everything I thought and felt and did was pushed and snapped along by the need of money. From Big Tom dropping down dead to Bill sitting at the ringside as I fought. From the sale at the horse fair to lying naked in Jem's arms on the heath. Even the reading and books, I thought, was all about money. Reading to better myself. Reading to pay Bill's fines.

Money: the need of it, the love of it, the lust for it, the fear of it. It was the reason I was sold and the reason I learned to fight. The reason I found Jem. The reason we were fleeing the noose to America. All I seen was them as had it, and them as did not have it, and there was no reason for it: only chance and luck and being born where you were.

Down on the steerage deck they set to a song, a sad and doleful Irish tune that floated up to us, and though I did not know the words, I could tell they were singing of broken hearts and the leaving of those you love.

And I wondered still, in the stiff breeze looking back at the coast of England. I'd once seen the underside of everything in an oak leaf. I'd known I was going somewhere. More important than the eighty pound strapped about my waist, I had new words and ways of speaking in my head and I could hear songs and music and see the meaning and intent.

I was out the other side.

Epilogue

Ithan, Pennsylvania
1906

The Missus had fallen asleep. Jeannie sat in the quiet room and watched. Her breathing was shallow and seemed to fit and start; the girl wondered if she should call Kenny to get a doctor.

Before her on the table, alongside the tray of empty teacups, lay the books the Missus had pressed on her and insisted she read. With the dark eyes closed, the face before her was less fierce; the head resting on the wing of the chair was small and childlike and the deep lines of the face had relaxed into soft furrows.

Jeannie looked at the two books. *Lyrical Ballads* and *Poems, Chiefly in the Scottish Dialect*. She'd never heard of them but she'd promised the Missus she would read them and come for a talk later that week.

With the gentle tick of the handsome steeple clock on the dresser and the rhythm of the Missus's gentle breathing and the golden sunlight slowly creeping from the room, Jeannie leaned back into the chair and felt herself slip into a kind of trance.

The clip of hooves and the rasp of carriage wheels on the gravel of the drive roused her, and Kenny opened the door, whispering, 'Jeannie, the lawyer is here for the Missus. Come now to fetch his tea and let her sleep.'

Jeannie picked up the two books and left the room.

A Note from the Author

Annie Perry was my great-grandmother. She was the granddaughter of William Perry – the Tipton Slasher (1819–1880). As children my brother and I were told countless stories about the Slasher, including the story of how his daughter Annie was offered up and sold at a fair when she was seven years old. These stories were all part of an elaborate family mythology spun by my grandmother, Mollie Kitson. Aside from the family lineage – as far as I have been able to tell – none of the stories she told were true. Mollie was an inveterate inventor of tales which she swore had happened and which had no basis in fact. When she died we discovered she was actually five years older than she claimed to be all her life, having knocked a few years off her true age sometime in the 1940s. She also maintained that we Kitsons were actually impoverished aristocracy, and even made up an entire branch of the family who owned vast estates and limitless wealth and were presided over by a mysterious (and entirely fictional) nobleman called Sir John Jeremy or sometimes Sir Jeremy John. She looked after my brother and me when we were children in a damp and lorry-rattled house opposite the chemical works on Corporation Road in Newport. And we adored her. I thank her for passing on to me the desire and ability to make things up.

Acknowledgements

I would like to thank everyone at Canongate for soldiering on with the publication of this book through the Covid-19 pandemic. I would especially like to thank Jo Dingley, Alison Rae, Leila Cruickshank, Megan Reid, Gill Heeley, Bethany Ferguson and Caroline Clarke for their splendid work. Thank you also to my agent Cathryn Summerhayes and to Keith Dixon for his excellent work on my books in France. I would like to thank and gratefully acknowledge the help of Creative Scotland and the Society of Authors for assistance during the Covid-19 pandemic.

Thanks to Paddy Kitson and Sheila Navas for helping me with the family connections of Annie's story. All my love and respect to my children Molly, Susie and Jimmy for their help and existence. And, of course, my muse, editor, inspiration and scone-making coach Jill.